I0741175

TIME FORGED

BOOK 10 OF THE GIFTING

TIME FORGED

The Gifting Series #10

Wren got screwed.

Earth Armed Forces promised her a fortune to use her elite coding skills to save kidnapped children—then denied ever hiring her. Arrested, stripped of her tech rights, and banished to a space station, she's forced to weld for a living. Her only thrill? Bungee-jumping off construction cranes with the best view in the galaxy.

Getting kidnapped?

Totally her fault.

Now trapped with alien tech she can't hack and women she can't protect, Wren becomes a test subject in a genetic nightmare. But she refuses to go down without a fight.

Cylo is an Etterian operative.

Saving kidnapped females for his people is his mission—until Wren crashes into his life. She isn't his, having not triggered the lifemate bond. But her fire, resilience, and raw courage leave him desperate to protect her anyway.

Wren should be unraveling, not evolving. The alien serum inside her is altering her DNA, awakening strange powers—and Cylo's the only solid thing in her world. But as her mind opens to the emotions and thoughts around her, even he can't shield her from the truth.

Cylo would give anything to claim her forever.

Too bad forever might not be an option.

Published by Sevannah Storm.

First Edition 2025

Cover Art by Sevannah Storm

https://sevannahstorm.com

Version_1

Also by Sevannah Storm

The Blood of Legends Series

The Huntress

The Healer

*

The Gifting Series

Soul Forged

Fate Forged

Sun Forged

War Forged

Star Forged

Shadow Forged

Earth Forged

Lust Forged

Fire Forged

*

Standalones

Xiaxan Fox

Ire of Silver

The Crucible of the Eternal

Inkoded

*

The Space Hunter Chronicles

The Shikari

The Justisaar

*

The Qaldreth Warriors

Sol Survivor

Dark Survivor

*

Plump Playwright Series

Plump Jane

Seducing Amelia

Loving Finley

Keeping Tessa

Kissing Navy

*

COMING SOON

Hope Forged

Stealing the Starstone

Rain Forged

Acknowledgements

I'd like to thank my beta team; you ladies are awesome:

Anuschka, Lanette, Leslie, Karen, Kristine

♡

Prologue

THREE YEARS, SEVEN MONTHS, two weeks, and two days ago, an old man in an overly decorated uniform had marched unannounced into Wren's loft apartment. Caught mid-step in her small kitchen, she'd blinked at him, unable to believe he'd simply strolled in. Her voice had lodged in her throat, and her skin itched.

A quick scan of her home for a weapon listed a butter knife, a still-hot kettle, and a dish towel. Not much she could defend herself with. And in her pajama pants, baggy, soda-stained T-shirt, her hair mussed, bloodshot eyes, and lack of sleep, she wouldn't offer up much of a struggle. She was on the tail end of a three-day coding project—without breaks, as usual.

She clutched a bag of stale popcorn to her chest with her forty-seventh cup of pseudo-coffee in hand. "What the hell?" she managed to say like an imbecile.

"Ms. Turner, Earth Armed Forces needs you." He crossed to her like she'd invited him in for tea.

She took note of his features. If she survived this, she wanted to remember every detail, from his buzz cut to the scar just below his jaw. His nose was crooked, his lips thin, and his chin had a tiny dimple mid-center. But what blinded her was the sheer number of badges marking him as high-ranking, but anyone could fake an E.A.F. uniform.

"Get out," she snapped, stomping to the door, then tried to open it while juggling the bag and hot coffee. "Wait." She set the cup on the nearest surface and faced him, finding he hadn't moved. "How did you get in?"

He waved a dismissive hand like her question didn't matter. "We need you to breach Pytheas Exploration's systems, and we're willing to pay handsomely for your services."

Her ears perked up at earning a little on the side. Any incoming tokens were squirreled away for her parents. Well, for Dad, to be honest. He lived for his welding job, loving the challenge of building bigger or faster ships for Everlast Shipwrights. She'd helped him on weekends, valuing the quiet time just working on a task...alone. He'd taught her everything he knew about welding—a fallback career she had no plans to pursue. If he won the global lottery, he wouldn't quit his job. Still, while he recovered from his last accident, he didn't earn as much. Every token she and her brothers could spare went toward keeping her parents housed and fed.

"Why me?" She gestured to the intruder's dark gray uniform. "You have agents with my skill set."

He arched a brow at her while meandering around her dust-covered living room-cum-office-cum-kitchen. "How humble of you to say." He smiled, all oily and sickly sweet. She shrugged back a shudder, her instincts clamoring for attention. "We're told you're the best."

"I doubt that." She waved her popcorn at the door. "See yourself out."

"P.E. is abandoning colonies, leaving these people to starve to death. Women, children..." He peeked at her, his beady gaze assessing. "We need to know where and why. Get me that info, and your father won't have to work again. Or would you prefer he lose an arm next time?"

He tossed a chip at her. She caught it mid-air then gaped at the flashing number. For that amount, she could ignore her screaming instincts... Just this once.

"P.E. will be tough to crack." She shuffled on her feet, the popcorn bag squeaking in dismay. The bigger the corporates, the harder it was to break into their databases. They hired the best to protect them. Could she do this? "Let me do a little digging."

At the first sign of any duplicity, she could bolt, retracting any evidence of her presence.

He clapped his palms together for a gleeful rub. "Excellent."

"Next time, make an appointment..." She waited for him to supply his name.

He didn't. And for a man of his age and girth, he made no sound when he headed for the exit.

"Wait," she said, throwing out her hand still holding the popcorn. A few kernels spilled out. "How do I get in touch—"

"I'll find you."

She gawked at the closed door, her mind reeling. No, he hadn't just said that. This was insane... Madness.

"Don't fall for this, Wren. It's too good to be true." She stared at the tokens he'd tossed at her. "Shit..."

She slipped the chip into her pocket then shoved a handful of popcorn into her mouth, chewing as she grabbed her cup and settled at her desk. It wouldn't hurt to do some research. Maybe only on what was public knowledge?

She huffed. How would that reveal anything other than that they had an excellent media department? No, she could risk a deeper delve, starting with P.E.'s import and export manifests. Not so public but not restricted information, either.

If anything sparked her interest, she could then decide whether she should agree to this bizarre request. She coughed when a kernel stuck to the back of her throat. A quick gulp of coffee helped, then with deft fingers, she reached out to her contacts. With any luck, she'd know who her intruder was by sunup.

Chapter One

Demeter Science Station
Year of 2254, August
Three Years and Seven Months Later

Wren launched herself off the tower crane, piercing the dark emptiness of space. She flew forward, her breath hitching while she waited for the whiplash of her ankle harnesses keeping her tethered. Below was the umber-periwinkle of Pluto, orbited by other stations, satellites, and tourist ships. Behind her was the Demeter Science Station, her home. For now.

Silence reigned, ruined only by her breathing. So she held it for as long as she could.

Some feared the nothingness around her. Others hated the loneliness. She relished both, savoring every moment spent in peace.

As many times as she did this, it didn't fix the state of her life. When her boots hit the station walkway, every horrible thought about her situation slammed into her.

Wrongly convicted of corporate espionage? Check.

One stupid hack... She'd gotten cocky. The stakes had been too high, but the rewards, had she succeeded, would've set her parents up for life. Of course, she hadn't covered her ass. What she'd done for the good of Earth had been twisted by an E.A.F. prosecutor.

Stripped of computer privileges? Check.

Her tech skills had defined her for most of her life. She'd had to find another her, dig deeper into her psyche. No matter what she did, a piece of her was missing. And she had two years left of her five-year tech ban before she might feel whole again.

Considered a snob by many because of her education? Check.

Sure, she'd landed her job with the welding skills her father had taught her, but thanks to her finishing school elocution, the maintenance staff didn't treat her as one of the crew.

Couldn't talk to scientists and engineers because of her criminal record? Check.

Not welcome in the slums nor among the science teams left her on her own. As she liked it.

But this... She drew in a deep breath and hummed in contentment. Few things kept her sane: bungee-jumping into space, tending to her bonsai, a long pull of splice, and her alien romance smut. Some poor E.A.F. agent had to read it, too—just to be sure 'well-endowed alien dragon shifters' wasn't code for something else. She giggled.

"Pony, get back here," Dallas snapped, then cleared his throat from a perpetual tickle—louder through her helmet's speakers.

She gritted her teeth. 'Rainbow Pony' had been her initial nickname, so named for her colorful hair. Unfortunately, that sobriquet had been too long for anyone to keep up.

"I closed out my shift. Can't you just leave me the hell alone?" She waited and prayed he was done talking to her.

"Seems like your usual suicidal dive has stirred up the tourists. A dozen calls to emergency services have the powers-that-be coming down on my head as your unlucky supervisor. Get your feet onto solid metal. I dunno how many times I've asked you to not do this when folks are awake."

She scowled, glanced once more at Pluto and Jupiter beyond, the sun's rays starting to reach her. "Shit," she muttered. "Gimme five minutes."

"You have two. Station-Sec's on their way already."

She groaned. "Thanks for the heads-up, boss."

Tapping the heels of her mag boots, she activated the boosters and spun, shooting toward the crane. If...she...could...just...reach—

"Ah, come on, Turner," Clemence whined on the maintenance frequency. "I thought it was you causing havoc again." Station-Sec slowed their shuttle beside her, its orange exterior too bright in the weak sunlight. He hung out of the gaping compartment, his focus on her.

"Sorry, sir. Forgot the time." She winced. *All lies.*

"I'll take it from here." Pierce emerged from behind Clemence and leaped out, crossing the short distance to fall in beside her. He maneuvered well with his boosters, making it seem effortless.

"Very well, sir." Clemence saluted him then double-slapped the inside of the shuttle.

She stared at its disappearing engines, choosing not to talk. Awkward silences were her domain and preference.

"Ms. Turner," Pierce said, his husky baritone tingling her ears.

"Captain," she said, smothering a grin. When she was younger, she'd nicknamed him Happy—Harold Antony Pierce.

He'd known her since she was a teenager, and she suspected he acted like her brothers expected him to. She had two and didn't need a third. There was no doubt in her mind that he updated Leon weekly. He had, in fact, chosen sides.

"Lovely day for a little sightseeing."

"Indeed," she said. "My apologies for disturbing your morning."

"I'd prefer it be you than a kid out on a joyride." His long-suffering tone sliced guilt across her conscience.

"I'm tethered, wearing certified ankle harnesses, with a full tank of oh-two," she hurried to say, aware they weren't alone on the comms.

She touched down on the metal frame of the tower crane, wide enough for her to walk along. Her boots' magnetic locks cut off the boosters and allowed her to stick to the structure. Sure, she was at a 67.3-degree angle, but up and down played no real part on a spinning station.

"Let me escort you back," Pierce said, pointing at the hatch more than a hundred meters away.

Giving him a glare had no impact when wearing a space suit. She'd hoped to have a few more minutes while she removed her harnesses and fixed them at the base of the crane. Instead, she grabbed the tether and pulled herself toward the anchor point. She cast a glance at the clasps she'd welded to the side of the station, hoping Pierce didn't spot them. To a layman, they looked like they belonged to the crane's support plates. If he knew she'd left clasps all over the station, her not-so-clean record would carry a warning she couldn't afford. Forcing a casualness she was far from feeling, she unclipped the tether from her ankle harnesses and the hook. With her gaze fixed on the distant stars, she looped the cord around her shoulder and elbow then, once coiled, slipped it over her head and torso. All this time, he hovered, his presence encroaching on her personal space.

"Is this necessary? I'm not a child," she snapped. He took his brotherly chore too seriously.

He said nothing, just nudged his head. He expected her to leap off and propel herself into the airlock the quickest way possible.

She gritted her teeth, deactivated her mag boots, and floated. Before she went too far, she used her toes to push off the crane. The momentum alone was enough for her to glide across. She caught the handle on the side of the round door then flipped to lock her feet to the metallic bulkhead. He did the same but wasted no time in opening the hatch. She crawled through, headfirst.

Once inside the hexagonal airlock, he sealed the hatch and smacked the re-pressurization button. When the red lighting flickered to white and their feet hit the floor with the full gravity the station could create, he unfastened his helmet, tugging it off to reveal his handsome features. Green eyes twinkled, and that silly smirk he always wore was firmly in place. Happy suited his ass.

"Up for a little breakfast?" he asked.

She removed her helmet and tucked it under her arm. With a puff, her bangs no longer blocked her vision.

"You mean dinner?" she teased; after all, she'd just finished her day shift when he was starting his. Day-night simulation meant everyone worked the day shift. It was always daytime somewhere on Demeter. "Doesn't seem like a befitting punishment for my 'joyride:' my steak versus your scrambled eggs."

Like she could afford actual meat, but she didn't mention that.

"True." The bay door opened to one of the station's many passages. "I bought you as much time as I could." He gestured to her to lead the way.

Her boots thunked on the metal grill, gravity weighing heavy on her limbs and soul.

Buying her time meant he'd known she was out there. She leveled a scowl at him. "How are you tracking me?"

"I have a man on Turner duty twenty-four-seven." He tossed a grin. "You can thank Leon for that."

She groaned. Even from Earth, her older brother had his way. "When I accepted your job offer, you didn't once mention this...perk." She'd hoped distance would, well, give her some peace and independence.

Pierce chuckled. "All part of our employee retention package."

"Coffee would be appreciated," she said, watching his expressions for even a flinch at the cost.

"Now *that's* an invitation I can't refuse."

Shit. She had to pay? Folding her arms across her chest, she tapped her foot while the elevator climbed to their level.

"Meet you at Coffeeholics in ten?" he said when the cage door opened.

"Sure." She stepped inside and held his gaze while the door shut on his signature smirk. "Damn it," she muttered, pinching her brow to ward off an impending headache.

The elevator door opened. She trudged out, heading to her unit. Six by three meters encompassed her privacy. A large porthole at the end looked out at pipes. At least she had an outside view. If she pressed her cheek to the glass, she might catch a glimpse of stars. She had to flip her bed up to shower. The kitchen was less than a meter wide, housing a rehydrator and a disposal unit. The toilet slid out when needed and was 'well-placed' beside her wardrobe. Whoever had designed these units was an idiot.

A light flashed above the 'kitchen,' announcing she had a voice message waiting. Few people checked in on her, and what friends she had, well, they'd vanished the second she was arrested. Which meant the caller was family.

She unlooped the cord, now having to get up earlier to return it to its clasps. A grin formed. A morning leap sounded like bliss—one way to test Pierce's system. Chuckling at her wicked plan, she removed her boots—keeping the ankle harnesses on—then peeled off her company-issued space suit to reveal a sweat-stained tank top and well-worn jeans that were butter soft. Station protocol stated that all personnel had to wear magnetic boots, even during downtime. On strippers, the clunky shoes made them look badass. She stomped hers on again, huffing when she clipped them in place.

Without time to shower, she swapped tank tops, deodorized, and ran a brush through her hair.

She caught her rainbow-haired reflection in the porthole above her bed. "Sorry, Mom, I'm not wearing clean underwear."

It was just Anthony Pierce she was meeting, and she wasn't about to get herself hospitalized or laid. Besides, coffee came first. She'd shower before bedtime.

She tapped the flashing light while considering whether she could risk a shot of splice.

Mom's voice stuttered on. "Are you avoiding my calls, Wren Marie?" Mom huffed. "Just make sure you're behaving. I wouldn't put it past you to sweet-talk poor Anthony into lying for you."

Anger tightened the knot in Wren's stomach. Her hand began to shake, her need for splice ramping with every word Mom uttered.

A scuffle sounded with Mom saying, "Wait, I'm—"

"Sweetheart," Dad said, his voice coming through stronger, kinder. "We called just to thank you for the tokens. Love you lots, as always."

Before the recording ended, Wren dug out a flask hidden behind a loose panel. She took two swigs of splice, tension easing as it slid down her throat. Sometimes, the splice was sweet, pale gold, and tasted of apple cider. Other times, she was lucky it didn't strip the lining off her stomach. Then it had the flavor of degreaser and licorice. Beggars couldn't be choosy. She tried not to think about her reliance on the stuff. When she was ready, she'd quit. That wasn't today. That wasn't until she could figure out a way to avoid her mother.

With her insides ablaze, she jog-walked, hurrying to reach the busy shopping level that was home to a quaint coffee stall. At this time of day, it would be busy, filled to the brim with those splurging on a good cup of joe from Ganymede. Pierce waved at her when she arrived. He'd managed to steal a seat by the solid glass windows staring out at the construction. Additional funding had fueled an expansion, with the science conglomerates needing more lab space. Blah, blah. It meant a job for her, and that was all she worried about.

"I ordered for you," he said when she climbed onto the bar stool.

"Thanks," she said, resting her chin on a palm and an elbow on the table.

"I'm glad you joined me. I wanted to talk to you."

She dragged her gaze away from the cranes, cargo-barges, and one-man hovers. "Sounds serious."

"It is. You've been doing these jumps more often. You okay?" He smiled at the waitress who served their black coffees. When she blushed, he beamed.

"I'm fine. Just itching to be free." Wren sipped her coffee, smacking her lips at the smoky flavor.

Not that he was paying her much attention, his focus elsewhere. She bounced her knee, frustration, a splice craving, and impatience hindering her ability to sit still.

"Get her number already," she snapped. "Life's short. Get laid."

"Whoa, that escalated quickly," he said after the waitress swiped her wrist across his, triggering his O.D.I. or optical data implant. It flickered a light just under the skin on his left wrist.

She had one, too—company policy and all that. Thankfully, that meant she *could* have one. But she could only use it for emails, banking, and reading.

"I worry," Pierce said, resting his boot on hers in yet another failed attempt to stop her fidgeting. "I don't want to tell your folks you've died. So be careful when you're out there, please."

"Staying on the station is more hazardous than off it," she said, hating to have to curtail the best part of her day.

"If your tether snaps—"

"I have my boosters. I can comm you, Dallas, Clemence... Now, quit it. I came for the coffee, not a lecture." She stiffened, her cup halfway to her mouth, her gaze locked on his.

He fell silent, lashing her with pangs of guilt. She was so tired of being watched, even on behalf of her family.

"I get it. Leon put you in this untenable position of babysitting me, and now you report my every move under obligation." She sipped her fast-cooling coffee. Another would be too much for her bank account to handle. "But see it from my side, please, Pierce."

He slumped. "I can't... I refuse to tell your family you died under my watch." He tossed her a lopsided smile. "Losing a limb? That they can handle."

"Do you really have a man on Turner duty?" She stared at her dwindling coffee, reminding herself that this was a treat, and those needed to be few and far between; otherwise, they'd lose their appeal.

"Yup."

She cradled the cup to her chest and gazed through the window, tears burning behind her eyes. "I'm sorry."

"Don't be. What E.A.F. did to you was brutal."

She laughed, on the verge of losing her shit. "It's Earth Armed Forces. They can do whatever they want, and the little people be damned." She set her empty cup down and rose. "You know my roster, what time I end my shifts. Send Clemence to my location."

"Shit, Wren. Please—"

"Goodnight, Pierce." She swiped her wrist over the paypoint and left him. As far as she was concerned, everyone could fuck right off.

The short shower did nothing to cool her anger. The few minutes pruning and spritzing her bonsai named 'Charlie X' did. She crooned to it, telling it how beautiful it was, what a wonderful green its leaves were, amid apologies when she clipped a few branches. Neither mentioned the nine that had died before it.

She sipped from a flask of splice as she read from her latest read: *Help! An Alien's Found My G-Spot!* Her cheeks flushed as the intimacy deepened, but she couldn't help the snigger when she highlighted sentences she was sure would draw the agent's attention.

Gailiqon spread her thighs, his forked tongue a gift from the gods. What he could do with it...

His dual-cock hit the G-spot every damn time, merging her breathless cries with moments of awe. Never had such pleasure saturated every inch of her body.

Wren sighed, wishing she could activate her O.D.I. and summon droolworthy images of Etterians—the only sexy aliens the news reported on. She gazed out her window with a smile twitching her lips, her mind filled with a bronze-skinned alien worshipping her body and summoning a wealth of orgasms. Hell, she'd settle for one glorious explosion of ecstasy not instigated by her own fingers.

But these days, what would she have to do to get a little action?

Chapter Two

Etterian Battleship Gladio

Comms Room

12254 Years, 8th Month

Cylo pressed a hand on either side of the spray's nozzle, tipping his head into the water and letting it pour over him. He gargled and flicked his head, his hair curling outward in relish. He grabbed his malehood, shivering at the touch. Attending to this task was required of all Etterian warriors, and this morning, a chore it was. A few quick pumps summoned the expected response—a lackluster fulfillment.

He was mid-dry when Afax's voice reverberated from Cylo's O.D.I. implanted in his wrist. "Asteroid incoming."

Eagerness exploded through Cylo, more than his chore had sparked. He tapped the blue button, ending the dryer.

"On my way." He marched to the replicator to order his armor for the day. "*Malia pa*," he muttered, catching his braided hair and snapping the clip on the end to stop it from unraveling.

Minutes later, he stood in the common, gripping the controller, his gaze on the tiny vid in his hands. Jerking to the right wasn't necessary, but in his many drone mining expeditions, he hadn't yet learnt to keep his body immobile and only move his arms. Still, the drone veered right, dodging a geyser of gas. Scans had shown the asteroid to be carrying gold. The chance of a nugget was too much to resist.

"Have you found anything?" Ronan asked, peering over Cylo's shoulder.

"Not yet," he managed through gritted teeth, not daring to blink, let alone glance at him.

Cylo's muscles ached from the constant tension. Not that he'd give up the experience for all the Maloidian steel in the known universe. A dot on the top right pulsed faster, indicating that he neared the target. Oh, to be able to inlay gold into a dagger's hilt...

A bright flash had him hitting the switch to halt the drone. A nudge to the left and right positioned it above the source. He tapped the center button then laughed. Excitement flooded his chest with warmth, reminding him to control his reactions better. He did but left a small smile.

In his quarters might have been preferable, able to soften his control. But the way his battle-bonds gathered around him meant they too shared in his enjoyment. He couldn't deny them that.

"By my calculations, this asteroid must have collided with another object to send it off its orbital path." Tias sipped his giyua juice, observing from across the common. "No planet nearby has a strong enough gravitational pull to have snagged it."

Cylo smirked. "So, you are saying I am lucky?"

Tias scoffed. "Luck is for the weak."

Cylo dismissed him, liking the idea that luck had played a role. Regardless, here, now, he could spend the next hour searching for gold.

"Cylo to the Hollow," Afax called through the intercom system.

"Alodon's balls," Cylo hissed, straightened, then forced himself to smother his disappointment. A summons to an interrogation could only come from his superior, Operations Commander Malo, and he dared not keep the male waiting.

Tias flicked his fingers. "I will get you your gold," he said.

As a data officer, Cylo trusted him to do so more than any of his fellow warriors.

"If I fail, we can follow this asteroid's path for a day or two longer." Tias slid the controller out of Cylo's grip then nudged him toward the door.

He marched along the passages to the Hallow—Malo's private interrogation room. Outside the door waited Trav.

"He is not in a good mood," he said by way of greeting.

"Why so?" Cylo asked, facing the door.

"Afax says we have been commanded to escort a Serratu Kayarra." Trav grinned. "She will be my first."

"She is Imarri ag Zennr, Operative," Malo snapped, stepped back, and gestured to them both to enter the room. "The favor is on behalf of Prince Citus. Any dalliance with the Maloidian operative would bring dishonor upon him."

"Not to mention that to do so would make us vulnerable to her skills?" Trav said, sliding into the room to lean against the solid Maloidian steel bulkhead.

"As pleasant as I imagine such an interlude would be, it is not worth the risk," Cylo said, standing beside Trav. Instead of relaxing, he chose to mimic Malo's stiff posture.

A five-by-five cube with gray walls, floor, and ceiling was impenetrable. Bolted to the floor was a steel table. For now, bright light filled the room, reaching into its dark corners. When needed, shadows could be enhanced enough to hide a warrior.

Malo paced the tight confines. "There are rumors of a Maloidian joining forces with Yithians. This does not bode well."

Cylo remained silent. Given time, Malo would reveal the reason behind the summons.

"Their addiction to bargains, the availability of billions of Earthians, and Earth's uncaring government enables an exploitation Maloidians would not be able to resist. I should have foreseen this though one Maloidian does not mean it should be a concern."

"We have battleships guarding their planet, do we not?" Trav asked.

"Indeed." Malo splayed his fingers on the table. "Still, we shall interrogate the Maloidian slave dealer and pray he values his life more than a deal." He tapped his O.D.I. "Bring him in."

The door opened to a yellow-skinned male. His tentacle-hair swayed as if underwater, serene in stark comparison to his dire circumstances.

"What is this?" he spluttered, glaring at Operative Ronan, who nudged him deeper into the room.

"Geffa, sit." Malo pulled out a chair with his booted foot.

The Maloidian hesitated. The spots from his brow to his hairline darkened. He sank onto the seat and clasped his hands between his thighs. "I...do not understand why I am here...with you." He snuck a glance at Malo then lowered it.

"This I cannot believe." Malo smirked for a moment before darkness consumed his expression. "King Xeus announced at the last Global Council meeting that Earthians are under Etterian protection." He tutted. "Of course, I am most surprised at finding a few in your care... And against their will."

Geffa blustered. "They agreed—"

Malo slapped the table, drawing a squeak from the prisoner. "Am I a fool?" Malo angled his head at Cylo. "What does the buzz say? Have I lost my well-earned reputation? Has the universe ceased to fear my name?"

"It must be so, Operations Commander," Cylo said, smothering a chuckle. "Perhaps you should demonstrate how well you protect Etteria?"

Malo grunted and withdrew his dagger, its blade glinting in the bright lighting. He spun it and offered it to Cylo, hilt first.

Cylo accepted and took a moment to admire the infamous dagger Malo's father had given him. The edge appeared razor sharp, typical of Maloidian steel. Even blunt, it would slice through bone with ease.

"Tell me, Geffa, who instigated your last mission?" Cylo leaned his hip on the edge of the table, hoping to convey a casual air. It might calm the Maloidian after meeting Malo.

"Um..." Geffa swallowed hard, a sheen of sweat forming on his brow. "I met a Yithian—"

"Where? Who?" Cylo studied the male. "And what did he say to entice you onto this path of death?"

"A slave ship threatened to blow up my little shuttle." Geffa sniffed.

Horror sent a chill down Cylo's spine. A male crying? He soothed an impending shudder. To feel is to fail—the Etterian motto they all embodied. Apparently, the Maloidians had no such creed. Well, not one that mattered. They lived for bargains. Thankfully, Cylo didn't need to deal with them like Prince Citus had to as Etteria's ambassador.

"So instead of fleeing, you formed a partnership with the most untrustworthy race in our known galaxy?" Cylo arched a brow.

"That is your opinion," Geffa snapped, showing some fire. "Maloidians find no fault with Yithians."

"Tokens are tokens," Cylo said, casting a glance at Malo with his arms folded across his chest. "You would sell your mother if she gained you an above-fair price."

Geffa spluttered.

"Do not bother denying it." Cylo flicked his hand. "Your Ambassador Barro has taught us much about your culture."

Geffa dipped his chin, averting his solid-black gaze.

"Nothing ill to say about such a prestigious male?" Cylo splayed his hands on the table, trapping the dagger.

"He is too ambitious, and *he* would sell his mother," Geffa spat.

"No lost favor between you two," Cylo mused.

"I do not know him, nor does he know me." Geffa raised his chin in adorable defiance. "We have not met."

"And yet, you united with Yithia in their quest to farm the Earthians. That sounds like an ambassadorial role."

Geffa scowled. "We took one female and returned her soon after. She was most unpleasant. I would rather face a sogair in a...room like this."

Cylo hummed at that bit of nonsense. "Are you saying a race known for its mercy delivered the female to her home? Did not jettison her from the nearest airlock?"

Geffa's yellow skin paled.

"It is as I thought." Cylo spun the dagger then passed it to Malo. "I am not in the mood to spill blood today, so if you would be so kind as to tell me everything I want to know, I will ensure your life is spared. Lie to me once, and your outcome will not be so positive."

"Good. Keep up the pressure," Malo muttered, too low for the Maloidian to hear.

"I am waiting, Geffa." Cylo flashed a charming smile. "Or would you prefer I hand you over to Malo to deal with? He is most anxious to demonstrate his skills."

"Oh, I am?" Malo growled.

"They offered me a choice. Help kidnap these females or die." Geffa scoffed. "I was forced into this. She was not our first, but she was the last. The two before her...died."

Ice coated Cylo's heart, eradicating any good humor he was in. "How?" he asked, his tone clipped.

"One punched the Yithian in the face and scraped her knuckles over his teeth." Geffa trembled, his lips flapping as if he was about to vomit. "The other...I was told, threw herself out of the launching shuttle."

Cylo scowled. What he'd heard of Earthian females was on par with the punch but not the plummet. They fought even when it was foolhardy to do so.

"I see you plan to die this day," he gritted out. "How did the second one die, Geffa?"

"I told you—"

Cylo stabbed the blade an inch above the Maloidian's heart. "How?" he whispered, bringing his mouth to the male's ear.

Geffa gasped, clutching his chest as blood spilled from between his fingers. With a perforated lung, he would live. "A soldier pushed her out."

"So why hide this?" Cylo frowned. "What do you gain by keeping this from me?" He paced, slicing glances at Geffa with every turn. "Unless she was not the second to die. How many before her? After her?"

He clenched his jaw. This disrespect for life grated him, especially when each female lost meant an Etterian male not saved from the void consuming their souls. The lifemate bond known as the Ethera wouldn't be triggered, and no damu would be born to save their species. Perhaps Maloidians and Yithians killed these females on purpose? Malo, no doubt, understood what motivated them. Cylo did, as well, to some extent. But deep down, there were hidden triggers that most were oblivious to. Even him.

"How many?" he roared, slapping the table.

Still clutching his wound, Geffa jerked back, his skin paling to a giyua yellow. "Six...teen."

Fury exploded through Cylo. He gripped the handle, on the verge of plunging the dagger into the male's chest again. This time, he wouldn't miss.

"Names, now, or you die squealing like the migtak you are." Cylo smoothed his lips, hiding the derision. He was failing, his lack of control unusual.

"But..." Geffa stuttered. "Names of the Yithians? Of the females?"

"The ship, its destination, how many were on board when we found you?" Cylo leaned in, bringing the shadows with him.

Geffa pursed his lips then muttered, "*Zannwar*, Mascroba, twenty-seven."

Cylo paused. A standard Yithian ship carried a crew of twenty. "Why seven extra?"

"I do not know," Geffa said. "I am not curious about their staffing."

"Do you know nothing about Yithian protocol?" Cylo snapped.

"No, only the bargain matters." Geffa raised his chin in defiance.

Cylo snorted. "And yet you gained nothing from this."

The Maloidian winced. "So it seems."

"Either you are the worst Maloidian at negotiating, or you are lying. Shall I disparage your name and that of your family, for surely, their skills are now in question?"

Geffa spluttered. "We are excellent—"

"Ah, so you are lying to me again." Cylo flicked out the dagger and sliced off a tentacle.

While Geffa screamed with his hand pressed to his scalp, Cylo tossed the squirming length onto the table.

"I will die at your hands, as you say." Geffa sniffed as if offended. "Etterians do not deceive though this is not what I would call honorable."

Cylo grinned at the male gathering his courage around him.

"Telling you anything more will only delay the inevitable." Geffa glared. "So...kill me and be done with it."

"Oh?" Cylo arched an eyebrow. "You die when I decide you do and not a moment sooner."

"I will not speak under torture." Geffa's voice was strong, but he dipped his gaze, not meeting Cylo's.

"I grow weary of this," Malo muttered. "Kill him. Inform the two Yithians of his death."

"As you command," Cylo said and thrust the dagger into the Maloidian's heart.

He died on a gasp.

"Seven extra? Mm, that has me intrigued." Trav scooped Geffa's slumped body off the chair and carried him out.

"Could be visiting dignitaries or operatives." Malo held out his palm for his dagger.

Cylo handed it to him. "Like the Yithian prince Lady Quin killed?"

"Indeed," Malo said. "You did well, Cylo."

With a bow of his head, he held the Hallow's door open for Malo. "Will you be monitoring the Yithians' reaction to the news?"

"Yes, from the comm." Malo nudged his head in the comm room's direction. "Task Trav to do the interrogation. I do believe you have an asteroid to mine."

Cylo fought to smother a smile. "I do."

"Thought so." Malo chuckled and sauntered off.

Cylo bolted for the common, praying the opportunity wasn't lost or that Tias had good news for him. He burst in and weaved between the males gathered to reach the data officer's side.

The expression Tias leveled on Cylo dampened any joy he'd relished seconds ago.

"I am sorry, my battle-bond. I lost the drone." Tias lowered his chin to his chest.

"It happens," Cylo said even though he wanted to rail at the universe. Whenever anger consumed him, he was never to reveal it. Malo expected stoicism, control, self-discipline—all three Cylo had abandoned this day.

"I deployed another and got you this..." Tias waved a palm-sized gold nugget.

Cylo grinned. "I can do much with this. My thanks, Tias."

The male laughed. "I am glad. There is still time if you wish to mine more." Tias slapped him on the back. "With two drones."

"That would be incredible." Cylo kept his body rigid when he ached to bounce on his toes. "Let us prep them for launch."

Chapter Three

Demeter Science Station
Year of 2254, August

"Hey, Pony, you joining us for drinks at Escape?" Dallas asked, pulling Wren out of her focus.

She switched off the torch, flipped her welding shield up, and leaned back on her haunches to admire the neat seam. With a sweeping gaze, from left to right, a swell of pride engulfed her. Sure, she had far to go, but with all the beams she'd already done, she could rest on her laurels.

"Undecided," she said.

"You say that every damn time we ask." He huffed. "We're not going to stop inviting you, so you might as well accept."

She frowned and ran her gloved thumb over the welded seam her father would say was a job well done. Or not. She smiled and raised her gaze to a tourist ship inching past her location. Behind them were a few other ships, some she recognized. Beyond those was the endlessness of space, calling to her.

"I promise to consider it if you'll shut up about it." She stowed the torch and stood.

A whoop bombarding her ears made her wince, but thankfully, he said no more.

Her shift was almost over. If she wanted to leap, she'd need to store her tank and gear to make it to the tower. Sticky sweat layered her skin between her clothes and the suit. She itched for a shower, to slip into a baggy T-shirt, and spend some hours doing research on her Cherry Blossom bonsai. It had yet to bloom, but one of the online groups she belonged to had assured her that it would be soon.

Or she could read the latest in her alien romances.

She smirked and guided herself along the makeshift scaffold, using gentle flicks of her fingers on the support struts to float back to the tool locker. While stowing her equipment, she nodded at her colleagues, not daring to make eye contact lest it encouraged them to chat. They mumbled about their plans for the weekend. She had none and preferred it that way. After latching a refilled bottle of splice-laced water onto her suit, she sipped from the straw hidden inside her helmet. The burn started on her tongue and slid down her throat to coil delicious heat in the pit of her stomach. *Yes, I needed this.* Without a backward glance, she launched herself toward the tower crane. It took moments to unclasp the cord and hook it to her ankle harnesses. All accompanied by sips from her cocktail. She didn't drink on the job, not wanting to risk getting caught. Possession of splice, though somewhat legal, would get her fired.

But she was off-duty now.

One more yank of the tether to the harnesses had her grinning. Along the crane she climbed, thunking along with her boots activated. Not that she heard a thing, just the vibration traveling up her legs from the magnets connecting and releasing. At the top, the crane stretched farther out. It must have been used that day. She laughed, grateful for the extended reach. This morning's leap had gone uncontested, without a single station-sec showing their faces. So much for Pierce's twenty-four-seven Turner duty.

Hooking the tether to the 'highest' cross beam, she straightened, closed her eyes, and drew in a deep breath. When she swept her gaze across Pluto, she pushed off, throwing herself at its moon, Charon. She spread her arms out wide like an eagle riding the air currents. If she waved her limbs, would it be considered 'making space angels'? She didn't know but did it anyway, giggling at her silliness.

"Urgent communication from Earth Armed Forces–Justice Division," a robotic voice, a little too feminine, droned in her ear. Before she could reject the comm, the automation continued, "Receipt documented for 0606/1806. Turner, Wren, Identification number: 222510180522081-A, age twenty-nine, on parole for corporate espionage."

"Yeah, yeah, get on with it," she snapped. E—e

The voice ignored her, programmed to deliver a message within set parameters. "Scheduled release interview delayed due to poor performance. Twenty-four months added to sentence."

She jerked back then cried out, "Two more years? For what?"

"Information classified."

Heat lambasted her body and not the good splice kind. "The hell it is. Declassify it."

"Message complete." A beep announced the call had ended.

She screamed, writhing in place as her anger poured out of her. No way would she stand for it. She'd log a call with her parole officer. Gunnar no more wanted her to be on his roster than she did. He'd know what to do. Maybe pull some strings to find out who the hell had done this to her and why? She'd been a good girl, damn it. She twitched her lips to snatch onto her straw for a deep suck but got nothing but air.

Of all the— She cursed. Her splice was gone when she needed it the most. Using the tether as leverage, she flipped onto her back, preparing to drag herself to the station. She needed alcohol and lots of it. But first, she'd shower, comm Gunnar, then drown herself in her sorrows.

"Dallas," she growled.

"What does my fair maiden require?" he asked, trying to mimic her elocution.

"Cut it out. If you're paying tonight, I accept your invitation." She locked onto the crane's metallic frame and headed for its base.

"Damn it, Pony," he grumbled. "By the sounds of it, you plan to drink us under the table."

"It's that or I, unfortunately, cannot attend." She unlatched her water bottle and gave it a shake.

A scowl formed. Did she have any splice stashed at home? She groaned after mentally running through her hidey holes. Nope. This had been her last. She'd need to head to the lower levels for a little...shopping. As a matter of urgency.

"Fine, I'll pay if you wear a dress." His mocking tone didn't make her wince, but the idea of not wearing pants did.

She grimaced. Never again would she dress up for anyone. "I don't own such a garment."

"I'll send one over." He hung up on a chuckle.

"Still won't wear it," she muttered and slid the bottle into its slot but fumbled, sending it spinning off into space.

Her name was stamped onto the metal flask. One sniff would tell anyone finding it what had once been inside it, guaranteeing her a one-way ticket to Mars' penal colony. Panic seized her. In one hand, she held the hook to her harnesses, glanced at the escaping bottle to judge whether she had time to secure the cord to her ankles, then cursed. She didn't. Praying her grip would hold, she launched herself after the bottle.

Splice vendors were by station law required to inform her that the consumption of splice was hazardous to her health, especially if she was pregnant. None had mentioned this scenario. She was running out of cord with the bottle blithely on its journey.

A sob lodged in her throat. Tears stung her eyes and splashed on her visor. *Now isn't the time to cry.* She clenched her jaw and extended her arm, her finger inches from the bottle. Each passing second sent it farther out of reach. Swinging herself out with one hand on the end of the tether, she tried again. She brushed the lid and sent it catapulting away.

For a split second, she considered setting it free, but space was a capsule, trapping everything in a 'time' vacuum. A decade from now, someone could find it and know about her little habit. Without considering the risks, she tapped her boots and shot forward, the power from her boosters forcing her to release the cord. She caught the bottle, trapped it to her chest with both arms, then tried to spin.

Pierce had made it look so easy.

Nothing was going her way today. She tumbled into a spiral. At least she headed to the station, but at this momentum, she'd collide with something if she didn't gain control. She locked the bottle into its slot then pulsed the boosters, slowing her 'descent.'

A grin formed despite the thundering of her heartbeat in her ears. Her breathing was ragged, and sweat droplets merged with her tears.

"Fuck yeah!" She laughed at the adrenaline punching through her.

Angling her body sent her toward the crane. She'd pull the cord in and head home.

What she needed was another splice. Her insides were jittery, and an unnatural thirst made her tongue stick to the roof of her mouth. A tingle spread from her stomach to the tips of her fingers. She frowned and brought her hand into her line of sight. Nothing looked abnormal; it was gloved, five-fingered, and steady.

Ice drenched her body, sucking the air from her lungs. One moment she was perspiring like a hover jockey at the races, then her suit was gone, and she was suspended in a yellow-lit room. Gray metal lined the walls, ceiling, and floor.

"What the hell?" She blinked, twisting in the anti-gravity cube to face a door. "How the hell did I get here, and where is here?" Had that last sip of splice killed too many of her brain cells? Had she lost her mind? She wiped her eyes and inched her ungloved hand away, hoping normality would surround her.

"Hello?" she called, swimming toward the door. It had a porthole and might reveal who or what was behind it.

She caught herself against the chilled metal to peer out. A passage? With grated flooring and other porthole doors? She pulled back to tap her O.D.I. Holographic letters flickered to life.

"Dallas?" she whispered, cleared her throat, and tried again. "About tonight. I'll come in the nude." She waited, sure he'd respond to that.

Her breathing grew heavier while the seconds trudged by.

"Pierce?" she squeaked, praying he heard her. When he too remained silent, she scanned the room again. It did look like a prison cell. Solitary confinement? Had E.A.F. imprisoned her? Was this part of their punishment?

Movement caught her gaze, and she glided toward the porthole. Something crossed it, the unexpectedness jerking her back. She evened out her breathing and closed the distance.

And hit the floor with a squeal. A whimper escaped when pain radiated out from her hip and knee. The door slid open. Thunk, thunk preceded the appearance of a set of military boots on massive feet. She squeezed her eyes shut. *E.A.F. The bastards.*

"You were adrift. It is good we found you," the man rasped in Galactic. "We saved you."

"Saved me?" She staggered to her feet, pausing to rub where bruises had to be forming. "Scared me is what you did. What the hell do you—?" Her voice lodged in place and formed a lump.

Before her stood a massive silver-skinned shark with his beady, black eyes, two slits for a nose, a super wide grin with sabertooth fangs pressing on his bottom lip, and a neck that reached his broad shoulders. He wore no shirt, but black cargo pants clung to his narrow hips. A black pistol-like weapon was holstered to his thigh.

A Yithian.

She gaped. Sure, she knew about them, Maloidians, and algris, but never would she have thought she'd get to meet one.

"My...thanks," she managed, years of manners bred into her.

"Lizu," he said, touching his chest with his three-fingered hand.

"Wren," she said. "I'm grateful for the rescue, but I do need to return to the station."

"That is no longer your home. You have another...destiny." His solid-black eyes twinkled, but her gaze locked onto a droplet of saliva sliding down a fang. *Venom.*

“I beg your pardon?” she said, dragging her focus to his eyes.

“We are testing our stasis chambers. Many of your females have died.” He ventured deeper into the cell, forcing her to stumble back or be touched.

The way fear prickled every inch of her skin told her she was in big trouble. Panic, worse than losing the bottle, had immobilized her muscles. “Did you say died?”

“Yes. The chemical that places your bodies in stasis needed to be perfected.”

She had to be dreaming, and if she knew that, then she was lucid. Maybe she could...

“Lizu, I do need to head home.” She flashed him a smile.

He twitched, then scowled. “I do not wish to mate with you, female.”

“I don’t want you either,” she snapped, stunned that her dream mind thought that. Well, after all her alien smut, she should have expected her fantasies to change. Maybe she needed to get laid? How long had it been anyway?

“Then do not smile at me.” He gestured to her mouth.

“Sorry. I was being polite. Regardless, get me back.”

“No.” He walked backward, his gaze fixed on her.

She followed but kept a little distance between them. “I insist.”

He chuckled, clicking and hissing.

“I mean it, Lizu. Set me free...or else.” She patted her hips, searching for her multitool still attached to the waistband of her space suit.

“I am glad you will live, Wren.” The door slid shut on his glee.

“Fuck,” she screamed and shoved against the steel.

There were no handles, which meant there had to be a panel to control access. She patted the sides, hoping to find something she could pry open and manipulate. Electronics had to be universal, right? Besides, she had to try.

She swallowed a whoop when the lid of a box slid aside. Colored buttons shone, and underneath them were letters in a language she didn’t know.

“Shit,” she whispered.

A Yithian had to mean a ship. Hell, this cell could be jettisoned for all she knew. Which meant self-contained with a set supply of oxygen? She wasn’t sure. Any of these buttons could do that. Or they could release a toxin and kill her. He’d said as much. A moment before her feet left the floor, an inactive button glowed blue.

That had to be gravity?

She hesitated, drew in a long breath, and pressed the button.

Her feet thumped down.

She grinned. *Well, well.*

They switched it on, and up she floated. Laughing, she hit the off. On, up. Off, down. Up. Down. On. Off.

The door opened to a scowling Lizu. He nudged her aside, snapped the panel shut, then welded it in place with a pen-like tool she couldn't help but admire.

"Before you go, what are the bad colors?"

His eyes narrowed. "Red, white, and green."

Again, he left her, sealing her fate as much as the locked door did. Up she floated. She let herself drift toward the ceiling. There had to be a maintenance trapdoor of sorts or a ventilation duct. Thin grooves marked square panels. The craftsmanship was next level because no matter what she tried, she couldn't get a good enough grip to peel a panel up. A hiss of air accompanied a sweet tang.

She grimaced and tucked her face into her tank top to possibly minimize inhaling the stasis chemical Lizu had mentioned. Already, the edges of her vision were tinged with black. She moved along the ceiling, panic making her hands tremble. Where she went, she left smears of blood, barely registering the sting from minor cuts.

Only her freedom mattered, as it had always done.

Her nose burned.

A brain fuzziness lured her, the kind that promised blissful, dreamless sleep.

An unusual warmth saturated her limbs, and any thought of escaping slipped away.

With a slow exhale and a dreamy smile, she succumbed.

Chapter Four

Etterian Battleship Gladio

Common Room

12254 Years, 8th Month

"What is *she* doing here?" Cylo didn't glance up from his drill—he was working through spear techniques. In a battle, he'd reach for his greatsword or a blaster, never a spear. But self-discipline required doing things he didn't like.

"We are to escort her to Argaxx. A favor for Ambassador Barro," Trav said, keeping his voice low enough for only those near to hear. "She is with us for one more day."

The 'she' in question was the notorious Imarri ag Zennr, a Maloidian operative and the leader of the Serratu Kayarra or Silent Sirens. She'd ordered from the rehydrator in the common and now leaned her curvaceous backside against the bulkhead, 'casually' observing.

For a female not Etterian, she was beautiful. Her pale-yellow skin glowed in the unforgiving lighting, catching her patterned markings fading into her swaying tentacles. He swept the room, focusing on all his males with their thick braids touching their heels. Etterian hair reacted to their moods, but Maloidian tentacles did not.

Somehow, her solid-black eyes seemed fathomless.

She caught him staring and smirked. "Careful, warrior," she mumbled.

He fumbled, almost dropping the spear.

Trav ducked with a grunt.

She pushed off the bulkhead and sashayed across the common. Silence gripped the room. Her garment exposed a little of her thigh—appearing smooth like the rest of her. What rumors Cylo had heard of her skill couldn't be true. Something about the rotation of her hips at the right moment, the way she could curl her tongue around a male's... He tried not to focus on the details when an operative should, but as an Etterian, mating her or any Serratu Kayarra would lead to his death.

Too late. He straightened and gritted his teeth. *To feel is to fail.* Malo wouldn't react as easily.

"Milady," Cylo said, keeping his tone cool. He dipped his head as a show of respect then offered her his back, once more spinning and thrusting the spear.

A huff preceded her exit, but he didn't allow the triumph surging through him to show. One small victory after his dismal failure? He threw down the spear and tackled Trav to the floor. They grappled, each trying to best the other, but he and Trav had been battle-bonds since the day Malo had chosen them for his brand of training.

Afax's voice breached the common. "Cylo and Trav to the Hallow."

Cylo slumped only for Trav to flip him over and pin him to the mat. The male weighed more than a fattened kreso and stank worse.

"I am surprised you only ask now," Trav said, leaping to his feet and offering Cylo a hand up. "She has been with us for a week or so."

Cylo huffed at the implication that he was unobservant or lacked curiosity. Both were poor traits for an operative. "This is the first time I have been able to gaze upon her."

"Indeed, she has been scarce. If I did not know of the wager among the Serratu Kayarra, I would almost believe she has spent the time finding her fulfillment."

The wager pertained to Malo. Cylo bit his tongue. What male would gamble his soul to lie with a female? Although, ten minutes with the renowned Imarri would surely expand the void's reach, especially in an elder, bringing them almost to the brink of death. He glanced at Durok, the older male on the verge of becoming a lima kuu, a great teacher. That he was reading from his tablet said much. No doubt some boring text on ancient Hatimaye techniques that most had forgotten for a reason.

That thought sent Cylo's mind into a spin. How had the Hatimaye, their fighting style, changed over the centuries? Perhaps there was validity in what Durok found fascinating.

"Hurry, Cylo. I wish to cleanse."

Cylo chuckled at Trav. "And risk Malo's wrath? Are you insane?"

Trav shrugged and jogged toward the barracks. Cylo veered left, striding down the passage to the room he'd been in a day ago. He slipped into a sweltering cell. Heat meant the prisoner was Yithian. Etterian armor regulated their internal temperature no matter the environment, but Yithians preferred the cold of space. A silver-skinned male sat at the steel table while Malo faced a display vid. The splash of red hair confirmed the female on the comm as Princess Oriana.

"Just be confident, courteous, helpful but not generous with the information, and they will reveal their intentions. Your contact is Director Adam Reyes. I have known him for a while. He's trustworthy." She peeked at her Eth, Prince Enyl, then flashed Malo a grin. "Oh, and Malo, do enjoy this off-time." The panel went black, but the sound continued.

"I do not like it when you talk to my males that way," the prince grumbled.

"Why not? Everyone knows only you rock my boat." There came a giggle, then a throaty moan before the sound cut out.

Malo chuckled, but when he faced the room, no emotion crossed his features.

Cylo stared at the blank vid behind him, marveling at the warmth and sweetness in Princess Oriana's voice. Earthians lacked control in all aspects of their lives. Like damu. And for a warrior species such as Etterians, their disorderly conduct was an attraction he couldn't explain. He frowned at the Yithian, one of the Maloidian's two companions. Odd that they would unite. Cylo had always thought Yithians were hated by all. Not that every one of them was evil. He didn't believe that when he should. As an operative, he only dealt with the soldiers. Somewhere in the depths of Yithia's green oceans were families, farmers, and who knew what else? They couldn't all want to corrupt the universe.

He stepped into the bright, white light which cast his face in darkness but spilled onto the prisoner, making him visible to the sec-vids. Malo taught that the battlefield was in the mind, and not fully seeing the interrogator added tension and fear.

The Yithian wasn't cowed. His broad shoulders, wide neck, and big head formed their own shadow across the table. His black eyes revealed no secrets, and as he sat there, dripping off a fang and onto his sleeveless tunic was a droplet of venom—cytotoxins, able to break down a body on a cellular level. Few knew that Etterian operatives suffered for years to build an immunity to most poisons out there, including Yithian venom. He made a mental note to check his virak, to refill all the vials, and perhaps sip a few.

He smothered a smirk. Malo's conversation with Prince Enyl while the prisoner listened in meant the poor male wouldn't leave the Hallow alive. Malo caught Cylo's gaze and gave him an almost imperceptible nod. Cylo drew his blaster and pressed the barrel to the back of the Yithian's head coated with sweat. Yithians couldn't abide extreme heat.

The male would dehydrate with his skin cracking and bleeding, followed by asphyxiation. For an average Yithian, from dehydration to death took twenty-two minutes.

"This is the last time I ask you, Smez." Malo glared at the Yithian operative. "What is Yithia's interest in Earthian females?"

"For the arena," Smez panted, his shoulders dropping an inch. When he shuffled on his seat, the movement cracked the skin on his arms and hands. Silver scales flaked off. Gray blood seeped out. The room filled with a salty tang along with the stench of raw kreso. He moaned in agony. "The arena, I swear, Etterian." He writhed, the smell of his sweat tainting the air further.

"I do not believe you, xemi," Malo roared and slammed his hands on the table, rattling it.

Smez jerked away, widening his wounds.

Malo's lip curled, a reaction Cylo hadn't expected to witness. "Earthians are weak, tiny, and easily killed. Their deaths have no purpose."

"Champion Ori served Yithia well," Smez stuttered.

All knew who Ori was. Prince Enyl had rescued her from the Yithian arena, and in doing so, discovered that she was his Dar Eth. The darkness known as the void within all Etterians would no longer expand for him, nor threaten to consume everything that made him Etterian: compassion, restraint, honor.

Smez slid out a thick and swollen dark gray tongue to lick his dry lips. "Water, please," he croaked.

He had approximately four minutes until death. When Malo stared at the male, his expression one of thought, Cylo withdrew a cannister from a hidden alcove. Malo scowled and glanced at Cylo, who obediently sprayed a fine mist over the prisoner. The Yithian sighed in bliss as a few of his wounds sealed themselves. A healthy shimmer returned to his skin. It wouldn't last.

"Let me understand you." Malo narrowed his eyes. "Yithia kidnaps females looking for another champion? All this expense? We know you have more females than what we have rescued. We have not seen them in the arena. Where are they, Smez?"

The Yithian smirked.

"You do not take this seriously, xemi," Malo growled then spoke to Cylo. "Your turn or mine?"

Cylo hesitated, the urge to kill the xemi or 'scum' pressing on his sense of justice. "Yours, Operations Commander."

"Truth?" Malo grunted.

"Yes, I dealt with the Maloidian, if you recall."

Malo retrieved the Maloidian throwing dagger he'd strapped to his upper arm. Cylo was in the process of crafting such a four-blade holster, the design ancient since it had been a gift from Malo's father before he'd died on Gikaet.

The Yithian stiffened at the sight of the compact blade.

Malo paused to study the gleam off the blade. "I have been most lenient with you, Smez, due to our history. I see you would prefer to take advantage of our bond. This is not wise."

"I cannot betray Yithia, Malo. They have my estuuba." Smez's eyes pleaded as only soulless, black eyes could.

Holding the dagger to Smez's finger, Malo whispered, "What family? I know you too well for that lie to affect me." He angled the blade to catch the light. "You only have three fingers. It would be a shame to lose one."

Smez pinched his lips in open defiance.

Malo sliced the finger in one clean stroke, the bone not impeding the blade. The Yithian screamed, curling his remaining two fingers into his palm. His silver finger lay in gray blood.

"I said I would not ask you again, Smez. What I *will* ask is which finger is next? I will allow you the illusion of choice." Malo arched a brow.

"You are a bastard, Malo." Smez clutched his hands to his chest.

Malo grabbed his wrist and twisted. The prisoner squeaked but couldn't prevent Malo from pinning his wrist to the table.

Smez's gaze followed the descent of the blade. "Iphara. There's a laboratory on Iphara."

Malo frowned, stopping the blade just above Smez's middle finger. "Why a laboratory? To what purpose?" He cast a glance at Cylo.

Blind fury consumed Cylo. He tightened his hand on the blaster, ready to fire.

"We seek to understand the attraction," Smez panted. "Why do Etterian males prefer Earthian females?"

"That is illogical. This does not serve Yithia." Malo brought down the blade.

Smez twitched his fingers. "Compatibility," he spat. "If Earthians are compatible with Etterians, they may be with other species."

"You wish to sell them." Malo blinked.

Sell Dar Eths? Cylo stepped closer.

"As pleasure slaves." Smez's shoulders slumped.

"Where on Iphara?" Cylo demanded, raising the blaster.

"In an underground chamber. Few Yithians are aware of it," Smez blurted.

"How many females are there?" Cylo roared and withdrew his blade.

Malo scowled. Cylo didn't care if his reactions disappointed his commander. Females were in danger, bartered like kreso, as...sex slaves.

"Seven," Smez stammered, his solid-black gaze riveted on Cylo. "They showed no warrior skills, were too weak. Nor did they resist the soldiers sent to retrieve them."

"How long have they been there?" Malo demanded.

"They were delivered four days ago," Smez mumbled, then trembled. Sweat dripped off his chin even as his skin paled under fresh cracks. "May Calzantu forgive me."

Cylo glanced at Malo, asking to kill this male. When Malo inclined his head, Cylo struck, slipping the tip between the Yithian's two vertebrae at the base of his neck. He fell forward. His death was swifter than Cylo would've liked, but finding these females took priority.

"Take a scimitar, liaise with the patrolling battleships, and save those females. Once you have them, ensure the laboratory is destroyed from within. There must be no indication of our involvement," Malo commanded. "And deal with this." He gestured to Smez.

Cylo hoisted the male over his shoulder.

"Leave the finger," Malo growled. "Have Trav deliver Uloz."

"Yes, Operations Commander." Cylo marched out of the Hallow and dumped the body on the first operative he came across. He spun on his heel and headed to the comm. Afax was in the pilot's seat, as usual. Males went about their duties. "I need a pilot, a data officer, a medic, and four operatives."

Afax didn't flinch. "Sending them to the scimitar *Kevol*."

Cylo released a long exhale. "My thanks."

"All of Etteria is with you." Afax's blessing reached Cylo long after he'd left the comm—the wonders of Etterian enhanced hearing.

Seven males waited for Cylo when he strode into the docking bay.

"I will brief you en route," he said as he marched up the ramp into the shuttle bay. Fully stocked, he wasn't surprised to find a kuta taking up most of the space.

Once they were inside and the bay doors closed, he addressed them. "Pilot Fyca, the destination is the island of Iphara. Data Officer Olin, monitor the buzz for any information on random Yithian ships heading to and from the island. We aim to rescue seven Earthian females."

Medic Qaff stiffened, spinning the med-gun between his agile fingers. "Are they unwell? Why would the Yithi—"

"Kidnapped while we guard Earth. This is unacceptable." Cylo met each one's gaze. "Malo ordered us to save them and destroy the facility. Any objections?"

"So, full fusion pulse?" Fyca arched a brow as he exited the common.

Within minutes, the battleship *Gladio* was behind them, and a critical task lay ahead. While sipping a giyua juice from the rehydrator, Cylo watched his males train, using the limited facilities the scimitar could provide. So far, only males of rank had met their Dar Eths. The buzz was that at this rate, it would be ages before the ordinary warrior would find his soul's salvation. He didn't believe that nonsense. Circumstances had interfered. Prince Enyl stumbling on the first Dar Eth from among humans had been the catalyst. Kanzo wasn't a commander or royalty. He was elite but a warrior whom the Maker had blessed.

Any operative meeting his female would prove that the superior ranks weren't keeping the humans to themselves. Desperation was behind these rumors, but to Cylo, that smacked of a lack of faith.

As a youngin, he'd often thought of his pairing. Then, it had required a trip to Issneen to attend a pairing ceremony in the hopes his Dar Eth would be there. If she was, what would follow was supposed to be mating once per day for three days and a chance to learn to love his lifemate. He would save her as much as she ended the void's expansion within him.

To find such a female was a blessing he'd never truly yearned for. It was rare. And required the right circumstances for every Etterian.

His breath hitched at the possibility of a human female being his. The few he'd seen had varied in appearance. They weren't like Etterians who shared the same hair and eye color. He didn't care what his Dar Eth looked like.

Hope blossomed like the Magnus sun dawning on his home village of Vahnal. He tamped it down with one thought. Whoever she was would change his life. It meant no certain death, but it also could mean leaving his chosen career. His position as an operative had been his goal for so long. Would she stay on a battleship with him?

Maker, I hope so.

Chapter Five

Unknown Location
Anti-Gravitational Cell
Year of 2254, August

Time blurred. Wren slid in and out of consciousness. She had vague memories of a sharklike man forcing her to drink water. Still, when she skimmed the edges of wakefulness, thirst bombarded her. Something seemed off, but she couldn't put her finger on what, nor did she care enough to bother about it. Sleep enticed her to linger, to sink into its blissful depths.

A full-body jerk forced her to open her eyes. Cold skin touched her bare arms then clutched her to a chest. She blinked at the face of a shark. A familiar odor assailed her, one she'd encountered too often on her splice shopping—piss. She grimaced. Had she soiled herself, and when?

He released her and stepped back, no doubt affected by her stench. Her skin was icky, too, as if she hadn't showered in a while. She ran her swollen tongue over her teeth that probably had moss growing on them, they were that furry.

"What's going on? Why have you taken me?" she demanded, but her voice was reed thin, raspy...from lack of use.

"Drink," he ordered, shoving a liquid packet at her.

She obeyed, uncaring if it was poison. Her tongue had stuck to the roof of her mouth. Unwilling to take the time to figure out how to open the packet, she ripped it with her teeth and drained it.

"Eat," he said, tossing a bar at her.

She needed answers, but she was starving. Four bites later, despite the plastic-and-bitter taste, she covered her mouth to burp. “Sorry,” she said. “Ate too fast.” Then scowled at her politeness. *He’s my...abductor, for fuck’s sake.*

“Good.” He inched toward the door.

“Wait,” she said, scrambling to her feet. Her gaze caught on the dissolving wrappers. One moment they were there, the next... Poof. “Um, where are you taking me? How...” She rubbed her face and winced. “How long have I been here?”

“We are descending. If you behave, I will not stun you.”

“Huh?” She frowned at him, unsure how bad a stun could be. Did he mean tase? “Listen here, Lizu, what the hell’s going on? I’m a human, and I have rights.”

He laughed, hissing and gurgling. “You are entertaining, little one. It is unfortunate that you will not survive what is to come.”

“What?” she squeaked, closing the distance between them.

He shuffled back, matching her movement. “You will be on Iphara. The kuliriji has not been successful so far, but as a Yithian, I do find you appealing. I hope he succeeds with you.” With his menacing black eyes, he ran his gaze over her body.

Her skin itched under his none-too-friendly perusal.

“So far, Earthians cannot survive our venom. But I am intrigued by your...kissss? Am I saying that correctly?” He shrugged.

“Lizu,” someone shouted. Behind him appeared another Yithian, a woman draped over his shoulder. “Do not tell her everything,” he snapped.

“She might live. I would like her to think of me favorably.” Lizu scooped up Wren and tossed her over his shoulder like a sack of dirty laundry, her hands dangling past his ass.

And without taking her wants into consideration. She pummeled his back then gave up when all that it gained her were bruises.

“This isn’t endearing you to me,” she said, holding herself up with splayed fingers across his fishlike skin. She tried not to shudder.

What he’d said awaited her and the other women sounded like experimentation. No way was she staying complacent for that.

“Iphara? Where is that, Lizu?” she asked, keeping her tone light even as panic clawed up her throat.

“A small island near Mascroba.” He juggled her, slapping her stomach against his solid shoulder. Each time, pain lanced outward and snatched her breath.

"And that is?" she managed to ask.

"The Royal City of Yithia."

"Fuck," she whispered, her voice strangled. She was heading to another planet. Not Pluto, Mars, or any of the ones she knew of. A foreign, hostile Yithia was their destination. She shivered when chills raised the goose bumps across her skin.

Focus. She drew in a breath. Island meant having to steal a boat to escape. But where was safe? How could she survive when the plant and animal life were unknown? Some planets had acid instead of water. Yithia could be one of those. Which left getting off-world her only choice. She'd need a ship. And a pilot, but the one ally she had was her abductor.

"Lizu, why me?" she asked, then frowned. "Wait, how long have I been with you?"

"Fourteen days," he said.

She swallowed her tongue. Two weeks? Her family would believe she was missing. All would know she'd been hitting the splice, and worse, the chance of a rescue was in the negatives. She doubted anyone had seen her get taken. But she refused to give up hope. There had to be opportunities, and when they arose, she'd grab them.

Staying friendly with her would-be suitor had to do, for now.

"Lizu," she whispered, peeking at the other Yithians. Their hostages were limp. *Shit.* No help from that quarter. And she wasn't sure she could save them either when her future was as bleak. "Will you let them hurt me?"

"If it makes you compatible with me, then yes."

She growled. *Strike one, asshole.*

"I do hope the formula works on you, Wren. I find your hair unusual."

Just her hair? She seethed, curling her fingers into fists. "Formula?" Oh, yes, an anti-venom to survive the cytotoxins in his saliva. "Like a vaccination or a chemical to trigger a drastic transformation?" Superhero powers right about now wouldn't go to waste.

"I do not know." He whipped her off his shoulder and shoved her against a bulkhead.

The shuttle's compartment was tiny, made crushing by the six Yithians crowding the space. The women were dumped on the metal floor though the Yithians had been gentler than she'd expected. With what she knew about this species, they were anything but considerate. They must not have wanted to damage the test subjects.

"Sedate her," a shark hissed, glaring at her through one scarred eye.

Lizu stiffened and faced the man. "The kuliriji said nothing about keeping them asleep."

One Eye smirked, adding a diabolical twist to his features, especially when venom dripped onto his sleeveless shirt. "He did say—"

"On the journey, which I did." Lizu stood firm.

"We will let him decide. I will not stop him when he kills you." One Eye settled in the cockpit and slapped a button.

The door shut, trapping her. Staying in her old cell or stealing their ship wasn't an option. Not anymore. Besides, she didn't know how many were on the crew. Though, taking it would have been ideal. Commandeer their ship and fly home.

Sounded easy.

She scoffed then lowered her head when a few sharks glanced at her. Now, if she could 'seduce' Lizu without dying from his spit, maybe he could be the pilot. Right, seduce a venomed alien who might not know how to fly anything, even this stupid shuttle?

She rubbed her nose to hide where she looked. His blocklike gun was within reach. Pickpocketing that without his notice would be damn hard, not to mention that it would focus all their attention onto her. No. She needed a knife—dagger, paring, butter—she didn't care. Yet none had such a weapon holstered to their belts.

In their boots?

She faked a sneeze, bending over to do so. *There*. Something glinted in Lizu's chunky boot. She smothered a smile. For all she knew, it was a buckle. No need to get too excited just yet. Rubbing a heel across her ankle brought the ring on the ankle harness to the forefront. It was all she could do without being too obvious.

She squared her shoulders then touched Lizu's arm. When he focused on her, she leaned in. "May I fix my boot?" She pointed down and waited, praying he didn't do it for her. He'd find out for sure she was lying. She clenched her jaw and kept her body lax.

"Yes."

With a slow exhale, she crouched and fiddled with the metal ring, her gaze on the glint in his boot. It *was* a knife. She chewed on her lip. He'd feel it if she tried to inch it free.

Think.

She made to rise. Faking a cry, she 'fell' forward, catching herself on his impressive calves. It took a second to wrap her fingers around the hilt. But to slide it ou—

He hoisted her up and pushed her against the bulkhead. "We are about to land."

"Oh," she said. "Thank you."

With the dagger between her forearm and thigh, she tried to tuck it out of sight. Where to stick it was the next dilemma. In her boot made sense, but when and how? Soon, he'd carry her over his shoulder again.

Had he said land? She ducked, slipped the dagger into her boot, then danced from side to side as if she wanted to 'see' through the windshield. Her heartbeat thundered in her ears while she 'misbehaved' like a child. She chanced a glance when he remained silent.

He scowled at her. "What are you doing?"

"What color is your sky? The land? Oceans? Let me see," she whined.

"It is good that you are curious." He grabbed her by her waist and lifted her, holding her like an offering to some nameless god.

But it gave her an unhindered view of his homeworld. She gaped at the pale-yellow sky with three suns. The ground was gray to black and the oceans an exquisite aquamarine to emerald green.

"It's pretty," she said, her voice breathless. She eyed the tiny island they were careening toward. *Shit.* She was running out of time.

"Our archive dwellers state that this world was once cold beneath layers of snow and ice. That Calzantu took pity on us and sent another sun. Since then, our lands dried up and our oceans shrank. The heat is unbearable, as would the loss of our cities be."

"The eventual death of our world is millions of years away," another Yithian said. "For now, our people are safe in our oceans."

"True, Diexa," Lizu said.

"Keeping her awake will not bode well for you," Diexa said, glaring at her like not being stunned was her fault.

She gritted her teeth, fury burning along her senses. They'd kidnapped and drugged her and planned worse. But if she lost her shit over their audacity, releasing all this pent-up emotion, she'd risk angering them. She wasn't that stupid.

The pilot spun around the hook-shaped end of the island before slamming down on a flat rock. She replayed the swift image she'd caught of the beach where no pier extended out nor boats bobbed alongside it. Why boat when they could shuttle? She swallowed a groan.

Jagged rocks broke the volatile waves, and off the shore were rows of trees with black bark and no foliage. She studied the ground and its lifeless soil where nothing grew, not even a random weed. Had a fire come through, burning everything in its path?

When Lizu tried to snatch her, she leapt aside. "I can walk," she said, raising her chin to meet his gaze.

"Lizu." One Eye pointed at her.

"She can walk," Lizu growled.

"The kuliriji will not be pleased."

"I do not know him other than displeased," Lizu said.

She coughed to hide a chuckle. Yithians could be sarcastic? Entertaining, but in this situation, there sure as hell wasn't anything to laugh about. A knife in her boot gave her a false sense of security. She wasn't an idiot to think she could take on seven sharks and remain unscathed. And Lizu had said 'stun.' She grimaced. That didn't sound pleasant.

The door to the shuttle opened, hitting her with a blast of sunbaked sea air. She breathed it in, having not smelled anything this good in ages.

With a nudge at her back, she followed the parade down the ramp and onto the rock. Her 180-degree view showed no buildings. They headed toward a clean section of the beach, only to halt.

"Truly?" One Eye asked, slapping the holographics on his wrist, then he gestured with a finger to turn.

Back they went, around the sleek, silver-gray shuttle—with a pointed nose and boxy ass—then into the trees. The ground crunched under her boots. She stroked a tree in passing, expecting soot to line her fingertips. But the bark was solid. With a stumble, she scanned them all. They weren't dead.

On they marched, no one paying the macabre scene any attention. Some of the women were beginning to moan; they, too, were ignored. Away from the shore, they continued, then around the hill and onto a worn path that cut into the rock. Partial shadows fell across them, granting a little reprieve from the three suns. Icky, sweaty, and smelly? She shuddered, wishing she could walk into the waves splashing onto the beach, willing to risk them being acidic for the chance to be clean. And she should've asked before they left that side of the island. But she doubted One Eye would've let her. *What an ass.*

They veered right under an overhang and onto a paved patio. Glass windows lined it and stretched along the structure built into the cliff. She admired the façade and smiled.

This was stunning. Typical of a science facility to be architecturally beautiful while death coated the walls within. A double door opened on silent wheels. She followed it with her gaze, noting the ridges of metal beside the grooves.

"About time you arrived," a yellow-skinned man demanded, striding toward them across a beautiful marbled foyer. He wore a long, purple tunic that brushed his booted feet. The flowing garment made her think of Earth's religious gurus.

"We lost many, Criass," One Eye said.

Criass jerked to a halt, scanned the group, then settled his solid-black gaze on Wren. "Why is she not sedated?" His strange tentacles swayed like a feathered headdress.

"I asked not to be," she said, dragging her focus away from his 'hair.' "Besides, I stink. No one should carry me."

Fire exploded across her cheek. She stumbled to the side, blood pooling in her mouth. Pain radiated outward, and she'd swear he'd shaken a few of her teeth loose.

"Why did you do that?" she asked, moaning when she poked her gums with her tongue and tasted the metallic tang of her blood.

"Do not speak," he snapped. "She will be first. Bring her."

Someone shoved her forward, forcing her to straighten or she'd sprawl onto the floor.

"She is right." One Eye sniffed the air around her. "Let us cleanse them before you begin your experiments."

She froze. Cleanse? As in bath? But the word 'experiments' gripped her thoughts and wouldn't let go. 'Hell no' formed in her mind, but she didn't dare say anything.

"You are done here, Captain. My people will take over." With a wave of his hand, more yellow-skinned aliens spilled across the 'hotel' foyer, their slippered feet not scuffing the polished stone floor. These aliens were skinnier than the Yithians, but still, with this many present, she wasn't about to try an escape. They'd recapture her and find her knife.

When a man swept her over his shoulder, she let him.

Now wasn't the time, but as soon as she could, she'd stab Criass in the neck. She was damn sure he didn't have a heart.

Chapter Six

Iphara Island
Planet of Yithia
Year of 2254, August

No one spoke as they hurried across the foyer. Any Yithians along the way kept their gazes down. That didn't give Wren a sense of peace. Shit was happening in this place that had to remain a secret. Why here, though? What was so special about this facility? The wide passages, decorated with tiny statues, narrowed until they reached an elevator. Its size was like a hospital's, able to take a gurney. Still, it wasn't huge enough for eight yellow men, their hostages, and Wren. The soil-scented air said they traveled far underground. She shivered, the cold seeping through her thin clothes.

The cage jerked when it stopped. Not that she had time to find her balance. In one surge, she was shoved out the door. She stumbled but managed to catch herself, splaying her fingers on the smooth wall to do so. She'd half expected to be in some sort of mine with rock-hewn walls, poor ventilation, and flickering light. The air was stale but had a chemical tang to it. Metallic panels and doors lined a narrow passage that headed left and right of her.

She had no doubts these men would go through with their threats. This place had a laboratory feel to its polished floors with sluice holes for easier drainage. No windows revealed what was inside each room; only narrow portholes high on the doors offered a glimpse. She couldn't pause long enough to peek.

They veered to the right as the rest of the group joined them. A sharp jab at her back drove her into a square chamber with a shelf stacked with white towels or clothes. Many drain holes ran along the other end. A coiled pipe that looked like a fire hose screamed this room's purpose. A hot shower would be preferable to what they planned. She gritted her teeth then winced when her fresh bruises pinged.

"Strip, and stand against the wall," Criass commanded. "If she gives you trouble, stun her." He smirked before leaving her alone with the other purple-robed men. They dumped the women with less care than the Yithians had shown.

She gaped. Pale yellow skin and tentacles for hair? Molods? Meloids? It didn't matter who these aliens were, but she had heard of their species. She frowned. Weren't they trade-faring people, dedicated to negotiating the best bargains? These men defied all she'd learned about them, not that it was much.

A few women moaned and sat up. Fear contorted their features; some sobbed or whimpered.

"Strip," a man said while uncoiling the hose.

Wren hesitated. The promise of a dousing, no matter how unpleasant, was too tempting to fight. Oh, to be clean again and not smell of piss... But she'd be naked.

"Turn around," she said, running her gaze across the voyeurs.

"Why?" One scowled, the black markings on his brow like tiny diamonds.

"For modesty," she said and waited, folding her arms across her chest. "Do this, and we will give you no reason to stun us."

"What?" a brunette asked, staggering to her feet. "I will not stand naked—"

"To be clean, I'll promise anything," Wren snapped at the woman. "Don't ruin this for me, for a chance to feel human..."

The others scrambled up, a few waking the last three still unconscious. All the women stared at the men until they offered their backs. Only then did they undress. Wren had never stripped faster. She was careful with the dagger, not wanting it to fall out and draw attention. With her boots set to one side and her dirty clothes draped over them, she faced the Hose Man.

A wall of foam descended, drenching her. Instinct had her closing her eyes, but a woman cried out. The shit had to burn then. Wren didn't dare peek. A click preceded ice-cold water blasting over her. It stole her breath. Goose bumps exploded into existence, chattering her teeth and summoning shivers.

She spun on the spot, hissing when the water reached warm parts of her. But at least it would wash away the foam. A few women pleading for the water to stop made Wren scowl. She said nothing, not knowing when next she'd get to be clean.

The spray shut off, leaving her dripping and trembling. Another man handed them each a garment while the hose was reeled in.

Wren yanked the robe on over her damp body, then slipped her feet into her boots, careful not to cut herself on the dagger. The others pulled on sneakers, boots, slippers, or sandals. None of the men stopped them.

Her hair wet the collar of the robe, but she didn't say a word, letting the men lead them single file to another room nearby. It had the look of a holding cell with a wide, metal bench lining the perimeter. A pale barrier formed the moment all the women entered the space. Wren studied it and grimaced—a forcefield of a sort.

"What's happening? How did we get here?" the brunette demanded, her face crumpling into a sob.

"We are Yithian prisoners on Iphara, their island," Wren said, sinking onto the bench. She cupped her cheek and worked her jaw.

"Yithians?" A petite blonde woman gasped, her eyes wide with fear. "I was in the park—"

"Fishing," a redhead muttered. "Took me right out of my boat. Name's Terry."

"Wren," Wren said, sprawling onto her back.

"Sandy." The brunette sniffed.

"Brenda," the petite girl whispered. "I was leaving my gym."

"We were all isolated," an older woman said, sweeping her gray-streaked hair back. "I'm Violet. Any chance of escape?" She whispered the last part.

Wren shook her head. "Unless you have a boat or a spaceship hidden nearby, we won't be going anywhere."

"You seem to know more than any of us." Terry strode closer, her gaze distrusting.

"I had a...kind jailor," Wren said, flicking a dismissive hand. "We're test subjects in the hopes of making us compatible for...sex."

Terry jerked back, her face twisting in disgust. "Why?"

Wren cast a glance at her. "I don't know."

"My children." A woman sobbed, rocking with her arms wrapped around her bent legs. "They'll think I abandoned them," she wailed, pressing her cheek to her knees.

Wren froze, ice colder than the dousing sliding down her spine. She swung her legs over the edge of the bench. Darkness engulfed her chest. If she could, she'd whisk everyone home. But all she had was the dagger in her boot. Even if they managed to overpower every man in this forsaken place, they were still trapped. Unless... One Eye had spoken to his wrist... He had an O.D.I., which meant they had to have some way of communicating with the outside world. Then again, sending out a mayday would probably bring down upon them the might of Yithia.

"Do any of you have weapons?" Wren rested her elbows on her knees and clasped her hands, praying she wasn't the only one armed.

Silence reigned with no one coming forward.

"Shit," she muttered, slumping. "Whoever they take first, your main focus is to stay alive."

Whimpers and mutterings fell across their little group. Their situation was dire.

"I could eat." An ash blonde offered a weak smile. "Call me Nora."

"Same. The bitter paste I last had coats my mouth." Terry shuddered.

The women mumbled among themselves, falling into natural conversation as if they'd known each other for years.

But they settled when a man strolled in, his gaze fixed on Wren. Criass had said she'd be first. She straightened and pushed off the bench, determined to face this madness with some dignity.

"Where are you taking her?" a woman with black curls demanded.

"Your turn will come," the man said.

The woman formed fists at her side, but Wren strode past her. "Don't worry about me. I'm glad I'm going first... I'll warn you—"

"You, with me." Another man pointed at the black-haired woman.

"I'm not a *you*. My name's Ronda."

"You females are always the same." The ass smirked, dragging Ronda across the forcefield after it shut off. "Your attitude will change once we are through with you."

Clammy fingers wrapped around Wren's upper arm. She glanced at them, sickly yellow against her skin. With a tug, he forced her to stumble forward.

"Come," he said.

He dragged her along the passage and through an open door, three rooms down. The steel table made her stop. It had a draining hole at one end, which didn't bode well. The sight of the four straps twitched her fingers. She wanted to grab her dagger and attack. Two men in purple faced her. A metal tray on a counter held many vials of colored liquid.

She swallowed hard and pressed her nails into her thighs, forcing the panic to settle in her stomach.

"On the plate," Criass snapped, gesturing to a disc sunk into the floor. Circular lights around its circumference pulsed in white, looking pretty and innocent.

"Why?" she asked, hesitating. If it was a metal detector, it would find the dagger.

Criass hissed and shoved her at the plate. She sucked in a sharp breath and stepped onto it. A beam scanned her, pausing across her pelvis, breasts, and head. Not once did it linger on her feet. A man pressed a device to her neck, pinching her arm to hold her still. The spike of a needle made her wince. Her neck didn't burn like he'd injected something into her. When he moved away, she glanced at him to confirm he'd taken a blood sample.

"We need a baseline," he said, his voice soft.

She stiffened, shocked to find some kindness. But she didn't thank him, when doing so might get him into trouble. Nice Guy slunk away to insert the blood-filled vial into a machine squatting on the counter.

Criass rattled off in a language she didn't understand, prodding her waist in the process. She could guess she was fatter than he'd expected, and sure, she had added on a few pounds since moving to Demeter. But the idiot didn't know that a single pound on a five-foot-four woman looked like five. She harrumphed, folding her arms across her chest. The glower she leveled on him had no impact. He tapped away on his tablet with far too much enthusiasm. The man derived joy from torture. She raised her gaze to the tiled ceiling. *Lord, please, if You're listening. Give this man a heart. Let him sob into his beer, or whatever the hell yellow aliens drink.*

"Excellent." He chortled. "Climb onto the table."

She shoved out her chin in defiance, not once glancing at the straps.

"You either get on by yourself, or I have someone do it for you." He gripped his tablet to his chest. His black eyes twinkled like tourmaline. The realization that he hoped she'd resist energized her.

"May I remove my boots?" She didn't wait for his answer and marched to a disused corner of the room. There she toed off her boots, bending to tuck the blade deep inside.

As short as she was, Nice Guy had to help her onto the table anyway. Gentle pulls stretched her limbs in place for him to fasten the straps on. She bit her inner cheek to silence the protests that jammed in her throat. Complaining would do nothing to help her escape. Spreading her legs when she wore no underwear inflamed her cheeks. She lay there, unable to move and vulnerable, but thankfully, the long, white robe covered her.

A ceiling tile above her head slid aside, revealing a gap to the floor above. An egg-shaped thing shot out on a hydraulic arm. It swooped down, flipped open to reveal a bright light, then ran over her from toes to head. She frowned. What was the point of two scans? Sure, standing on a plate might be like a scale, but what had the white beam done? The egg blinked, changing from white to ultraviolet. She shut her eyes just in case. Some stations had such mist sprays for sterilization, especially on those closest to mining colonies.

But when the warmth cooled, she peeked. The egg glowed red—infrared? She stiffened, so glad she'd removed her boots. The scan couldn't penetrate metal, but a dark-shaped dagger might have shown. Into the silence, her stomach gurgled.

Nice-guy gasped and hovered his hand above her torso.

"That's normal," she said. "I'm hungry."

"We are done," Criass snapped, spinning on a heel to storm out of the room. "Test her blood," he called.

"I am sorry, female. Food is not a priority. If you die, the Yithians will bring another." Nice Guy's lips curled down in what looked like distaste. His unibrow mirrored the movement.

"My name's Wren," she said, meeting his gaze, hoping a personal detail might gain her an ally. "What about water?" There'd been stories over the years of people living on nothing but water for twenty-four months. The sheer idea of it twisted her gut.

"I..." He glanced over his shoulder at the sealed door. "Let me see what I can do."

"Thank you," she said, a wealth of gratitude summoning the sting of tears.

Then he left her...lying there.

She gaped at the door. *What the hell?*

And worse, splayed out like a spatchcock chicken, her nose began to itch.

Chapter Seven

Cylo blinked at the message from Malo. "Detour to Mascroba? When females are in danger, and we are this close?"

"What is it?" Olin asked, raising his gaze from the mini war table set to the side of the comm.

"We are to sneak into yet another facility and steal a Durn." The insanity of the command irritated him. Cylo gritted his teeth, wishing he could decline the assignment.

"Should take an hour at the most." Olin tapped the 3D holographic of Yithia and zoomed into the mother city. "Ah, Tias has shared the location. It is near the throne room. Slipping in undetected might be challenging."

Intrigued despite his frustration, Cylo studied the model. "What if we came up from below?" He ran his finger along the path they should take. "That chasm runs deep, does it not?"

Olin hummed. "Indeed, if the kuta could make less noise."

"Then let us travel deeper."

"What? And have the Durn plummet to us?" Olin chuckled. "Endangering such a rarity would not be well accepted."

Cylo smirked. "He can climb down, can he not?"

"I suppose." Olin swiped his wrist over Cylo's. "Comm this Zucis. Set it up."

"Why me?"

"Malo instructed me to collect the Durn? I was not aware I was entrusted with this." Olin chuckled. "Fyca, were you aware of my new responsibilities?"

Fyca glanced away from the display vids while his fingers flew across the console. "It is well deserved."

Cylo scoffed at their teasing. "Enough. I shall comm our target and have him prepare for our arrival."

"Should I secure it? If secrecy is required?" Fyca gestured to the biggest display vid dominating the forevids.

"Wait. Let me ensure he is not surrounded by an enemy." Cylo typed a quick message from his O.D.I. and settled into the nearest comfy. A zing shot up his arm. At a glance, he caught the gist of the message and signaled to Fyca to make the connection.

"Greetings, Etterian." A blue-skinned, white-haired, and white-eyed male bowed his head. "How may I assist?"

"I have been instructed to escort you off Yithia." Cylo rose out of the comfy, clasped his hands behind his back, and squared his shoulders.

"Indeed." Zucis smiled. "Your Sub-Commander Aaro is honorable."

Cylo wasn't about to claim all Etterians embodied that trait when it was far from the truth. "Data Officer Olin will share our plan. See to it that you are in place at the correct time."

"I will be there."

When the comm ended from the Durn's side, Cylo had no right to hiss in offense. A Durn was to be revered, but like Etterians who didn't all value honor, so, too, should Durns not expect instant respect.

"How long?" he muttered.

"In four hours, we will breach Yithia's atmosphere." Olin angled his head. "At midday. Might be wise to let the weaker sunlight of 'night' shade us."

"And give those Yithian xemi a chance to hurt the females?" Cylo leveled a glare at Olin. "No. Time is crucial." He gripped Fyca's shoulder in passing. "Just fly the kuta lower than their suns' light can reach."

He headed along the passage to the common. Operatives Nhyht, Unher, Durok, and Koddo gathered around the table. "We have a short, important mission above and beyond the Earthian females. Prepare for battle. You have four hours."

Nhyht leapt to his feet. "Stealth?"

"In a way. I am hoping we do not need to leave the kuta."

"But plan for the worst," Durok said, lowering his chin to his chest. "This may be a chance to die for Etteria."

Silence fell upon the room like the numbing effects of Foutas venom.

"The void cannot have you just yet," Koddo said, patting Durok on the back. "We save the females first, then you may claim your honorable death."

"Dying on Yithia?" Cylo forced a smile. "Let us find you a worthy opponent. We shall hunt the galaxies for such a creature."

"My thanks," Durok said, gazing at the males gathered.

Cylo tapped the med-gun in his pants pocket and nudged his head at Qaff in a silent request for Durok to get scanned. If the male's void threatened to consume him, Cylo needed to know how soon. At Durok's nod, Cylo abandoned the common for his quarters in the barracks. Irritation had him pacing the narrow confines when what he wanted to do was roar at the delay. Instead, he controlled his breathing and willed himself to calm. In four hours, this issue would be behind him, and if all things went well, a Durn would be aboard the scimitar.

Fully armed, Cylo's arms gleaming with the mini daggers he'd strapped there, he strode into the kuta's compartment and settled behind Fyca. Shooting out of the bay was done in silence, with the shuttle's well-maintained engines humming.

"If we had stealth," Olin said into the quiet.

"Indeed." Cylo grimaced. "Maloid has perfected it."

"That is recent. We have yet to adapt, to learn how to detect them."

Cylo scowled. "Not good."

Blinding sunlight highlighted every corner within the compartment. There'd been a buzz about Yithia harvesting their three suns and selling the sunlight to planets in need, but that had fallen through. Not many wanted to do business with the Yithians when there were far more hospitable planets out there.

Olin rubbed his nose then gripped the support strap when the kuta shuddered. "They would have to hide their heat signatures as well as visuals. An intriguing challenge: becoming invisible in its entirety."

Cylo remained silent at Olin's awe. This development marked a change in the power dynamics. Etterian led the way with their sheer numbers and combative approach to life. Yet they could not penetrate the seas to reach Yithian's underwater cities. So, Maloid introducing stealth when Etterian relied on honest dealings with their allies... Worse, if Maloid chose to share this technology with anyone other than Etteria, it could tilt the balance. But all this was unconfirmed. Unless he 'saw' it with his own eyes, he wouldn't worry about it.

King Xeus had prepared for a war, nonetheless, bringing the Gika into the fold. Now, that had been a change in centuries of tactics. Etteria had once used the Gika battlefields as a rite of passage. Making them allies meant Etteria's aging males could no longer find their deaths at the hands of eight-legged creatures.

Cylo rubbed his chest in remembrance. Images flashed in his mind of red mandibles and razor-sharp pincers. He'd used his great sword to dismember them while dodging their acidic saliva. It had been a long time since he'd last visited Gikaet. Perhaps, once the females were safe...

Even imagined battles fired his blood.

When Fyca steered the kuta into a ravine, darkness consumed the compartment. No one panicked at the loss of light, not when Etterians had excellent vision, even in shadow. The temperatures dipped, too.

Cylo grimaced when the kuta skimmed the side of the chasm, a screeching scrape that deafened him. "May I remind you that this is our only kuta."

"It is made of Maloidian steel," Fyca called, dropping the shuttle. "Should be wider from here on out."

Tension tightened Cylo's shoulders. Something...a sense, had him on high alert like they were flying into a trap. He studied his males. Only Qaff was on board the *Kevol*, and he wasn't enough to storm the facility. No, they had to survive this mission, no matter what awaited them.

Fyca navigated the zig-zagging chasm with ease. Dark green plants clung to the black rock. And despite his excellent hearing, Cylo couldn't pick up anything past the engines.

Which meant, if any Yithian was listening, they would hear them approach.

And yet, his males' heartbeats were steady. He glanced at Unher whose stomach gurgled.

Fyca punched the console and yanked on the lever. The kuta careened to a halt—its backside rising before settling. "Sensors."

Cylo peered through the forevid at two discs mounted to the chasm walls. Almost as black as the rock, they would have missed them if not for a telltale shimmer.

"Koddo, shoot the left on my command." Cylo opened the door to a flood of heat, smelling of organic material and water. "I will climb over the roof to reach the other."

Without waiting for a response, he gripped the top edge of the doorframe and swung himself up and over in a single move, his arms bearing his weight without issue. Sprawled on the roof, he scanned the wall on the right. A strip of sunlight above almost blinded him, forcing him to adjust his eyesight. He shouldn't have looked up, because when he focused on the shadows, it took him longer to find the device.

"Do not destroy them," Olin said, peering over the edge at Cylo. "Stun them. Yithians may believe the devices have malfunctioned."

"Agreed," Cylo said. He leapt to his feet, spreading them wide for balance, and unholstered his blaster. A smack of the yellow button on the side set it to stun. He drew in a breath then exhaled. "Now, Koddo."

The shots almost deafened him. The shimmer ceased. He strapped the blaster to his thigh and swung into the compartment.

Olin sealed the door behind him.

Fyca launched the shuttle forward.

"Let that be the only obstacle," Olin said.

"You are troubled, too?" Cylo met his gaze.

"It seems too easy. Why the extraction when we can fly in and collect him without a fight?" Olin peered through the forevid.

"I agree," Durok said. "Stealing a Durn should garner more resistance than this. Unless..."

Cylo scowled. "If he is a spy, then we shall deliver him to the *Phoenix*. I will not endanger the females any further." He pinched his brow where a dull ache pinged. "I would prefer this task to be a disaster than the rescue of the females."

"We are nearing the meet point," Fyca called. "Five minutes."

"Any movement on the rock face?" Olin asked Fyca when the male glided the shuttle to a stop.

"Nothing yet." Fyca touched the console, flicking the forevid to infrared. "No heat signature either."

"We will wait," Cylo said then glanced at Durok. "Head onto the roof. In case he needs assistance."

Olin smacked the button that opened the door. Durok swung out and up.

"Nhyht, Koddo, go with him." Cylo nodded at his males.

They followed while Olin crowded the console. Cylo fired off a message to Zucis, and of course, no reply was forthcoming.

Gritting his teeth, he stomped to the door and swung out, landing on the roof with a thump. Koddo met his gaze from his position guarding the rear of the shuttle. Durok peered up one rock wall, Nhyht the other.

Cylo tapped his O.D.I., summoning the meet point. It was closer to the right. He burst into action and threw himself against the side of the chasm, digging his fingers into gaps to hold himself in place.

"Cylo," Nhyht called. "Be careful."

Durok paused beside Cylo, gave him a slow nod, then started to climb. Up they went, taking the time to find grips and footholds. The light brightened the higher up the chasm they traveled and, still, no sign of the Durn. Cylo paused at the bright stream of sunlight across the rock. If he continued upward, he'd be revealed. Meters above him was a platform. Durok hesitated, as well.

"I do not like this," he said.

"I agree. We do not know what awaits us." Cylo glanced into the depths of darkness, picking up the clear outline of the shuttle. He wanted to abandon this stupid mission. Now more than ever.

A steady tread approached. He stilled and raised his gaze to the edge of the platform. He released one hand and twisted to unstrap his blaster. Plastering himself to the rock face, he glanced at Durok, who'd drawn his weapon, too.

A face appeared, and the sight of it whooshed air out of Cylo's lungs.

"My apologies, Operative," Zucis whispered. He adjusted his carry-all across his chest and shoulder, then leapt over the side.

Cylo hurried to holster his blaster, anticipating that he might need to catch the Durn's arm. But the male caught ahold of a jutting rock and hit the wall with an 'oomph.'

"I could not slip out as quickly as I wanted to," he said, starting his descent. "Nor could I respond to your message. My thanks for waiting for me."

Cylo grunted but said no more. He hurried past Zucis, needing to reach the kuta before the male did. A glance at Durok conveyed the message to trail the Durn. Durok nodded. The lure of a mission completed flooded Cylo's limbs with energy, and he touched down. Koddo and Nhyht faced ahead and backward while Cylo gazed upward. The Durn climbed without hindrance in his open-toed footwear. Not an easy task but he did it well.

Moments later, they were in the kuta, the door sealed.

"Flipping," Fyca called.

Cylo grabbed a strap and gestured to Zucis to do the same. In time, too, for Fyca yanked the nose up and somersaulted the shuttle, rolling them to head back the way they'd come. Cylo hung while the shuttle rotated, his booted feet touching the ceiling a second before the shuttle righted. Fyca strapped to the seat didn't need to hold onto anything. Their braids whipped, though, showing the movement.

"Heat signatures ahead," Olin called, once more peering through the forevid. "They are repairing the sensors."

"Alodon's balls," Cylo grumbled. "Drop as low as you can. Let us wait them out." He activated his O.D.I. and messaged the *Phoenix*, warning them to anticipate their arrival and who they were escorting. No one spoke, their gazes fixed on the two Yithians glowing blue-green on the forevid. Their nearby shuttle hovered, its single engine glowing red.

It didn't take long for the repairs to be completed considering the devices had been short-circuited and not destroyed. Fyca didn't bring them closer to the sensors until there was no doubt the Yithians were out of range. Only then did Cylo and Koddo re-stun the devices before Fyca shot them off-world.

"Anything on the buzz?" Cylo asked Olin, who'd been staring at his O.D.I. since they'd left Yithia and headed toward the orbiting battleship *Phoenix*.

"Nothing so far."

Cylo allowed his shoulders to slump. Thankfully, Zucis did not speak. Cylo had nothing to say to the Durn, nor did he want to inadvertently reveal their Iphara plans.

He gazed at the male, not even bothering to offer a polite smile. "Welcome to the *Phoenix*," he finally said, gesturing to the battleship filling the forevid.

Chapter Eight

Leaving the atmosphere of Yithia felt wrong. Where Cylo wanted to be was on an island in the middle of the Knaetian Ocean. He kept his gaze on Zucis, trusting Fyca to steer them true. No one spoke except Fyca announcing their impending docking, the battleship *Phoenix* their destination.

Impatience twitched his fingers. He gritted his teeth and willed his body to submit to his control. This task was almost complete. He activated his O.D.I. and messaged Jokta, sharing his concerns about Zucis. Caution was advised.

After the kuta touched down and the door opened, Cylo waited. He had no intention of disembarking.

Durok caught the edge of the doorframe and swung out. "Delivery of a Durn?"

Ending it in a question tempted Cylo to smirk.

"Greetings, Operative," a male said, stepping onto the ramp. "And welcome, Zucis. I am Supreme Commander Jokta."

The Durn bowed his head at Cylo and strolled out of the kuta. "My thanks, Supreme Commander." Zucis glanced over his shoulder at Cylo then trailed Jokta out of the shuttle bay.

"Fyca, head to the *Kevol* for pick-up." Cylo grabbed the strap hanging from the compartment's ceiling. "I want no more delays."

On the *Kevol*, he gestured to his males to head to the comm for one last check-in. As soon as Qaff gave up the pilot seat, Fyca sank into it. Cylo gazed at the males gathered around the holographic of Iphara. Afax had chosen well. Cylo could trust these males with his life. That mattered on an important mission such as this. Each one would act with honor—well, as much as being an operative would allow. Olin had done his research, with the underground facility fully known. Cylo tapped each room that was a possible location.

"These are single laboratories." Olin flicked the holographic to display the layout of a room. Cabinets lined one wall, and in the middle sat a table with straps at the corners.

Cylo grimaced, his imagination adding a squirming victim. "Find one female and free her. Seven have been taken. If the Maker blesses us, seven will be saved." He met their gazes. "This is a Malo-sanctioned mission, and I have every intention of destroying this facility. Fyca, as pilot, you will remain on the *Kevol* as our exit strategy. I need you all to gather what data cubes you can. Any information gained will be crucial in discovering what the Yithians are up to. But rescuing your female is your priority."

"As far as I know, Iphara does not have a port-dampening shield. I could port you in and out with minimal fuss," Fyca said.

"I prefer that option," Durok said, palming his med-gun.

"As do I," Cylo said, "but it is one way to miss someone. We cannot allow them to send comms outside of the island. Which leaves us sweeping the facility and eradicating any who seek to stop us." He grinned. "Let us teach these Yithians not to steal what does not belong to them."

"I agree." Nhyht folded his arms across his chest. "We do not know for certain where these females are. Porting in might put us at a disadvantage and place our targets in harm's way."

"We go in on foot," Olin said. "I will start a body-heat scan. Fyca will run continuous surveillance and share the results with us all. I would prefer not to waste time on empty rooms."

Cylo couldn't help but be impressed by his males' ingenuity. "Excellent, Olin, I did not want to wait while the *Kevol* ran another diagnostic."

Fyca typed on the console. "What manifests I have found have one ship landing on the island within the last ten days. It is no longer planetside, but that does not mean our breach will be uncontested."

"They anticipate our arrival?" Koddo asked, a frown forming.

"I hope not," Cylo said, stroking his jaw. "Anyone who runs such a facility should not be complacent. They would be fools. And these Yithians managed to pass our defenses with females onboard."

"Indeed," Olin said.

"Once you have returned with your female, see to her well-being. If she has serious injuries, you know how to work the med-E.D." Cylo bowed his head, praying the females were well.

Olin gripped Cylo's shoulder. "You have considered all the variables, and we have planned accordingly."

"We will succeed. These females need us to," Koddo said.

"We depart in ten. All of Etteria is with us," Cylo said as they parted, leaving him staring at the 3D holo.

To slip in, they'd enter through the front doors then descend into the lower levels. He didn't believe the Global Council or G.C. condoned whatever happened down there. If they managed to learn anything, King Xeus would take the evidence to the G.C. and insist Yithia cease this nonsense. Etterians needed humans. King Xeus had made that clear. Not to mention, he'd placed Earth under Etteria's protection.

And yet...

Cylo clamped down on his simmering anger.

There had to be something Etteria could use to force Yithia to comply. King Urio claimed that Yithia had no interest in Earth. Which either meant he lied or was ignorant of what his males got up to. Etterians informed Xeus of everything. Perhaps King Urio was kept in the dark on purpose? No, that made no sense. Cylo couldn't believe such a strong male could be anyone's puppet.

"What is the worst you are expecting?" Olin asked, zooming out to reveal the island and its many caves.

Cylo tapped a cave system, more out of curiosity. "We are overwhelmed, are unable to find the females, or they are dead."

"And your plan for each of these?" Olin peered at him, patience in his still stance.

Cylo grunted, aware of Olin's strategy to ease his anxiety. "We fight, we tear the facility apart, and we bring their bodies back to Earth." He prayed, out of all the adventures he'd been through and would go on, that this one was the easiest with the best outcome.

Olin took over from Cylo to fiddle with the map, entering and exiting the caves without bothering to study them. "Every male on board would die for the good of Etteria. Females in danger does not change that."

Cylo spared a nod before striding from the comm room.

"Cylo, I have a concern," Durok called, forcing Cylo to stop. "Where will they sleep?"

"Anywhere we can find. They will be with us for the time it takes to reach the closest battleship."

"True." Durok inclined his head. "We shall ask the females. The narrow confines of the barracks might be too much for them after their ordeal."

"Wise." Cylo smiled, thankful that Afax had added Durok to his crew. They needed a male who considered the females' comforts *before* they were onboard.

Cylo headed to his room which he shared with Nhyht. It didn't sit well with him to use the only officer's quarters when his rank was above any male on board. The door sealed behind him, granting him a small measure of privacy. Spread on the table were all his daggers. He'd brought his entire arsenal, even the tiny ones he was in the process of crafting. Not sure what he'd need, he hadn't taken the time to decide. The new gold nugget Tius had mined for him was center stage. He palmed it.

Tension tightened his body, making blade smithing too intricate for him to handle in his current state. He flicked the gold into the air and caught it, falling into pacing as he did so. Energy pulsed along his veins, stealing his peace and sleep. No doubt, Malo would've been commanding this mission had Prince Enyl not sent him to Earth.

Cylo smirked. Malo as an ambassador would've been entertaining to observe. The Malo he knew would struggle with diplomacy. All Etterians would when it required a tongue used to deceiving or spinning the truth in a more favorable light.

"Fyca, comm the nearest battleship orbiting Yithia." Cylo waited, his gaze on his O.D.I. He flipped the nugget and caught it.

"Supreme Commander Jokta," a male answered. "Operative Cylo?"

"My apologies, Supreme Commander, I did not wish to discuss my mission with Zucis nearby. Have your males noticed a change in the shipping routes—from Earth to Iphara?"

"Days ago, a Yithian trade ship left Iphara for Maloid."

"Maloid?" Cylo frowned. Geffa's involvement was no coincidence—something Malo didn't believe in. "Will the *Phoenix* be remaining in Yithia's orbit?"

"We have not received instructions otherwise," Jokta said.

"Excellent. Prepare quarters for seven human females."

"Seven?" Jokta cleared his throat. "Of course. How long will they be remaining with us?"

"That is for them to decide." Cylo shut his eyes for a moment, hoping one of his males would find their Dar Eth among these females.

"All will be as asked. In addition, my pilot, Msar, will ensure the next battleship en route to Earth will detour to Yithia."

"My thanks, Supreme Commander." Cylo ended the comm then winced. As an operative, his rank wasn't above Jokta's. The right to 'end a comm' belonged to the superior officer. What he knew of Jokta, the male would not take offense and report Cylo to Adviser Kanzo. He swung his braid and caught the tail, stroking the tips. Dishonor would cost him a foot of his hair.

He swapped the nugget for a dagger. Time to choose what he'd carry with him. He also needed a clear path. Strolling through the front doors was a bold move. With three weak suns, Yithia had eternal daylight. There'd be no cover of nightfall to hide them. Fyca's suggestion to port had merit, but Cylo didn't want to admit to any of his males that his fury simmered just below the surface. He wanted to storm the place and cause the biggest destruction possible. Then erase any sign they'd been there. If the buzz claimed it was an accident with few casualties, that would be a job well done.

Any Yithian he encountered would die—no justification existed to excuse what they had done and were doing.

He grimaced, prepared to do what he must. "Olin, can you still not pick up anything—no comms, access to their data cubes?"

"It is frustrating, Cylo. I have never faced such resistance." Olin almost sounded impressed.

"Keep trying. If we can harvest what we need before the strike, I will be less reticent in my actions."

"I will consult with Kemt on the *Phoenix*."

Cylo waved a dismissive hand Olin wouldn't see. "Let me know the findings, no matter the hour."

"As you command, Cylo."

The comm ended.

The door opened to Nhyht bearing a plate of kreso. He placed it on the table, shoving daggers aside. "Eat. We must be strong for what is to come."

Cylo scowled at his disappearing back, not liking that the male spoke the truth. He sank onto the chair, grabbed the closest dagger, and sliced through the soft steak. He was careful when he peeled the sliver off the blade with his teeth. While he chewed, he mentally planned the route he and his males would take. They'd start at the beach and work out which doors to open first, which rooms to check, what the quickest escape would be. Porting then? Yes, if a male found a female, then porting would be the safest. He killed imaginary Yithians with a blaster or his sword. Upon locating a blurry-faced female, he'd toss her over his shoulder and port. If he retraced his steps to the beach, they might encounter a swath of Yithian soldiers, all intent on taking her back and killing him.

If they couldn't port...

He tapped his O.D.I. "Olin, is there a male on board who can strap the *Kevol's* Chokaars to the shuttle?"

"Their combined weight would hinder the kuta's ability to take off. Perhaps one will do?"

"See to it as a last resort should we be surrounded."

"I shall speak to Koddo. I like this plan." Olin ended the comm.

"Durok," Cylo spoke into his wrist, twisting to do so and dripping momaberry sauce off a sliver of steak. "Ensure each male carries two med-guns. Should a female require immediate healing, a faulty med-gun is unacceptable."

"Agreed," Durok said. "Like I said earlier, you have considered all variables."

For minutes afterward, Cylo sat there. The impossible still had to be considered. What if the females were well, safe, and did not want to leave?

He shook his head. With what he knew about humans, they were impulsive, stubborn, and almost damu-like in their emotional range. He didn't think male or female would take too kindly to being taken.

Still, if a hostage chose to stay, he would accept that was her decision to make. He pushed aside his half-eaten meal. *Maker, I hope that is not the case.* In two days, he'd know if all their efforts were in vain.

He pocketed the nugget, grabbed his plate, and carried it to the common's waste disposal.

Chapter Nine

Iphara Island
Planet of Yithia
Year of 2254, August

Wren needed to pee. No way was she going to go on the bed when she'd just gotten clean. Parts of her were beginning to go numb, tingling to her toetips. How long had it been since Nice Guy had left? She'd dozed off and on, throwing her concept of time out of whack. Her stomach twisted, spiking a sharp pain in her abdomen.

She grimaced. If she could eat anything, it would be pizza or a grilled cheese sandwich. Iced coffee? Soda? Hell, a chilled bottle of water.

She had one thing to be grateful for, though. Gone was her craving for splice. Still, if she ever got back to Demeter, she'd be imprisoned for going A.W.O.L. while on parole. The sharks had made things worse for her. The two-year extension on her probation was nothing compared to what E.A.F. would do to her.

"Hello?" she called, straining her ears to hear.

A sneaky thought silenced her. What if the labs were soundproofed? After all, no footsteps came from the passage, no screams or chatter from staff or victims. She peered at the walls, trying to assess with her non-X-ray vision whether the walls were flimsy or filled with dampening foam. Not that she was an expert, by no means.

No windows meant no weaknesses, but the gap between the ceiling panels and the floor above could be an option, *if* she could free herself from the restraints. Even then, she wasn't sure she could climb into the gap.

What would it buy her anyway? Delayed experimentation? As nice as that sounded, she needed a better plan. Making it out of this place would mean fresh air and nothing more. They were on a friggin island, one she didn't know at all.

A cave would be good for hiding, where she could starve to death. No, the best bet would be to kill her way through these assholes. She'd at least have freedom, shelter, and food. Anyone landing some sort of shuttle could be taken out. Then she would have to figure out how to fly the damn thing. There were too many obstacles she'd have to surmount to survive. And on top of that was the question of whether she could take someone's life.

Hell, it's them or me, isn't it?

She grimaced.

The alternative was to let them do to her what they wanted, but by what One Eye had said, not many of their previous victims had made it. Her only opportunities were in transit, if she could get her hands on one of those gun-thingies they carried. Except the scientists and Criass sported no such weapons. She grinned. Stabbing them with their own concoctions would be justice served.

She pinched her thighs together. "Listen. Anyone, I need to pee. Seems like humanity and dignity do not extend outside our galaxy. Let me pee, you bastards. Stealing women for your experiments," she sang at the top of her lungs. "This is gender-based violence, but I'm human, a woman, and this bullshit is done."

She caterwauled with no tune in mind and probably sounded like a drunk space pirate way past his splice fix, but her bladder was making her desperate.

"Drug her," Criass said, striding in as if he'd just enjoyed a leisurely tea break.

Nice Guy slunk past her, his gaze averted. The coward. His back was to her while he fiddled with vials. Swish went one purple liquid into an injection gun then the gurgle of another. She squirmed, shifting to the opposite side of the table, as far as the straps would let her.

She cast a pleading gaze at Nice Guy, but he pretended not to notice and kept his chin down.

The cold of the gun's nozzle on her neck made her yelp. She had nowhere to go, nothing she could do to stop this. She was alone. Definitely not the way she'd expected to die.

At the sharp bite of the needle, she hissed. Fire blazed outward, clenching her teeth. She keened, arching off the bed with her heels hitting the table in a rapid beat. When the burn traveled to her chest, she screamed. Dying sucked.

"Wake her," reached her through the fog clouding her mind. Thoughts followed, too fast for her to grasp. "Return her to the others, and bring the next one."

She vaguely registered the releasing of her limbs. When Nice Guy tried to help her, she threw out a hand and glared at him. She staggered to her boots. Yes, she'd kill these fuckers, and she'd use her knife to get a gun. Her determination hardened when the dampness between her legs told her she'd wet herself again. The indignity of it. The urge to stab them both gripped her when her fingers brushed the hilt.

Could she do it?

Nice Guy held the door open. Criass had his back to her. So arrogant.

She hesitated. Her veins blazed with whatever shit they'd put in her. And they were about to do it to the other women. She made to follow Nice Guy, wrapped her fingers around the hilt, and swung it. The blade sank into the back of Criass's neck like a fork through cake. He slumped to the floor, his face contorted, his mouth opening and closing without a sound escaping him.

She blinked at him then faced Nice Guy. "Get in here, or I'll stab him again." She nudged Criass's prone form with her toe.

Nice Guy obeyed, sliding inside the room and shutting the door.

'Kill him' zinged across her mind. She tried to silence the shock, to focus. "Help me escape, or I'll kill him. I mean it," she snapped.

Nice Guy inched deeper into the room. "There is no way to go." He pointed at Criass with his chin. "We will just heal him."

"Shit," she muttered. "You're immortal?"

"No, but he is losing blood, nothing more." A smile teased his lips. "Our hearts are where your livers are."

She scowled. "Why are you telling me this?"

"I despise him, and the longer we wait, the more he will bleed out." He tapped a spot on his torso. "Here."

"And you don't think I'll use that knowledge on you?" She eyed him, trying to ascertain whether she could trust him.

"No, because I can get us out of here."

Her brow furrowed. "Why?"

"He is my uncle." His gaze showed not an ounce of love. "A male I have hated, resented, and served all my life. I am nothing more than a slave to him."

"Hiossu," Criass croaked, green blood spilling through the fingers he pressed to his neck. "Fetch the med-gun. Now."

Without warning, Hiossu snatched the dagger from her hand and plunged it into Criass's heart. "Done," he said, offering her the knife. "I shall escort you to your females as if nothing has happened."

"But aren't there others like your uncle?"

Hiossu winced. "Yes, I am sorry. Some of your females would have already received Gamma 7. Let us hope this is a good batch. If you wish to save them, we need to 'follow' protocol."

"Get me a gun and a ship."

He blinked at her. "First, we must kill any who oppose us."

She eyed him, not sure she could trust him. But what choice did she have?

"What about a distraction? A way to spread them out and give us a fighting chance? Taking out so many all at once..." She stared at the door, half expecting company. "I'm not one for killing." She swallowed hard and focused on Criass. "Can't we just...sneak out?"

"Go where? There is a cave system south of here, but..."

She pinched her brow, a mother of all headaches forming. A few of her fingers had started to tingle, and her toes had an unfamiliarity to them, like she had borrowed someone else's feet. "It would be the first place they look."

His pursed lips said that was true. "Shuttles do not often visit here when the resort is not open during winter."

"Huh, resort?" She almost laughed at the ingeniousness of it all. Having a medical facility beneath a hotel? Any comings and goings could be attributed to supplies being delivered or guests arriving or leaving.

"We need to wait for one and ambush it."

All the deaths would be on her hands. Maybe if she enlisted the women... To be fair, she'd only stabbed Criass. Hiossu had finished him off.

"Okay, what do you have in mind?" she asked.

He shoved her through the door. "Walk, Earthian," he spat.

Doubts hit her like a sledgehammer except his grip was gentle. Screams reached her from all sides. Her breath caught, tears forming. He was right. They had to plan this well with the women scattered. He steered her into another small lab. Terry was yelling and fighting the restraints.

A purple-robed man spewed orders to the lab assistant then glared at Hiossu. "What is the meaning of this intrusion?"

"Criass sent me," Hiossu said, slipping the dagger into her hand he clasped behind her back.

With surprising force, he pushed her at the assistant. She pretended to stumble, using the man to 'catch' her balance. When he did, she quietly slid the blade into the area of his heart. His gasp was lost amid Terry's ruckus, which cut off when Hiossu slit the other man's throat with a scalpel.

"What the hell?" Terry cried out, scrambling off the bed when Wren cut through the straps. She leapt back until her ass hit the wall. "You killed them?"

Wren winced. "Are you in or out?

Terry scanned the room, straightened, and squared her shoulders. "In."

Before they hurried out, Wren said, "This is Hiossu. He's—"

Hiossu collapsed to the floor, tripping her.

"We are not fools, Earthian." One Eye smirked, his bulk dominating the passageway. "You have made the situation worse for you and your females. Do you think you are the first to try for freedom?" He hiss-laughed, nudging his gun at her to follow. "I do so enjoy showing you how superior we are to your...kind."

Surrounded by a wall of sharks, Wren mouthed, 'I'm sorry,' to Terry, then with a growl, she flung the dagger at One Eye.

That was all kinds of stupid. Not only had she lost her only weapon, but the damn thing bounced off his chest like a breadstick off a table. With as much damage.

Yithians tackled her, slamming her to the floor, bruising every part of her, so she screamed, unable to register what hurt where. She clenched her jaw, fighting the waves of agony stemming from all directions.

Terry made demands, but her cries dwindled like she was being carried away.

A Yithian dragged Hiossu into a lab, propped him against a wall, and manacled him.

The sharks restraining her hoisted her onto the bed, then all four of them pinned her limbs down. Their cold grips were worse than the straps, less forgiving and more soul-destroying. A purple-robed yellow-skinned man strolled in, his eyes narrowed in hatred.

"For your foolishness, I shall inject Criass's prototype. If you die, then justice will be served. If you survive, then we are closer to our goal. We win either way." He smirked, tapping the rainbow-colored fluid in an injection gun. "Hold her still."

She squirmed.

"I shall take pleasure in harming you, female, if you do not behave," One Eye snapped, raising a wicked dagger.

Fear coursed through her, along with anger. "And what will that gain you, asshole?" She bit her lip. Antagonizing him wasn't helpful.

A sting registered on her left forearm, a thin line of blood forming.

She glared at the one-eyed bastard circling the table. "See... Nothing. Pointless. I never gave it much thought, but maybe Yithians are dumb?"

Another sting followed, summoning a hiss.

"Easily led by these Malods." She nudged her head at the Purple Robe who hovered, injection gun extended.

One Eye's face darkened to a dull silver. "An alliance does not make us the weaker, Earthian. It is you who should be concerned." More flicks of his dagger heralded minor bites like bee stings, all while his gaze remained fixed on her. He relished the hurt he inflicted.

What a dick.

"Do it, kuliriji," One-eye spat.

She blinked. Ah, so kuliriji must mean scientist? Like Frankenstein? But when Purple Robe squeezed beside the Yithian holding her in place, she shuffled back though it would buy her no more than a few seconds.

The fire exploding outward, from her neck to her toes, was nothing like before. Ice and heat took turns to flush her body. Muscles spasmed and cramped at random. Memories and darkness sputtered on and off. Emotions bombarded her: glee, curiosity, revenge? It had to be her imagination, her tortured mind grasping for sanity while her body became...something else.

"She lives? Intriguing." Purple Robe turned his back on her and fiddled with things unseen on the counter. The four Yithians tightened their hold on her limbs.

"Stop this," Hiossu demanded.

"Gag him," One Eye said, hiss-laughing. "Nothing pleases me more than a silent Maloidian."

"Do not overstep," Purple Robe muttered.

"Yes, kuliriji," One Eye said, but his black eyes twinkled with an eagerness that summoned a shiver down her spine. He frightened her more than anything the *Maloidians* could inject into her.

Chapter Ten

It was too quiet. Cylo hadn't expected the Yithians to post guards, but no one hindered their approach. No movement or light showed life. Nhyht's frown said it all. The front doors were unbarred, swishing open on silent puffs of air. With blasters drawn, they spread out, ensuring no one hid. In the process, they planted incendiaries and set the timer for 'twenty.' In the foyer, they reunited then hurried along the corridor, their steps no more than a whisper. They dared not use the pod lest it drew attention. Down they scampered: ears on heightened alert, armor maximized, and blasters raised.

No life signs on the second level made planting the explosives simpler, then downward they went.

Chaos on the third floor had Cylo wincing, but he didn't adjust his hearing. "Scan," he muttered to Olin, who waved his O.D.I.

He pointed at each room they passed, sending a male in to investigate. Cylo stayed in front of a distracted Olin locked on his O.D.I., keeping him safe. When they neared the end of the passage, Olin tapped his wrist, swiveled his gaze from left, center, then right at the last three doors. He pointed to the third door.

Cylo inched it open. Sprawled on the table was an unconscious female, her hair solid black, her limbs not strapped to the table. Without hesitation, he fired, killing the two Maloidians unaware of his presence. On the counter was a data belt charging two cubes. He tagged them, porting them to the scimitar. Slapping the explosive to the wall, he hoisted the female over his shoulder and met Olin in the passage.

"One more," Cylo said, heading to the left room. Inside, a damu-like female lay alone.

Olin slipped past him and, with one arm, held her against his body. He dug out an incendiary and tossed it onto the table. No data cubes were visible, and they didn't have the time to search.

"There is another," he said, his tone unfazed as he nudged the female over a shoulder.

Cylo blinked. "Do you mean an eighth female?"

"I believe so. She is in a central room with walls almost too thick to scan through." Olin paused in front of the middle door. "Six additional life signs spell trouble. Her core temperature is elevated: stress, pain, fear... I cannot say." He gestured to the black-haired female Cylo was carrying. "Give her to me."

Cylo did, gently scooping her onto Olin's spare shoulder.

"Do not do anything foolish." He held Cylo's gaze. "I will hand these two to our males and return."

"Very well, my battle-bond," Cylo said, though he had no intention of waiting.

A second could mean the death of this unexpected female. Deception was against Etterian honor, but he was an operative, trained to lie if it served his mission. When Olin almost reached the stairwell, Cylo faced the final hurdle.

Eight? So Smez had lied. Cylo harrumphed. That shouldn't have surprised him. He brought up his blaster, checked the red kill button was set, and cracked the door open enough to assess the larger room. A female writhed and yelled on a metal table, her tears soaking into her multi-colored hair. Four Yithians held her limbs in place. A Maloidian sat on the floor, bound. Another in a purple garment focused on an injection gun.

"You're insane," she screamed. Exposed parts of her body showed bleeding cuts, bruises, and the side of her face had swollen, now dark blue and black. An eye was half-shut.

Yet she fought on. Cylo admired her determination and strength of will.

The bound Maloidian met Cylo's gaze but said nothing. *An ally?*

Cylo gathered the meager shadows around him as Malo had taught him and hid behind the closest Yithian. He flicked out his dagger, sinking it between the two vertebrae at the base of his neck.

When he slumped, one glanced up and hissed, "Etterian." His reaction was swift: a kick to Cylo's knee.

Fiery agony exploded outward and dropped him to the floor, and he hit it hard. He spun his dagger and, in an icepick strike, buried it into the Yithian's thigh. As he fell, Cylo tackled him to the floor, stopping with the male pinned beneath him.

The other two Yithians released the female and lunged, their weapons drawn. The tap-tap of a blaster button being activated warned Cylo. He rolled the Yithian over him, letting him take the lethal shots. With the full weight of the dead Yithian on top of him, he couldn't avoid the flare from the shots burning him. His upper arm went numb, and the smell of his blood saturated his nose. He shoved the male off him enough to fire his blaster in rapid succession, killing the last two Yithians.

He staggered to his feet, his knee and arm displeased with him. If the building wasn't about to blow, he could've used his med-gun. With time not on his side, he faced the room, pretending that blood didn't drip from his fingertips and that his knee didn't want to buckle.

The purple-clothed Maloidian held the injection gun to her neck.

Ice added to the sensations lambasting Cylo.

His O.D.I. vibrated with Fyca's voice. "A Yithian ship is inbound."

Alodon's balls. No one was meant to see a single Etterian anywhere close to the destruction zone. "Is everyone on board the kuta?" he asked.

"Olin has returned for you," Fyca said.

"Call him back and leave. We will port."

"Acknowledged," Fyca said, ending the comm.

The Maloidian laughed. "You have trapped yourself, Etterian. The facility dampens all porting when a ship is en route."

Cylo smothered a grimace. They needed to escape the blast zone first. It would take an hour to reach the safest side of the island. Doing so injured and with a female in tow would be hard enough. He didn't dare glance at the female or the bound male. He couldn't afford the distraction. Unsheathing his greatsword had the Maloidian flinching. Cylo balanced it against the table's leg. Placing his blaster on the table, he sidled to the right of it to cup the female's knee in a 'casual' pose while giving it a reassuring squeeze.

"The building is gutted. No one is alive. Do you truly wish to test your skill against an operative?"

The Maloidian paled, squared his shoulders, then lifted his chin. "I am dead anyway."

With the last of his energy reserves, Cylo struck, slamming into the male and sending them colliding against the wall. There, he held the Maloidian in place. Vials clattered to the floor, shattering and spilling their chemicals across the gray floor. Movement on Cylo's peripherals caught his attention for but a moment. The female grabbed his greatsword and dragged it to the bound male. Her arms quivered, but she held it still for the male to cut himself free.

"You cannot hope to stop us, Etterian. Earthians do not belong to you or your King Xeus," the Maloidian gritted out, straining against Cylo's weight.

He smirked. "They are called humans, xemi." He snapped the male's neck and stepped back, allowing his limp body to slither to the floor. For extra assurance, he flipped out his dagger and sank it into the corpse's heart.

When he faced the female, she met his gaze, unflinching. Time slowed; so did his breathing. Nothing mattered at that moment. Underlying the steady pulse of pain was a tingling and a tightening of his chest as if to still his beating heart. She broke eye contact and rummaged through a Yithian's armor to withdraw a green-stained knife. Despite the greatsword's weight, she'd returned it to where Cylo had left it.

The counter on the perimeter was clean of data belts, but in a room this large, this important, there had to be some recordings. "I need data cubes we can use to unravel Yithia and Maloid's interest in humans."

The male pushed off, hobbled to a cabinet, and took out a data belt stacked high with cubes.

"You are coming with me, milady," Cylo said to the female while he tagged the cubes with his good hand.

"Not without Hiossu." She raised her chin, exposing the graceful column of her neck. "They'll think he's a traitor."

"I will stay," the male said, clasping his side where blood stained his tunic.

Having run out of tags, Cylo eyed the remaining cubes, considering leaving them behind. But since the data wasn't on a central system, Olin hadn't been able to syphon the information like every battleship did passing any inhabited world.

Before Cylo could ask, she stretched past him to shove them into her pants pockets and one down the front of her sleeveless tunic. He was taken aback by her intuitiveness.

Realizing they waited for his response, he growled, "You cannot stay. It is not safe." *Not with the explosions imminent.* He sheathed his greatsword down his back and tapped his O.D.I. "Fyca, three to port." He clasped her wrist—the skin there incredibly silky. Clearing his throat, he quickly grabbed the male's shoulder.

Fyca's voice crackled. "Signal unstable. A Yithian K-class is on the way."

Proving the dead Maloidian's threat as true.

"Inform Olin to draw back until the area is clear." Cylo clenched his jaw. "We will head to the surface."

"Eleven minutes remaining, Cylo," Fyca said.

"Until what?" the female asked.

"Now is not the time." Cylo took his blaster and headed out the door. "Stay close."

She did, on his heels, but Hiossu hesitated.

Cylo clutched his tunic and yanked, bringing their gazes in line. His patience was nonexistent. "We are destroying this place. Do you wish to remain?"

"No." Hiossu stumbled back then fell into position behind the female.

Along the passage, they hurried, with Cylo casting glances over his shoulder to ensure they trailed him. The Maloidian favored his side, as expected. The female seemed unstable on her feet, but she didn't utter a word of complaint. When they breached the second level, an alarm blared, proving someone had lived. He cursed. It didn't matter. Getting the female to safety did. Hiossu hadn't been part of the plan, but he might serve some purpose if the data on the cubes was useless.

"There's another way out," she said, stopped on the second level's landing, and slouched against the wall.

Cylo gazed into her good eye then lingered on the daintiness of her nose and her enticing mouth. "Are you certain?"

"I saw a map of this place." She moaned, rolling a shoulder. "And when we got here, the Yithians first took us toward the beach."

"She speaks truth," Hiossu said.

Cylo cupped her unblemished cheek, soft despite what she'd endured. A data cube made her tunic bulge. His arm hung limp at his side, and his knee threatened to collapse. Hope sparked to life. The beach was perhaps far enough for them to not suffer the brunt of the explosions. "Lead the way, ensa."

Her chest rose in a sharp inhale, then she bolted, bumping into walls like her balance was off. With Hiossu between them, Cylo could do nothing to help. At one point, she doubled over and vomited. When Hiossu reached out to her, she straightened, wiped her mouth with the hand holding the dagger, and took off again.

The cascade of her vibrant hair lured Cylo, serving as a beacon he was compelled to follow.

When she ducked, revealing an armed Yithian, it wasn't enough time for Cylo to react. The blaster shot hit Hiossu in the chest, sending him to the floor and skidding back. She screamed, threw herself at the Yithian, and plunged her dagger into his eye. He roared and thrust her away, granting Cylo a chance to fire. He didn't hesitate.

She scrambled to Hiossu's side and raised wide eyes to Cylo. "Is he dead?"

Activating his O.D.I. with his nose, he scanned the Maloidian. It didn't heal, but it could diagnose. With a grunt, he said, "Step back. Let me lift him."

How, he didn't know. He clenched his jaw when he rested on his knee. Then, with a dip and her help, Hiossu draped over Cylo's shoulder. She clasped his elbow, helping him to stand.

"Let us go, ensa," he said, flashing her a smile.

She blinked, swiveled, and snatched the blaster from the dead Yithian before pushing onward. Her steps faltered more often. The skin around her bruises had taken on a deep purple tinge. What had these xemi done to her? He was tempted to awaken Hiossu and pin him to a wall, to extract every painful secret he harbored.

She halted in front of a Maloidian steel door. No amount of yanking on the handle opened it. Cylo leaned against the tunnel wall and slid Hiossu to the floor. He clambered to his feet, swallowing a groan at the renewed agony locking his knee, and joined her. He nudged her to the side and handed her his blaster. With his good hand, he clasped the lever and pushed. The door cranked open on silent hinges.

Salty air hit him in the face. He grinned at the female resting against the door's frame, clasping two blasters to her chest. A weak smile teased her lips, but her blinks were lazy, her eyes glazed. His joy faltered. She needed a med-E.D.

"Come," he said, lumbered to Hiossu, and wormed him onto his shoulder.

They entered the cool tunnel with bright sunlight at the end. The floor changed from metal to black sand. Waves crashed onto the shore, their gentle hush soothing his hearing and enhancing her ragged breathing.

He tapped his O.D.I. and caught her hand. "Fyca, three to port to medical."

"Head to safety." Fyca's voice broke up. "Explosions in seven. Kuta has..." Crackle. Hiss. "Recalled with Yithian ship... Find shelter."

"Shit," she muttered. "You planted bombs?" She whipped her gaze away, but he caught her glower.

"Yes. We want to stop the—"

"I get it," she snapped. "We need distance, so where to now?" She stomped ahead, leaving him to follow. "Hiossu mentioned a cave, but I have to tell you, we'll be sitting ducks."

"Ducks?" Cylo's O.D.I. hurried to share images and details of a strange bird. "Is that bad?"

She stared at him then giggled. Running a hand over her face wiped away her mirth. "It means we'll be fixed targets."

"Ah," he said. "Under the circumstances, we must be far from here." He scanned the beach, noted its shape, and headed south.

The sand made running harder, his knee pinging with every step he managed. Her heavy breathing trailed him, her uneven gait a concern. He chanced a glance over his shoulder at her pale and glistening face and pinched his lips. On the horizon was a jagged line of rock, pitted from centuries of waves crashing against it.

Sweltering heat pouring off the sand added a layer of sweat to his battered body. His armor's automatic temperature adjustment must have failed. As they neared the cavern's entrance, he swung Hiossu off his shoulder and rested the male against the warm rock wall. Through a narrow crack, a breeze cooled his skin.

"I'll go ahead and check. I don't want any surprises," she said, dropping a blaster at his feet then hefting the other with both hands.

He stared at the discarded weapon then glared at her. "I will do it."

"Why?" She met his gaze even as she swayed on her feet.

"I am a trained warrior." He tried to fold his arms across his chest, but his left arm didn't budge.

"Fine. We'll both go." She pointed her chin at Hiossu. "Drag him inside." And through the gap she slipped.

"Cursed female," Cylo muttered.

He scooped up the blaster and tossed it in after her. It clattered across the rock floor and ended with a splatter. Grunting, he grabbed Hiossu by the wrist and pulled him across the sand. The moment he stepped into the cave, Cylo swallowed a moan of relief at the lower temperature. His eyes adjusted in an instant, granting him a clear view of the interior. Toward the darker rear, yellow, curl-like plants glowed from the ceiling in what he assumed was some sort of bioluminescence. They wouldn't be in complete darkness, not with the cave opening on the ocean to the right. After propping Hiossu against a natural pillar, Cylo ventured farther into their temporary haven.

Tiny echoing footsteps marked her location in what sounded like a series of caves. Silence fell, only marred by the ocean's waves lapping at the rock floor. Had something happened to her? Panic cinched his heart, stilling his breathing. He found her on a rock-pool's ledge, staring out at the horizon. She fiddled with her boots, cast a glance at him, then removed them. Into the water she shoved her feet, throwing her head back on a moan. The delicate arch of her throat drew his focus again.

"If I didn't think I'd pass out, I'd go for a swim."

He angled his head, unsure he'd heard correctly. "It is best that you find a place to rest. The blasts could—"

Booms thundered—too loud for comfort. A wave of hot air and sand hit him. He raised his arm to shield his face, then froze. Whirling in her direction, he lunged for her. Protected by his armor, he could bear the brunt of the abrasions but not her soft skin...

A splash halted him in his tracks as the ground trembled beneath his boots. Chunks of rock broke off the ceiling and clattered down, a few hitting the pool she'd dived into.

A white light consumed his vision, almost blinding him. He wasn't sure it was a symptom from the explosions or...fear since he'd never experienced the latter.

"Female," he roared, stumbling to the pool's edge. Wedging his hips against the side, he shoved his good arm into the green depths, caught something wispy, and yanked it up.

"Ow," she said when she breached the surface.

Cylo scowled but released her hair. He wasn't about to admit she'd scared him. "What are you doing?"

She met and held his gaze. While he waited for her to respond, red blood trickled down her temple. His heart lodged in his throat. He looped his arm under hers and hoisted her out of the water. She squeaked but clung to him, her wet clothing cooling his body further.

"You are bleeding," he whispered, setting her down. A quick dig in his pocket had him taking out one of two med-guns on his person. "Stand still," he said as he ran it over her temple.

She tilted her chin up, her gaze traveling over his features. Her breathing evened out, and so did her heartbeat, but her pallor remained the same. With the shush of the waves and the tensions thick post-explosion, he couldn't drag his attention from her. The wound sealed, so he wiped away the blood trickle, not liking the sight or smell of it. That she'd been harmed had barely restrained anger threatening his control. He focused on the bruises across her face and the tiny cuts along her arms. The purple changing to a horrid yellow brought him some peace. The smooth skin when her wounds healed deepened his gratitude.

"Any more explosions?" She peered over his shoulder in Hiossu's direction.

"No," Cylo said. "I will not apologize for it. We had to hide our presence."

She harrumphed. "Did you get all the women?"

"Seven?" He arched a brow and waited, content to admire her unusual beauty.

She chewed on her bottom lip, her focus distant. "Yeah. There weren't others?"

"According to the heat signature scans, no. You were a surprise."

Her eyes narrowed. "Which means you could be wrong."

He studied her stiff posture. Could Olin have missed more when they hadn't known of her? "The Yithian I interrogated mentioned these women and no others."

"Well, it's too late now. At least they died swiftly." She weaved around him to kneel beside Hiossu. "Why is he still out?"

"The length of unconsciousness depends on the strength of the blaster's stun." He passed her to peer through the crevice to the beach beyond.

A massive section of the cliff and the building built into it were missing; detritus littered the grounds around it. Flames meters high licked the sky, serving as a beacon for the incoming Yithian ship. More would arrive soon.

They had to move.

"We cannot stay here," he said, facing her. He jerked back when she held out her hand. "What do you need, milady?"

"Your medical device."

Thinking she meant to run it over Hiossu, Cylo placed it on her palm. "Press and hold the button."

She brought it within inches of her face to study it, then she did as he instructed. "Where are you injured?"

Heat rippled over his skin at her concern. "My left arm and knee. I can do it."

She hesitated then shook her head. "Show me. It's best I learn how. Just in case."

She crouched to run the med-gun over his knee. The relief was instant, eradicating the constant throbbing that had shot shards of agony up his thigh. Until it had healed, he hadn't realized how much pain he endured.

The med-gun pulsed.

"Why did it do that?" she asked, once more holding it an inch from her face.

He swallowed a smile. "It has completed its task."

"Oh, well, that's good." She beamed and moved onto his shoulder.

Close to him, he watched her expressions and the marvel of her shifting eye color: gray to green to blue—as alarming as her purple-colored skin and rainbow hair. The salt tang of seawater teased his nose, along with a subtle sweetness that was her natural scent. He drew it in though hid that he was doing so by keeping his breathing shallow.

Life returned to his fingers, along with a violent sweep of tingles. Those faded, too. With a mumbled thank you, he rolled his shoulder to test its mobility.

She ran the med-gun over Hiossu then nudged the male. He groaned, and a moment later, jerked to the side while throwing out his hand.

"Come. We need to hide somewhere else. Any ideas?" she asked, standing to her full height which reached Cylo mid-chest.

Hiossu frowned at the cavern. "Yes, they will look here first." He scrambled to his feet.

She offered the med-gun to Cylo.

Just in case? He liked her caution. "Keep it," he said.

She shoved it between the waistband of her pants and her bare skin. "So where to?"

"No help from your males?" Hiossu gazed at the beach. "Mm, the Yithians will come."

"Exactly. We must find somewhere else with a clear signal for..." She peeked at Cylo. "Porting, right?"

"Yes." He tapped his O.D.I. "Fyca."

"Dampening shield activat... Separate mission to destro—" The sound cut off.

Into the silence, Hiossu said, "The emergency power hub is to the east of the island."

She touched his forearm. "Could we make it there unseen?"

A flush of fury gritted Cylo's teeth. He stepped between them, breaking the contact. "It is our best option. If we reach the hub in time, we could board the kuta."

"I assume that's a ship?" she asked.

"A shuttle." Cylo hurried into the cave to gather the blasters.

He knelt to strap one to his thigh before shoving the other at Hiossu. Without another word, Cylo slipped through the crevice and winced when the sunlight, the hot sand, and the heat hit him. More evidence that his suit had to be malfunctioning. Despite the logic, he spared a few moments to adjust its temperature controls. He skirted the rocks along the beach until he could break away and head inland. He didn't use the zedali trees for cover. What mattered most was reaching the eastern beaches. Random glances confirmed they followed—the female between him and Hiossu.

"You're not thinking of running, are you?" she asked the Maloidian.

"You are an odd Earthian," the male said.

She walked backward while she spoke. "Will your people welcome you home? Or are you a traitor now?"

Hiossu stumbled, his cheeks darkening. "No, not many know of this...agreement between Yithia and Maloid."

"But Criass was your uncle." Her pale face flushed a bright purple when she caught Cylo's gaze. She didn't look away, though.

"Was." Hiossu nudged her from behind. "If you are up to it, let us increase the pace."

She nodded and caught up to Cylo. Her unsteady steps made him frown. Her breathing was harsher, more ragged. The med-gun should have helped her. That it hadn't meant her condition was worse than anticipated.

In the distance, an odd-shaped rock seemed out of place. With a kuta in front of it, that had to be the 'hidden' power hub. A small flash of white silenced a low hum that had been growing stronger with every step he'd taken.

"Cylo, acknowledge." Fyca's voice snapped Cylo's attention to his wrist.

He hesitated. Taking the shuttle would leave them open to further mishaps. "Can we port? We are sitting ducks." He smirked, enjoying the humor warming the female's face.

"Ducks?" Fyca asked.

Cylo caught her hand. "Come." He gestured to Hiossu to draw nearer, then gripped his shoulder. "Three to port to medical."

Chapter Eleven

THE MOMENT THEY APPEARED in the *Kevol's* common, Cylo scooped the swaying female against his chest. She squeaked then held his gaze as if she decided something. He hesitated mid-stride, the weight of her in his arms, her softness against his body, all imprinted on his senses. She buried her face into his chest, her eyelids fluttering shut. If time wasn't an issue, he'd savor her trust in him. Instead, with her health on the line, he marched to the med-E.D. and lowered her onto the bed.

She tried to sit up.

He cupped her shoulder, keeping her in place. "Let the med-E.D. work," he said. "It will heal you."

She slumped, wiggling in place like she searched for a comfortable spot. He stared at her bare feet, realizing she'd left her boots on Iphara then hiked across the coarse sand without him noticing. He stroked the underside of the closest foot then sighed when he met smooth skin.

Flashing skin, she reached inside her tunic and pulled out data cubes, holding them against her stomach. Taking them from her meant touching her, the heat from her body warming his fingers. He handed them to a passing Nhyht with a whispered, "To Olin."

"Please...keep this safe for me." Her husky voice snatched Cylo's attention to her then to where she held out the med-gun.

He took it, his fingers brushing hers and sending a shiver up his arm.

Qaff typed on the console, sealing the dome.

She lifted off the bed to float in mid-air. Her eyes widened. "What—"

"I'll be here when you wake up, ensa." Without breaking eye contact, he slid the med-gun into a pants pocket.

Her lips parted. Glancing behind him, she asked, "Hiossu?"

Cylo clenched his jaw. Was this female insane? Why did the Maloidian matter after what had happened to her? "He is being attended to and will be here when you are well."

She frowned at Cylo. "Promise?"

He forced a smile he was far from feeling. "Yes, ensa."

She held his gaze until the med-E.D. shut her eyes, and she drifted off.

"I do not know what they injected into her, but it took three variations of our usual sedatives to bring on sleep." Qaff scowled at the female. "You best see to your promise," he said, pointing his chin at Koddo running a med-gun over a pale-but-otherwise-fine Maloidian. "And have him heal you, too. We only have one med-E.D."

Cylo harrumphed but approached Hiossu. "How do you feel?"

"I am well, Etterian," Hiossu answered. "When the female is, too, I will share all I know."

"Fair enough." Cylo hesitated, not liking the Maloidian having free reign of his scimitar. "Koddo, escort Hiossu to the barracks."

The Maloidian opened his mouth then snapped it shut. "You do not trust me. I understand why. I shall be patient, Etterian."

"Operative Cylo," he said, tapping his chest. When Koddo took the male away, Cylo returned to the med-E.D. "How long?"

Qaff held his gaze but said nothing.

With a huff and a last glance at the stubborn female, Cylo marched to the comm. "Fyca—"

"That was the brightest cloud no doubt seen from every surrounding landmass," the pilot said, casting a glance at Cylo then grimacing. "I smell blood." He rose out of his seat and removed his med-gun.

Cylo waved him aside. "And the women?" he asked.

Eight had better survive this.

Informing Malo of the loss of even one female wouldn't be well received and might cost Cylo many feet of honor. Losing his hair wouldn't be sufficient punishment to assuage his guilt. A dead human meant a doomed Etterian, male or female.

Fyca grinned while pocketing his med-gun. "They are in the officers' quarters ordering meals off the rehydrator and cleansing. Qaff has tended to their wounds and neutralized the chemicals injected into them."

"That is indeed welcome news," Cylo said and tapped his O.D.I. "Olin, are you certain we did not miss a female?"

"There were no additional heat signals after we found Lady Eight. I made sure to rescan at the highest setting."

"My thanks." Cylo dipped his chin to his chest, having to accept Olin had done his best. The male was a respectable and experienced data officer, but Wren had planted doubt and mistrust in Cylo's mind. "Fyca, please comm Supreme Commander Jokta."

Fyca dropped into his seat and pressed the glowing keys on the console. "Connected."

"Operative Cylo, I hear the mission was a success."

"Indeed, Supreme Commander." Cylo bowed his head when Jokta's face dominated the display vid. "There were eight females, not seven. One is in critical condition in the med-E.D. I do not believe we can move her."

Jokta hummed. "Medic Qaff has already communicated his findings. The medical council in Issneen is your only option. Deliver the females to the *Phoenix* and head for home."

Just what Cylo wanted to hear. "I will send them on a kuta since we are not in porting range yet. I dare not waste a moment."

"Agreed. We shall meet them with the full might of Etteria." Jokta glanced down. A kaleidoscope of lights from his O.D.I. painted his chin. "A few scimitars are departing now to escort the kuta."

"I have an additional request, Supreme Commander. Please task Data Officer Kemt to monitor the comms. I need to know if human bones were found among the debris. Also, start the search for other such facilities."

"You believe a female was lost?" Jokta scowled.

"No, we did multiple checks, but if we missed one, then we will know to do a more thorough reconnaissance."

"Mm, or perhaps improve the equipment utilized. I shall personally discuss this with Kemt." The screen flickered to black.

"My thanks." Cylo gripped Fyca's shoulder, fatigue sending a ripple of weakness through him.

"I will let you know should we pass an asteroid."

At Fyca's offer, Cylo bowed his head in thanks and left.

"See to your female," Koddo said when Cylo entered the common.

He should have reported to Malo, but that could wait. Instead, he glanced at the rainbow-haired female a little obscured by the opaque dome.

"The females are asking for her...Wren." Durok squeezed Cylo's upper arm.

"Wren," Cylo said, rolling her name over his tongue. He crossed to her. The bruises were almost gone, but the purple tinge to her skin remained. "Findings?" he asked Qaff.

"It is difficult to summarize." Qaff stayed silent for a few moments. "The chemicals they gave her are attempting to change her genetic code. The other females were not administered the same chemicals. Hers are more potent. Perhaps she was given more than one dose?" Qaff stared at her, his brow furrowed.

Cylo splayed his fingers across the dome when her limbs twitched. "Will she live?"

"Yes." Qaff was swift in his response. "But as what, I cannot say. I have shared the data with the medical council and all medic lima kuu."

Cylo grunted, having all this confirmed. "How long will she sleep?" He stroked the dome as if he could tuck a floating turquoise curl behind her ear. She seemed so small—nothing like the fierce creature who'd used his greatsword, stabbed a Yithian in the eye, and challenged him post-explosion.

Qaff shrugged. "The sedatives must be modulated constantly to ensure she remains unconscious for the med-E.D. to complete its analysis."

"So not the normal doses required for humans?" Cylo smothered a wince when she jerked again, the movement rippling through her vibrant hair. He turned away. "Durok, fetch the females. Perhaps their voices will be calming."

"As commanded." Durok hesitated, meeting Cylo's gaze with ice-blue eyes.

Cylo froze. "Durok?" He caught the male by his shoulders to stare into his changed irises.

"It is true." The male beamed.

Joy exploded through Cylo like a sunburst, snatching his breath. "This...is wonderful."

"I must warn you. A fem...*woman* is a mother and is calling for her damu, claiming they are all alone." Durok dipped his head in sadness. "The women are asking for our aid."

Cylo jerked back. '*Woman' instead of 'female?'* What Durok said registered next.

Anger was swift to dampen his happiness. "The xemi took a mother?" He clenched his jaw as violent fury burned through his veins. "Supreme Commander Jokta is sending scimitars to guard the kuta transferring the...women to the *Phoenix*. One of them can be diverted to Earth. Comm Adviser Kanzo. A battleship orbiting Earth must send a few warriors to protect or retrieve her damu."

Durok smiled. "I will do so."

"Good," Cylo said.

Under the circumstances, that was all they could do from so far away. Exhaustion weighed every limb as if he carried slabs of Fuyra rock. He struggled to remain upright. The med-gun had done its job but hadn't revived his energy levels, and as Fyca had noted, the scent of his blood still lingered.

He glanced over his shoulder at the eighth woman.

Determination curled his fingers into fists. Since she was unexpected, she was a gift he had to treasure. He headed to his quarters in the barracks. There, he stripped and stepped into the cleanser, moaning when the hot water drenched him. He caught the tail of his braid and removed the Maloidian metal clip. Tossing it aside, he raised his face to the spray while his hair unraveled itself.

His mind replayed every second since he'd met...Wren. She'd shown remarkable strength after what she must have endured. And she'd been commanding. Without her suggestion, they might not have escaped the explosions in time. He smiled while spinning for the blast of air from the dryer.

"Malia pa," he said and waited as his hair braided itself.

He caught the tail and snapped the clip in place. Taking long strides, he crossed to the small replicator and ordered fresh armor. He dressed, with the final task the latching of the magnetic straps on his boots. A row of daggers sat on the table, tempting him to slot them into their loops along his belt. He hesitated. Being that armed on board was illogical, but the compulsion to do so was strong.

The memory of Wren touching Hiossu's forearm had Cylo sliding a hunting knife into his boot sheath. Its heaviness offered some comfort and calmed his anxiety. Hiossu escaping his quarters was slim, and even if he managed it, overpowering the operatives on board wasn't conceivable.

Cylo chose a meal then sat at the table with the lump of gold at its center, his virak of poisons, and an array of daggers to the side. Re-ordering the tools to make a knife in the time it took to reach Issneen was a foolish waste of resources. Besides, with how unwell Wren had been, he doubted he'd have a free moment.

He chuckled. A rainbow-haired, purple-skinned woman with indecisive eye color? None of his fellow operatives on board the *Gladio* would believe him. And since a few women had triggered the Ethera, then so could Wren.

That realization dismissed his good humor. Losing her to another male... A pairing was progress for Etteria, and yet, the thought didn't bring him joy like Durok's salvation had. And what if these changes she'd undergone on a genetic level did make her compatible with Maloidians? He groaned. *Hiossu*.

Why was that male waiting for Wren to be well before revealing what he knew?

Cylo shoved aside his uneaten meal and flipped open his virak. Rows of black, glass vials sat on the top drawer. He lifted that out to reveal the stash below. To know the contents was to uncap each one. The unprepared dared to sniff. Poisons assaulted the senses: touch, taste, smell. Some affected the mind: perception, self-awareness, sight, speech, beliefs. With the right combination, he could make anyone believe he was the Maker.

Since he need not fear an uninitiated accessing his virak, he'd carved tiny symbols into each vial: | for smell, || for taste, and ||| for touch. He stroked them, and depending on the marking, he inhaled, sipped, or smeared the liquid or dusted powder across his inner wrist. Nuances of scents told him what they were, from the Uikl lizard to the gagoni from the planet Durn—the rarest of them all and the sweetest smelling.

A warm buzz settled in his bloodstream as the poison took effect. He grinned, remembering his first time sipping just one vial. Determined not to ask for healing even as he swore his blood bubbled, he'd endured. Switching the bottom tray for the top told him which vials to sample. That way, he kept his immunity at its peak against all known poisons.

Flicking the lid shut, he marched to the *Kevol's* makeshift confinement—a room opposite to his. He entered without chiming.

"What is Wren to you?" he demanded, then clenched his jaw at the revealing question. It wasn't what he'd intended to ask.

Hiossu sprawled on the bed, stiffened, then sat up. "A victim?"

"She seems too familiar with your person," Cylo growled. He glanced away, fighting to gain control. *To feel is to fail*.

"I do not know the ways of these Earthians. Perhaps they communicate with touch." The Maloidian shrugged and lay down. The sickly-sweet aroma of genkoo hung in the air, so he had at least eaten.

Cylo folded his arms across his chest, not believing Hiossu's air of indifference. "Then why insist she be well before your interrogation?"

"You seemed distracted, Operative Cylo," he said with a dismissive flick of his hand. "You needed time to gather your thoughts."

Cylo grunted. "How many women have passed through that facility? Why her? Why now?"

Hiossu smirked. "Because she had somehow managed to find a dagger." He chuckled. "She had hidden it in her boot. It was our steel, and yet, she had not cut herself." Sliding an arm behind his head, he gazed at the ceiling. "The other females screamed, cried, made threats. This one had courage. Had the Yithians realized this, they would have done far worse to her. I do not think you would understand how precious such fearlessness is." His lips curled downward. "She has strength where I am weak. I never once raised my dislike of my uncle's methods, of his insane goals. I suppose you could say she inspired me to rebel."

She *had* made Cylo question the efficacy of his males, their equipment—something an Etterian never did but an operative should do.

"I suppose you are hoping she is your Dar Eth?"

A weight crushed Cylo's chest in a vice grip. He did his best to hide his reaction. "Finding my pairing is a constant hope. It would be a blessed gift if she is mine."

"For the part I played, I am indeed sorry." Hiossu bowed his head. "You need not fear that I am an abingu, ready to strike."

"Such an attack we prepare for," Cylo mumbled, the weight of the dagger in his boot lying heavy on his conscience. The venom from a slithering abingu was the dangerous part, which meant Cylo couldn't relax his guard around the talkative Hiossu just yet. "Tell me, how do the Yithians manage to steal these women without us or Earth's forces noticing?"

Not that Cylo had respect for Earth's detection systems. Supreme Commander Ulriq had been able to land and enjoy a meal on Earth without trouble. Well, excluding the Yithian attack. That too had gone unnoticed. At that stage, Earth and Etteria had yet to negotiate a treaty. Ulriq had risked much.

Too much.

But when King Xeus had learned of humans triggering the Ethera, nothing had stopped him from conquering Earth—through treaties or war. Thankfully, the latter hadn't been necessary. It had been close, though, with Medic Teric insisting on returning with his Dar Eth to her planet when nothing had been finalized. Had Earth declined Teric's relocation, King Xeus would have used all Etteria's battleships in a show of force.

Hence Malo's new appointment as ambassador and engineer. It didn't help that Princess Oriana didn't trust her own people.

Cylo smothered a laugh. He'd have to reach out to Garix and find out how Malo was doing.

"Well?" He faced Hiossu. "How do the Yithians succeed?"

"That I do not know. Do Yithian ships have stealth?"

Cylo stiffened. "No." Though, if an agreement had been made between Maloid and Yithia, perhaps Maloid had seen fit to share this? "Comm me if there is something you recall."

"Of course." Hiossu didn't glance at Cylo when he left.

He paused in the passage while the door sealed. "Olin," he said into his O.D.I. "Investigate whether Yithia has Maloid's stealth technology."

"Mm, when they have refused to share that with us? I shall task Data Officer Tias to prioritize this."

Cylo pursed his lips. Tias was one of the best and a dear battle-bonds, but the more eyes on this, the better. "Excellent. Perhaps ask all data officers in orbit around Earth, Maloid, and Yithia."

"Wise. I will keep you informed."

"Share your findings with Adviser Kanzo, as well." Cylo ended the comm and headed to medical.

Chapter Twelve

Cylo glanced at Qaff and opened his mouth to ask—

"No change," the medic snapped.

"Can we get her showered?" A red-haired woman settled beside Cylo. Other women gathered around him.

He ran his gaze over Wren's leggings accentuating well-sculpted legs. A sliver of her belly was exposed, but the sleeveless tunic appeared clean. Her hair was as vibrant as when he first met her.

Qaff turned, tablet in hand. "The med-E.D. sterilizes—"

"Nothing compares to a shower; it makes us feel human." The redhead swept a hand down her body.

Cylo frowned. "She cannot be moved. Not in her present condition. I have just informed Supreme Comma—"

"She has to be," the redhead said. "It's her greatest wish."

"Other than health, Terry?" A brunette scoffed.

"I will not allow it." Qaff stepped between the women and Cylo. "Not at this stage. A cleansing would awaken her; she must do so on her own. Interrupting the analysis could be hazardous."

Terry glared at Qaff. "Listen here, Etterian—"

"Please." A black-haired woman placed a hand on Terry's arm. "A shower can wait."

Terry pulled away. "Ronda—"

"I will ensure she is well and receives whatever she needs." Cylo pressed his fingers to the dome. "In the meantime, those who have not met their Eths—"

"A what now?" a young woman asked; her damp hair, almost brown, soaked her tunic.

"When an Etterian meets his soul mate, it triggers what they call the Ethera." An older woman grimaced. "It changes his eye color to neon blue. He becomes your Eth and you his Dar Eth."

"Soul mate?" Ronda squeaked.

"Yes," Cylo said, silencing their gasps and murmurs. "He will kneel for you. I must apologize. This is your Eth's responsibility to inform you, but the situation is dire. A shuttle will fly you to the battleship *Phoenix* where you can decide your destination. A scimitar or two will meet you halfway to escort the mother to Earth—"

"Donna, did you hear?" the woman with the damp brown hair split the crowd to hug another.

"Truly?" Donna asked, raising her green gaze to Cylo.

"Indeed. Etterians do not lie, for it is dishonorable. The scimitar will speed you home, and if you speak to any supreme commander orbiting his battleship around Earth, he will ensure your damu are rescued or guarded as needed."

Donna crumpled to the floor with a sob.

Cylo's chest cinched tight. Alarmed, he took a step—

"Thank you," the woman chanted, rocking back and forth amid her weeping.

He flicked a hand at the common. "For those remaining—"

"Why would we stay?" Terry gripped her hips, challenging him.

"An Eth cannot be separated from his Dar Eth. It is certain death for him. Together, you may choose to stay or leave. When he approaches you, I only ask one thing: please, show him kindness. To find one's mate is a gift from the Maker. You hold his life in your hands."

Terry folded her arms across her chest. "You say Wren will be secure, safe, but why is she inside this machine? How can you promise she'll recover?"

"The chemicals the Maloidians injected into you were easy to eradicate. Wren has too many and too much." Cylo gazed at Wren, amazed at how she still breathed. "Our only hope to save her is for our greatest medical...teachers to assess her. We bring her to Issneen where we can best help." She was his to guard; that was all he could focus on.

"Her vitals are stable, but the med-E.D. cannot slow the modifications happening to her genetic code," Qaff added.

"I vow to you, milady, that Wren is under my protection. I will defend her with my life." The compulsion to be by her side was beyond anything Cylo had experienced, driving him to admit he'd die for her. Not just any woman, but Wren herself.

"What those assholes did to us was barbaric," Terry growled. "Thank you for saving us." She faced the women. "I've nothing waiting for me at home. I'll stay."

That the female insisted on remaining with Wren like he wasn't good enough? Anger erupted so fast, Cylo struggled to control it. "Do you not trust me? Believe I lack honor?"

Terry staggered back, her hands raised. "No... Not at all. I just thought a friendly—"

"I am hostile?" Cylo roared. He gathered the shadows around himself and loomed over the argumentative and insulting woman. "Can you tell us what was injected into any of you? Is your Earthian medicine far superior to ours? Would we harm her in any way?"

"Violet is my Dar Eth. She will remain with me on *Kevol*." Durok weaved among the women to stand behind an older woman with a lovely gray hair color.

She lifted her chin, clenched her fists at her sides, but didn't glance at Durok over her shoulder. "Seems I'm staying."

"Then this matter is resolved." Cylo turned his back on them and took a few seconds to calm the volatile emotions simmering under the surface. He focused on Wren, trying to gauge whether her skin was less purple.

"Operations Commander Malo on comm." Fyca's voice snapped Cylo from his daze.

He rolled his shoulders then tapped his O.D.I. "Patch him through to medical."

Malo appeared on the display vid mounted to a bulkhead. "Cylo, I have read the report. Well done." He glanced at the med-E.D. "May the woman survive."

"I pray so," Cylo said, resisting the urge to look away from Malo.

"Data Officer Olin has assured me that you have made the necessary arrangements for the women, and that a few of our males have found their Dar Eths. Indeed, King Xeus and I are well-pleased."

A few males? Who else? Cylo bowed his head. "I could not have done this without my males. Olin is trawling through the data retrieved. Perhaps, soon, we will have a better understanding as to what the Yithians and Maloidians are up to. In addition, this..." He gazed at Wren. "...Woman befriended a Maloidian who is on board the scimitar and is willing to share what he knows."

Malo grinned. "Excellent. Since she serves as a distraction, ensure Olin continues to update me." The comm ended.

Cylo grimaced. As a reprimand for not attending to the report himself, he'd endured worse. He activated his O.D.I. "Olin, my thanks."

"None needed," came the male's response.

"Yet a favor is owed." Cylo disconnected the comm and faced Qaff. None would mention how costly favors for an operative could be.

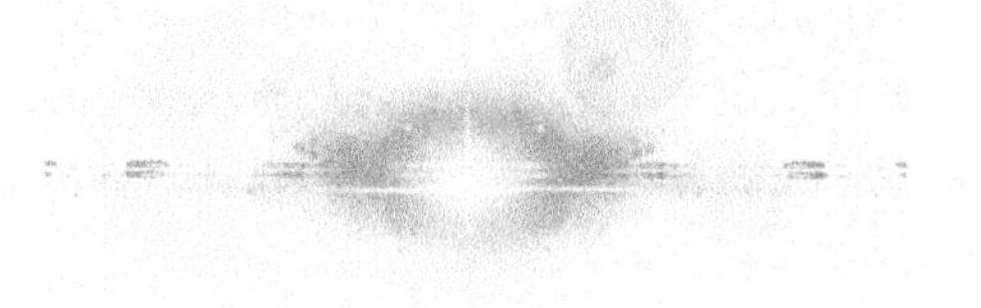

WREN WAS WARM, COMFORTABLE, and yet, not herself. Something was odd. No pain twinged through her, disturbing her sleep. It almost felt like it was her off-day and she'd slept in. She stretched then wiggled her backside, searching for a comfortable spot on her lumpy mattress. That spot was elusive, so she gave up.

How many hours....no, *days*, had she been asleep? Time felt different, distant. A sense of weightlessness lingered. She was no doubt on a leap. Her eyes wouldn't open to let her gaze upon the beauty that was Pluto. Splice zinged through her veins, adding a little heat. Images flashed like memories, but they were so far-fetched, they had to be fiction. Silver sharks with fangs, yellow-tentacled, black-spotted aliens, and a purple liquid. She shook her head, trying to shove them aside. No, she wanted to remember the hero who'd stormed in to save her. Piercing dark blue eyes, the kind she could drown in. Long, black hair in a thick braid that swayed across his tight ass when he moved. A sharp jawline, even lips, led her gaze to his long nose and low-arched, black brows.

When he'd touched her knee, peace had descended, calming her frantic heartbeat. Why was she scared? That didn't matter. He'd gotten her to follow him. Probably with his smile hinting at a dimple in his left cheek. She'd never seen a more attractive man. What a weak-assed description. He was a stunner, she'd admit that. But what the hell was he doing strolling through her dreams? No such men existed on Demeter, well, except for Pierce, and he didn't count.

She snorted. Not that she'd met every man on the station. Her stomach churned into a hot, tight, mess when her dimpled man called her 'ensa.' The tone had the sexiness of 'sweetheart,' so she leaned toward it meaning that.

A gasp tore through her.

Was he Etterian?

She'd read about them in digi-mags. In person, any of them would be quite impressive. Still, what had made her mind conjure this specific man, down to the details? Her overactive imagination couldn't have brought about her nightmarish adventure. Which meant...

Shit. Yithians and Maloidians *had* played a part. And her hero was real?

Her eyelids fluttered open. A tinted bubble surrounded her but not so clouded that she couldn't see beyond it. The place was empty, with a nighttime atmosphere if she judged the silence. Only the beep-beep of a machine registered.

A face appeared, familiar... She gasped, blinking at her hero, his handsomeness sending a flush of warmth through her and liquifying her limbs. Her lungs forced her to suck in a breath. *Wow.*

"How do you feel?" he asked, pressing his palm to the dome as his deep baritone rolled over her.

"Where am I?" she managed, her voice hoarse. At least she could speak. The delicious sight of him made her swallow her tongue.

"On the *Kevol*. We are rushing you to Issneen."

"Where's that?" She frowned. "Why?" Wiggling her limbs only got her spinning within the pod until her ass pointed at him. Heat exploded across her cheeks. Flaying her arms didn't help either.

"Qaff, is the med-E.D. done?" he asked another Etterian she hadn't noticed.

Air whooshed out, and she found herself face down on the bed. Before she could flip over, her man gripped her by the hips and hoisted her into a sitting position, her legs hanging off the edge. He slid his fingers from her hips, along the sides of her thighs to her knees. Had he done that on purpose?

Intrigue hit her, an emotion not her own. She pinched her brow at the ping of a headache forming.

"Issneen is Etteria's royal city. Our best medics await your arrival," he said.

Anxiety trickled into her when he swept his gaze over her face.

"What are you worried about?" she asked, attempting to scoot off the bed.

His arm across her waist kept her in place and flooded her with a splice-like zing.

"Until Qaff assures me you are well—"

"She is well...for now, Cylo." Qaff turned away, tapping on a tablet.

Silo? That was her man's name?

"But...she is purple," he said, swiping his hand over her forearm, summoning goose bumps.

"Huh?" She scrunched up her nose then glanced down. "What the hell?" With a muffled squeal, she scrambled back and toppled off the other side of the bed. Into his arms. They encompassed her like steel bands. She fought the urge to burrow into him. "Sorry," she said, her shoulder pressed against his chest. He smelled so damn good, too, like something spicy and sweet.

Focus, Wren. You're lilac.

She stared at her arms, familiar yet not.

"How? No, scratch that. Can you fix it?" She raised her gaze to meet his. "And can you put me down, please?" That he liked holding her was too distracting when she had other things to deal with like how long would she be lilac? And how could she sense his emotions when Etterians were known not to have many? Where had she read that?

He lowered her feet to the floor, his hands lingering. When she swayed, dizziness spinning the room, he looped an arm around her waist again. She prodded her pastel purple skin. It was still her, just a different color.

"A side effect of whatever the Maloidians did to me, Qaff?" she asked the doctor just to confirm her suspicions.

"We believe so, milady," he said without glancing at her while he flicked through symbols on a wall-mounted screen. "Only in Issneen will we know the truth and perhaps how to undo it."

"I see," she said, tossing a tentative smile at Cylo.

"Do you wish to cleanse?" he asked, his gaze intense.

She gaped for a moment. How had he known she'd kill for that? When her stomach wrenched, she cleared her throat. "Please, and food?"

"Can you walk?" he asked, drawing back his hand in a caress across her abdomen.

"Of course I ca—" One step and she slithered to the floor but found herself once again in his arms.

"Use my quarters," Qaff said, his focus elsewhere.

Cylo veered to the back of the medical bay and into a room. A bed was to the left and an open-plan bathroom to the right. Dull-gray metal walls added no cheer to the depressing space.

She fixed her gaze on what looked like a shower cubicle, made noticeable by being white-walled. Excitement exploded through her but merged with his butterflies. She stared at him, trying to read an expression on his stoic face.

He halted *inside* the shower.

"What are you—" A spray blasted her, drenching them both. She spluttered, spitting out water, then wiped away her wet hair to glower at him. "Now my clothes are wet." Visions of him yanking her out of the pool came to mind. Then, he'd been furious with her. She'd been soaked and smelling of the sea. It had been incredible, though, to at least wash the stench off her. And sure, salty ickiness had coated her skin until he'd let the med-E.D. enclose her.

"Forgive me, you are too weak to stand. I will order you whatever you wish to wear, ensa."

Shit. The way he said 'ensa' was like a drug on her senses. His emotions saturating her were of affection and admiration, mixing with her desire and anticipation.

"Um, Cylo." She peeked at him.

He dipped his chin to meet her gaze. "Yes, milady."

She hesitated, unsure how to explain what was wrong. "Something weird's happening to me."

He stiffened, his stance widening, concern and determination exploding from him. "What is it?"

"I can sense—" She bit her lip, not wanting to sound like an idiot.

He lowered her, then faced the room, trapping her in the corner by pinning her in place with his body. "Do you feel in danger?"

She couldn't see over his broad back or around the width of him. But...it wasn't something physical she feared. Deep inside, it was as if voices roiled, climbing into her mind, and whispering half-truths—some she ached to believe. How could she put that into words? Where he wouldn't think she'd gone insane? "No, not at all. It's just that... Maybe I should tell Qaff?"

"You do not trust me?" He spun, the front of his body touching hers, but his ferocious scowl couldn't compare to his fury hitting her like a sledgehammer to the chest. She bowed under the weight, fighting to find who she was amid his reactions.

Wincing, she tried to drown him out, to think. But with his sadness, disappointment, anger clouding her mind, she was fast becoming overwhelmed. She gripped his upper arms, tempted to shake him. "Cylo, please... I can't..." She drew in a shaky breath and peered into his eyes. "I can feel what you feel."

He frowned. "Like an empath? Can humans do that?"

Surprise, puzzlement, and intrigue whiplashed her. Needing to be grounded to this moment and place, she fixed her gaze on where she clasped him. The strength beneath her fingers soothed and...bolstered her. "Some humans can, but I wasn't one of them." Her voice broke, and tears pressed the backs of her eyes. *Fuck, I hate these aliens. What gives them the right—*

"Ah," he said, gathering her against his rock-hard chest, a tentative smile teasing the appearance of his dimple. "Another side effect?"

Holy shit, he's gorgeous. "I think so. I'd have to test it to be sure."

His eyes narrowed, and in a gentle voice, he asked, "What can you sense in me?"

Oh, she could write him a book. When he waited, expectant, she pressed her temple to his armored chest to focus, but the action only brought his smell closer. "Humor, relief..." Meeting his gaze, she whispered, "desire."

He sucked in a sharp breath. "I cannot risk my void to mate with a woman not my Dar Eth," he said. "But you tempt me, ensa."

An almost orgasmic wave of heat not her own hit her, hardening her nipples. She shivered despite the hot water pouring over her.

He whipped her out of the shower and stood still for a lengthy blast of air. Stuck in his arms, she didn't move, content to be held. After her ordeal, she'd probably have let Dallas hug her for hours. Yet, Cylo embraced her like he cherished who she was.

Knowing he wanted her and wouldn't do anything about it sank like a splice-detox in the pit of her stomach. A little sex would have done wonders for her mood, but it might complicate things between them when now wasn't the best time. He wasn't for her, and no matter how attractive he was, she'd have to let him go.

Then again, since when had she listened to reason?

Chapter Thirteen

Cylo didn't want to release Wren, even when the air dryer could do no more. Their garments were damp where their bodies met, but the swirl of colors in her eyes—from green, to gray, to blue—mesmerized him. Her accurate reading clarified what coursed through him. He *did* desire her. Wanted nothing more than to kiss her, to taste those lips that uttered his name, especially when she scowled at him.

To feel is to fail.

Maker. He cradled her close, unable to resist her softness.

She yanked out of his arms, swayed, but pressed her hand to his chest, holding herself upright. "Hiossu?"

Her concern calmed a little of Cylo's ardor. "He is well, ensa. Dress, eat, and I shall take you to him."

Her smile was blinding. "Good. He was my only ally when I needed one." She stilled and raised a wide-eyed gaze to Cylo. "I'm his only ally now."

She spoke the truth. Cylo could admit that. And having an empath in the same room as the Maloidian would be helpful, not to mention test whether her new skill extended beyond him. But not as she was. A glance confirmed her garments clung to her, accentuating parts of her he didn't want Hiossu to notice. Even as he longed to run his palm along every curve.

"Come, choose what to wear, to eat." He caught her hand and ushered her to the replicator and rehydrator. A few commands altered the menus to Galactic. He stepped aside for her to browse without him hovering.

"Jeans, T-shirt, boots...underwear," she muttered while she ordered. After the items materialized, she shifted to the rehydrator. "Coffee? I wish. Start with something small...

Soup. Argh." A bowl appeared filled with steaming brown liquid with a savory aroma. A bottle of water followed.

She snatched up the bundle of garments and faced him. "I need to change."

"Why?" he asked, fascinated by the play of light across her hair.

"Into these." She tightened her arms.

He frowned. "What is stopping you?"

Her purple cheeks darkened. "Could you give me a few minutes alone?"

"No," he snapped. "If you fall—"

"Fine," she huffed. "Turn around then, and no peeking."

What a strange command. "Why?"

She raised her gaze to the ceiling before meeting his. "With your back to me, I can dress. No peeking means don't look at me, not even if you're tempted."

Silence settled between them. Ah, she waited for him.

"Leave or turn away?" He swiveled on his heels. "Like this?"

"Yeah, thanks." Fabric shuffled, slithered, hitting the floor in a range of thuds. Her muted moan urged him to look, but he resisted. When she thumped her booted feet, he chanced a glance.

Her hair was dry, wisping outward, yet the colors appeared less vibrant. Again, she wore blue leggings that hugged her legs, and this time a dark blue, short-sleeved tunic that covered more of her.

"I like these boots," she said, scooping up the bowl and bottle of water before sitting. She yelped but didn't leap up when the comfy conformed to the shape of her backside. Her eyes remained wide for a few seconds, then she settled.

"My apologies for not warning you—"

"How were you to know I'd never encountered an adjusting chair?" She flicked a dismissive wrist, the bottle in her hand.

"Is that enough food?" he asked, crouching in front of her.

"I don't know when last I ate anything solid. I've heard to start slowly when reintroducing food." She tucked the bottle between her thighs and cradled the bowl, bringing it to her lips.

He lowered his gaze, trying to smother the anger rising within. That she had suffered so, that other women had, too...

"How are they?" she asked between sips.

He jerked back. How had she known where his thoughts had gone? "If you mean your women, they are well. Some have triggered the Ethera in my males."

"Ah, yes, the soul-mate thing." She smiled. "I'm happy for them. And Donna?"

"The mother?" Cylo ran his thumb along the shell of his ear, wishing he could do so to Wren. "We are speeding her to Earth."

She grinned. "Thank you. I remember something about them leaving this ship?"

"Yes, those not paired. Only two remain on board."

She stiffened, a glower forming, sparking an answering fire in his belly. "Their choice?"

His chuckle was too hoarse for his liking. "Etterians are not in the habit of forcing women to our will."

Her cheeks flushed a deep purple. "I can imagine how persuasive you can be." She set the empty bowl aside and took a long draw of water. The angle of her jaw led his gaze to her lips wrapped around the bottle's mouth. "Now, let's visit Hiossu and find out what the hell his people and the sharks are up to."

Cylo offered her his hand. When she slipped her fingers across his palm, a frisson of heat uncoiled in his core. He enclosed her delicate grasp and guided her to her feet. "Want to stop by Qaff to mention the empathy?"

"Sure, then we can test it on Hiossu. Might be my imagination acting up."

"You have been correct so far." He brushed a curl off her temple—the strands cool and clinging to his fingers.

"You said fucking a woman—"

He growled, his fingers twitching to yank her against him. The vulgar word sent a tsunami of need through him.

She froze. "What's the matter?"

Not willing to go into why he found her harsh edges appealing, he cleared his throat and asked, "What about mating a woman?"

"Well, you said you risked your void if you...*mated* with a woman not your Dar Eth. Is it the physical act that's the trigger, or is just being with me like this?"

"I suspect it is tied to physical interaction and emotional fluctuations. When I tend to my chore, it does not expand the void. If you were to—" He swallowed hard when images of her running her hand along the length of his malehood pulsed fiery lust through him.

"Chore?" Her nose twitched, then her mouth parted on a gasp. "Not what I would call an orgasm." She threw back her head and laughed.

He found himself smiling. "When your fulfillment is by your own hand, it does become...monotonous."

Her mirth faded, but her cheeks had darkened, and her eyes sparkled. "How is your void now?" she asked, inching closer to peer at him.

Her subtle scent tantalized him. Her question sparked his curiosity. He turned his attention inward, prodding the solid nothingness at the center of his chest. "It is as normal."

Movement snatched his focus. She rose onto her toes, cupped his jaw, and brushed her mouth across his, stunning him. Warmth, softness, and sweetness registered. His lips tingled. He blinked while hunger, craving, and compulsion urged him to kiss her like he longed to do. Gripping her hip, he planned to do just that.

"And now?" she asked, snapping him out of his daze.

He glared, releasing her. "This is not a game—"

"Cylo, just test it."

He sighed and did so. Again, no change. He whipped up his head, shock locking his limbs. *Kissing her is safe? How... How is this possible?*

Without hesitation, he looped an arm around her waist and lifted her. She gasped and clung to him. Her heartbeat thundered in his ears, and silence stretched between them as his body noted the feel of her in his arms and the heat of her hands clutching his shoulders. Her cheeks warmed when he dipped his head. He took his time to drown in her ever-changing eyes. When her focus shifted to his lips and her nostrils flared, all caution disintegrated.

He slashed his mouth across hers, thrusting his tongue between her plump lips. Her taste, though flavored by the broth, rattled his control. His breathing labored, his heart thumped against his rib cage, and everything else faded. Only Wren remained, filling every one of his senses.

Her moans, the way she dug her fingers into his hair, the stroke of a caress along his jaw, made him Fuyra hard. He'd never been this...stimulated.

Keeping a hand on her shoulder, in case she was as dizzy as he was, he broke away.

Her eyes had narrowed with a need that mimicked his own. "Test it," she rasped.

With a struggle to rein in his thoughts, he focused on the void, then stumbled back. It had shrunk. "How did you know?" he managed, probing the dark mass that had been his constant companion since he was a damu.

She huffed hair away from her face. "I don't react like this to any man. It must mean something." She strode to the door.

He curled his fingers into fists to stem the urge to drag her back to him. "Where—"

"Come." A beautiful smile blossomed across her pink lips. "Have Qaff scan you."

"Why?" he asked, adjusting his armor's temperature in a silly attempt to cool his arousal.

"You, my doubtful Cylo, need facts to believe." She left him standing there.

"Believe what?" he muttered. That she was an oddity? A mystery?

"Qaff, tell me, why can I now sense emotions?" She leaned over the bed, resting on her elbows as she waited for Qaff to respond. The position angled her backside in a sensual way, snatching Cylo's focus repeatedly.

"What did you say, milady?" Qaff took out his med-gun. "Could you not do so before?"

"No. You're intrigued, puzzled, and amazed." She patted her chest. "And eager to unravel this new development."

"I am indeed." He chuckled. "The chemicals are flipping through your genetic code like a damu's game. Hence your uncertain eye color."

"My what?" she gasped, then crossed the med bay to peer into the reflective surface above the counter. "My eyes." Her pulse ticked at the base of her jaw. "Lilac skin; now this? How are my organs?"

"They are well, if not more efficient." Qaff summoned a graph flickering up and down. "The chemicals toy only with your code—"

"As if it's searching for something specific." She growled. "To make humans compatible with Yithians and Maloidians."

"And perhaps incompatible with Etterians," Cylo said.

"Losing humans as our Dar Eths would doom our species to a dwindling death." Qaff grimaced. "You may be correct, Cylo."

"I made Cylo kiss me," she said like they were discussing their next meal. "Check his void, Qaff. It hasn't worsened."

"Truly?" Qaff's brow furrowed in thought. "Although, more than a kiss might be needed to affect the void's expansion."

"It shrank," Cylo muttered, too low for Wren to hear.

"Impossible," Qaff snapped, circling medical to run his med-gun over Cylo. "Status marked. Kiss milady again."

Cylo ached to but not with an audience.

She looped her arms around his neck, pressing her body to his as she rose onto her toes. He grabbed her hips, lifting her in place, then lowered his head. This time, he took each second gifted to him to explore every corner of her delectable mouth. The soup's flavor had vanished, intensifying the essence of her. He succumbed, needing everything about her to fill him, like a light eradicating darkness.

"Mm," Qaff hummed. "Unusual. Since you have not knelt for her, she is not your Dar Eth, yet she affects you as if she is."

Cylo drew away, pressed his temple to hers, and sucked in ragged breaths.

"While Qaff tries to figure out what the hell's happening to me and you, let's see how Hiossu's doing?" Her cheeks were flushed, her eyes glazed. "And if you could hide some of that arousal, I'd appreciate it."

Chapter Fourteen

Appreciate? Wren almost scoffed. The man had no idea what he'd ignited in her. *Wow*. She tingled better than any splice buzz. And where he ran his hands, from between her shoulder blades to clasp her butt cheeks, her senses were on high alert. Need consumed her core, drenching her fresh panties. She shouldn't be reacting to him this potently. They'd kissed twice. Her first peck hadn't counted. And if what Qaff had said was true, she'd get to be horizontal with Cylo soon. Her nipples pinged in eagerness.

"I smell your arousal, Wren." His breath feathered across her ear.

"I can't control it," she said, then glanced at him, almost brushing her mouth across his, he was that close. "Do you want me to not be aroused, Cylo?"

Navy and neon swirled in his eyes, like the forming of a dwarf star. "I want you as you are, whatever that may be."

"Good answer," she said, then gestured to the common. "Lead the way."

He did, his tight ass still in damp uniform. Why didn't that bother him? She'd itch to change into dry clothes. When she'd stripped, she hadn't bothered to check whether he snuck a peek. The conviction and determination controlling his desire were admirable. Damn, knowing people's emotions sucked and didn't at the same time. She'd have liked a bit of mystery when he was too obvious. Still, the certainty of their attraction was also calming. She didn't need to worry her advances would be rebuffed or he was just stringing her along. Although, she doubted Etterians played those kinds of games.

He took her down a narrow passage, then stopped in front of one door among many. "The barracks," he said. "The scimitar houses ten warriors and one officer."

"How many stayed instead of going with the women?"

"Five, including myself," he said, studying her upturned face.

"Which women?" She hesitated, pretty sure he'd mentioned two were on board. The thought of being the only human and facing this experimental fallout by herself... She shuddered. "Or am I alone?"

He faced her, his expression intense. "You, Brenda, Fyca's Dar Eth, and Violet is Durok's."

When the door swished open, he paused in the doorway, blocking any possible attack. The man didn't know Hiossu, not well enough to risk her life. Or so it seemed. She peered around Cylo and smiled at her ally sprawled on the bed with his fingers laced across his belly. Nothing marred his lemon-yellow skin. Not that she expected Cylo to have beaten him up, but a tiny part had considered it.

Hiossu sat up and smiled at her. "You are well?"

She scoffed. "I'm purple but, other than that, weirdly okay." When she made to go around Cylo, he threw out his arm, catching her across the stomach. She narrowed her eyes at him. "Hiossu's had many chances to kill me."

"Let us not give him another," Cylo said, his gaze running over her face.

He thinks I'm beautiful. The realization exploded bubbles in her belly like sparkling wine.

"I will not harm her. I vow." Hiossu clasped his hands between his knees. "You want answers I hope I can give you."

"First, thank you," she said, settling into a seat Cylo flipped down for her. When she took it, he stood beside her, close enough for heat to pour off him and summon a shiver.

Hiossu grimaced. "I did not help. Look at you." He gestured to all of her.

"Do you know what was in those chemicals?" Cylo demanded.

She touched his arm. His drive to heal her flooded her with warmth, but she needed to focus on what Hiossu was feeling. If she could, that was. Focusing this...skill could be like trying to steer a broken cargo barge. "Have there been similar results? As in other purple humans?"

Hiossu dipped his head. A 'shadow' stretched out to bathe her in sorrow. "Purple, yes, but they died. You...are a miracle." He leaped to his feet to pace the small space before sinking onto the bed. "I assume the other females are well?" He held Cylo's gaze until he nodded. "Which would mean either my uncle's sample had no effect on you, or the double dose did. Or still nothing until Jniaa injected his formula. Each kuliriji..." Hiossu frowned. "What is the common word in Galactic, Etterian?"

"Scientist," Cylo gritted out.

"Yes... Each scientist has perfected their own mix in a race to bring Earthians...humans to our planet."

"Why?" Cylo loomed though how he did that without moving, she wouldn't be able to explain. "You do not need them other than for slavery or as products."

"In a way, you are correct. At first." Hiossu ran his gaze over Wren, summoning a shiver. He liked the look of her. Her skin crawled, unlike her reaction to Cylo's admiration. "A vid of Lady Ava and Ambassador Barro showed a species softer, intelligent, and capable of such emotional intensity that it piqued the kuliriji council's interest. When further news reached us that Etterians had found Dar Eths among these Earthians and that Yithians hunted them for the arena... Well, it was a business opportunity we could not pass up."

He offered her a weak smile.

"How many women?" she asked. Darkness formed a shield around Hiossu's soul as if he couldn't share this with her.

"Before I was enlisted, I cannot say. You were part of the third delivery." He threw out a hand. "I truly am sorry for what my people did...*are* doing." He grabbed his temples. "I would be naïve to think there is only one facility. Yet, I have never heard my uncle or the other scientists mention another."

"Could you help Qaff figure out what's happening to me?" She gazed at Cylo. "Whether I am dying?"

He scowled. "Issneen—"

"Is still our destination, but let's not waste time. Additional diagnostics from Qaff and your machines would better inform your doctors." She rose, desperate for a moment alone. To be caught up in this when she'd have an E.A.F. shitstorm to deal with? "Speak with Qaff, please, Hiossu. Offer what insight you have."

"Liaise with Olin, as well. Perhaps you can help him locate other testing facilities. You are free to leave your quarters." Cylo typed on his O.D.I.

He was hot on her heels when she left. Even his presence, though it had calmed her before, was a little too much to handle.

She faced him, splayed her fingers across his chest, and met his gaze. "I need...a place to just be me. I was taken because I had a habit of leaping into space with only my ankle harnesses tethering me to the station." She feathered her fingers along the velvety skin below his collarbone exposed by the 'V' of his chest armor. "Please, can you help me?"

"I will not allow you to launch yourself out of a bay door," he said, inching closer to cup her elbows, determination pouring off him. "And the scimitar is traveling too fast to risk it. But I do have an idea." He caught her hand and laced their fingers with a familiarity that was awe-inspiring.

She followed him to the common, then along a passage to what she assumed was the bridge. The door was shut, but Cylo faced the opposite side. He pressed a wall-mounted square to the right, and a narrow panel opened onto a ladder.

"Up there is an observation deck. Use it for as long as you need to."

She cupped his cheek, ran her thumb over his bottom lip, then climbed before she succumbed to the desperate need for a hug. A glance confirmed he watched her. The thought of her ass filling his field of view flooded her with delicious warmth. Yet the moment she stepped onto the deck and the hatch sealed, all emotions not her own faded. She crossed to the thick glass to press her temple to it. Before her...or rather, the scimitar, was the vastness of space with bright stars and constellations in the distance. This... Somehow, he'd known this was exactly what she needed. How could a man be that intuitive? Considerate? It couldn't be just to get into her pants, right?

Her thoughts drifted to what awaited her at Demeter Station, which brought Pierce and her family to mind. *Shit.* She shimmied down the ladder and winced when a wall of emotions hit her, like she waded through quicksand. She swallowed, wrestled with her inner self, and managed, just, to tamp down the cacophony. Enough to think. With a trembling hand, she tapped on the door to the comm.

It swished open to a petite blonde sitting on an Etterian's lap. They had to be Brenda and Fyca. Violet was the oldest woman among them with her lovely silver-gray hair.

"Um," Wren said, her nostrils filling her with primal urges she wasn't in the mood to deal with. "I need to contact my parents or someone on a station orbiting Pluto."

"Not an issue, milady," Fyca said, brushing aside Brenda's hair. "Do you require privacy?"

Since only lust saturated the bridge, she could speak to Pierce without issue. "No, not really."

Fyca pressed a button on the multi-lit console. "Cylo to the comm."

Damnit. That wasn't what she meant. There had to be a way to call Pierce without bothering Cylo. She pursed her lips and swiveled on her heel, planning on meeting him in the passage.

His strong thighs carried him toward her, his braid swinging behind his forceful strides. "What is it, ensa?" His concern preceded him like a force field.

"Can I speak to my family? I need to let them know I'm alive." She wrung her hands. How could she have forgotten about them? She grimaced. Because the moment she made contact, she'd get arrested and imprisoned indefinitely. Her parents had dealt with so much when she'd first gotten arrested.

"Of course." His hand at the base of her spine sent a shiver of heat through her. He escorted her through a door into large quarters. "Address the display vid with the full name of the person you wish to speak to, and it will connect you using their closest communication device."

She faced the screen and tried to regulate her breathing.

"Do you require privacy?"

She shook her head. "Anthony Pierce, Demeter Station." She held her breath as an image flickered and formed.

"Pierce here." His handsome face was as clear as day.

"So much for Turner duty," she said past the lump in her throat.

He whipped his gaze up and gaped at her.

In all the years she'd known him, she'd never seen him speechless. Her ordeal was almost worth it. *Not.*

"Wren? Where the hell have you been?" He glowered. "Your folks, your brothers, everyone thinks you're dead or worse. You've got the entire station wondering where you went with your empty suit still tethered to the tower crane."

She shrugged while pretending tears didn't threaten to fall. "I got kidnapped," she rasped.

"Leaving your suit behind? And why's your skin purple? You better get your ass back here, missy. I'm done babysitting you, too. Do you have any idea how much shit you dumped on me? E.A.F. interrogated me as if I'd smuggled you away. Parole violation means imprisonment, y'know. For what? Some sort of joyride?"

"She does not lie," Cylo growled, coming to stand behind her, coating her back with warmth. His fury made her square her shoulders, despite the swell of gratitude swelling her heart.

Pierce fell silent, nor did he blink. "Well..." He cleared his throat. "Who took you?"

"Yithians and Maloidians...for experimentation." She waved her hand. "Hence the purple. Cylo rescued me and other women. I'm heading to the Etterian royal city in the hopes they can heal me."

"I did say your jumps might get you killed." Pierce rubbed his face. "I'll inform your family."

"Thanks." Facing her parents would turn her into a blubbering mess. "If I survive this—"

"You will," Cylo said, determination rolling off him.

She rested the back of her head against his chest. "I'll deal with the fallout then."

The ship shuddered, shimmering Pierce's image.

Crushing her against him, Cylo looped an arm around her to tap his O.D.I. "Fyca?"

"We are being pursued."

"And fired upon?" Cylo roared.

"Affirmative."

"Call ended." Cylo dragged Wren with him, ushering her to the bridge. Concern but not panic hit her from every man she passed. "Yithian?" Cylo asked, settling behind Fyca.

Next to a wide-eyed Brenda, Wren sank onto a chair. She reached across the table between them to squeeze her shoulder. Relief was short and sweet before her fear filtered through the air like the sour stench of curdled milk.

"Yes." Fyca's fingers flew across the console. "The ship's trajectory is from Mascroba. Do you think they know we destroyed—"

"We left no trace," Cylo said. "Hail them but no visuals."

Fyca cleared his throat. "Yithian vessel, this is the Etterian scimitar *Kevol*. What are your intentions?"

"Etterians, so arrogant," a Yithian hissed. "Your orbit around Yithia was most curious."

"A meeting with the battleship *Phoenix*, nothing more," Fyca said, casting a glance at Cylo.

"And yet you fire upon us without provocation." Cylo gripped the back of Fyca's chair and glared at the console. "I am not in the mood for this. Do not test me, Yithian." He mumbled something Wren couldn't catch, sending Fyca into a flurry of activity.

She shut her eyes, hoping to catch their emotions. An indomitable control smothered everything except what Brenda released in a steady flow.

"Come, I'm hungry," Wren said, rising to her feet.

"But—"

"Fyca and Cylo know what they're doing." Wren took Brenda's hand and tugged her out of the chair. "What do you feel like?" she asked, hurrying them to the common.

"How can you eat at a time like this?"

"Considering I had a bowl of soup?" Wren met her gaze. "A grilled cheese sandwich sounds amazing. Do you know how to work the food thingy?" Of course, she'd already figured out how to navigate the rehydrator and replicator, but giving Brenda something to do might distract her. "Oh, and a coffee with cream and sugar. I'd kill for that." While Brenda ordered the food, Wren settled onto the bench. "Why aren't you purple?" she asked when the woman slid a plate onto the table. The aroma of melted cheese made Wren's stomach gurgle.

Brenda gave a delicate shrug. "I was for a short time. Qaff caught the effects in time."

"But not mine." Wren bit into her sandwich and moaned. She chewed slowly in case this many carbs so soon would upset her stomach.

"Yeah. Fyca said you had a triple dose of unknowns." She pushed off and returned with a plate of fries which she picked at.

The ship lurched, drawing a yelp from her.

"Felt like we fired at the Yithians." Wren sucked on a thumb, then rotated her sandwich to find the best bite.

"A battle?" Brenda squeaked.

Wren laughed. "Do you think the Etterians can't fight well? Have you seen their muscles, their technology?" And without going into detail, Cylo's confidence still pressed in on her.

Brenda gave a tentative smile and took another fry. "You're right. I'm being silly."

"And you're okay with being Fyca's soul mate?" Wren drew her coffee nearer for a sip, then abandoned her sandwich for a gulp. The hot, sweet liquid warmed her belly. In an act of gratitude, she pressed a kiss to the mug.

"I was curious. It's always been a fault of mine. I explored the ship and found him on the bridge. At first, he didn't glance at me, just answered my questions." Brenda giggled. "Until he swiveled his chair and faced me." She shut her eyes on a hum. "Wow. Seeing the Ethera hit him was amazing. He didn't hide his eye-color change, but his expression of awe won me over. No man has ever looked at me like that." She met Wren's gaze. "Is Cylo yours?"

Wren opened her mouth to answer, but that very man approaching her silenced anything she was going to say. She ran her gaze over him, lingering on his long legs, his massive feet, then up to the width of his shoulders, the strong column of his neck, and his chiseled jaw. His gaze was fixed on her. As well as all his attention. He spared Brenda a glance. Wren couldn't answer her anyway. He wasn't her Eth, but he acted like he was.

He assessed the half-eaten sandwich. "You are eating. Good."

"And?" she asked, gesturing to the bridge. "The Yithians?"

"Dead," he said, sliding onto the bench beside her.

"That's my cue." Brenda bolted, returning to Fyca.

Cylo pulled her plate across to him and picked up a fry. "I fired the Chokaar." He bit into the fry then dropped it in distaste.

Wren smothered a chuckle at his reaction. "So," she coughed, "I assume that's some sort of weapon."

"Indeed. If you are done with your meal, let me show you to your quarters."

She grabbed her coffee and scrambled after him. Back to the barracks they headed—the same place as Hiossu's cabin.

Cylo gestured to a panel beside a door far away from Hiossu's. "Place your hand there. It will allow only you and security to enter."

"Security?" she asked, pressing her palm to the cool glass. It scanned her then slid the door open.

"Me," he said, a smile twitching his lips. "I am to your right. Olin to your left. Should you need either of us..." He paused. "We have increased propulsion to reach Issneen sooner." Inching closer, he cupped her cheek. "I do not want you in danger again."

"Um, thanks," she said, unable to bear the onslaught of his chaotic emotions: honor, desire, concern, determination, anger...

He dipped and caught her lips in a sweet kiss, not lingering despite his aching need to deepen it. "When you awaken in the morning, I will ask Qaff to insert an O.D.I—"

"I have one," she said, touching her wrist without spilling her coffee.

His grin was brilliant to behold, snatching her ability to think. A swipe of his arm across hers sent a zing to her elbow and broke her from her daze. "Comm me if you need me."

The door swished shut on his handsome face, and she was once again alone with her own thoughts. More importantly, her own emotions.

CHAPTER FIFTEEN

CYLO WANTED NOTHING MORE than to force Wren to step back, to let him into her room. One glance at the bed behind her almost made him succumb. She wasn't his. And doing anything with her, no matter how much he longed to, wouldn't be honorable or fair to the male she truly belonged to.

He'd allowed himself the barest of kisses, enough to inhale the unusual beverage she consumed. It hadn't been enough.

When the door shut, a blast of anger had him punch the Maloidian steel bulkhead. His knuckles split, but the sharp pain couldn't compare to the agony within. How could this woman invoke so much when she wasn't his Dar Eth?

He headed to Qaff's quarters in medical and chimed the door.

"What is it?" the male asked, ushering him inside.

"Why is she not mine?" Cylo fell into a pace.

Qaff sighed, halted Cylo, then scanned his bleeding hand with a med-gun. The dull throbbing ceased. "All of her must be seen to trigger the Ethera, and what you are seeing is not who she is. Not her true hair, eye, and skin color."

Cylo sank onto the comfy. "If we return her to who she was, then I will kneel?" *Maker.* He hoped so.

"I cannot say, especially when we might not be able to stabilize the genetic modifiers."

Cylo froze. She was his but could never be due to the Maloidian chemicals. He was doomed to die on the battlefield, unpaired. But this knowledge also meant she would be no other male's Dar Eth. For the same reasons applied.

He tapped his O.D.I. "Olin, investigate Wren. She is wanted by the Earthian authorities. Get me the details."

"You could just ask her," the male grumbled then ended the comm.

Cylo planned to, but truths could be manipulated, and most viewed their past through their perspective. Regardless, he'd battle anyone attempting to take her against her will. Including himself.

"Get some sleep." Qaff gestured at his door.

Cylo smiled at the blatant dismissal. "My thanks."

He headed to the comm to check on Fyca. The giggling alone implied he needn't have bothered. In the barracks' passage, he stared at Wren's door. If he chimed, would she let him in, let him—

He entered his quarters and let the door shut behind him. Sleep. Qaff was wise to suggest it.

"And do not mate with her," Qaff said via Cylo's O.D.I. "The addition of your DNA might play havoc with her condition."

Cylo glowered at his forearm. "So only kisses?"

Qaff hesitated. "Yes."

"Alodon's balls," Cylo muttered and sat on the edge of his bed. Exhaustion pummeled him, his emotional state in turmoil. He tried to control his thoughts, the urges she invoked, but that only circled his focus to her, to their future.

"You used the Chokaar?" Adviser Kanzo demanded, his face appearing on Cylo's display vid.

He leaped to his feet. "I had no choice. The Yithian vessel fired first; not to mention, they were suspicious of our presence on Yithia."

Kanzo's expression turned to confusion in the narrowing of his eyes and crinkled brow. "The facility, I see. I hope this will appease our king. He does not take too kindly to the unjustified use of the Chokaar."

Cylo clasped his hands behind his back. "I have three women aboard; two are Dar Eths. It was justified."

"You are correct. Thank you for the information." The comm ended.

Cylo slumped, then faced his room. A cleanse then rest; both would do much to strengthen him for what was to come. "To feel human," Lady Terry had said. He unlatched his boots, stripped off his armor, and stepped into the cleanser for the third time that day. He raised his arms above his head, splayed his fingers on the bulkhead, and let the water stream over him. The constant ache in his groin would have to wait until the morning chore to be dealt with. He stroked his hard malehood, his breath catching when images of Wren flooded his mind: a flash of a perfect breast, the smoothness of her inner thigh. And in his visions, her skin was still purple, but her hair was a pale blonde. A gasp not his own came from his O.D.I.

"Enough, please, Cylo," she whispered.

He froze, and the imagery vanished. "You can sense me through the bulkhead?"

"Apparently," she said, yawned, then hummed. "You're affecting my dreams."

"My apologies, ensa." He squeezed his eyes shut to soothe their burning.

"Night," she mumbled.

He released his malehood and left the spray. The water cut off. He ignored the air dryer to sprawl on his bed. His wet braid soaked the linen, but he didn't care. Controlling his thoughts mattered, so he focused on his breathing and on what tasks awaited him when he returned to Malo's side. He flicked his gaze to the lump of gold on the table. Finding that couldn't compare to Wren's kiss. Coercing information from a prisoner didn't affect him like the perfume of her skin did.

He tucked an arm behind his head and willed his mind to clear. It was harder than he expected, not used to having to keep his thoughts off a female. He pictured a drone, navigating it to a passing asteroid. In his mental hand was the console, allowing him to shift the drone's direction with his thumbs.

"I can't sleep," Wren said, ruining his descent into slumber. "Talk to me. What are you thinking about? It...feels boring."

Far from it. He exhaled. "In my spare time, I drone-mine asteroids."

"Oh?" Her voice perked up. "Not dull at all. You were picturing this?"

"Yes." *Or trying to.*

"Do you have a drone on board?" Her excitement sparked his.

He chuckled. "Yes, only one. I left the others on the *Gladio*. Finding you was more important."

"So, all we need is a passing asteroid?" she asked. "If we get lucky, that could be fun."

He tried not to focus on the excitement raising the hairs on the back of his neck. That she might share his enjoyment of his favorite pastimes hadn't been something he'd thought he'd value.

"Tell me, Wren, what did Anthony Pierce mean when he said imprisonment?" He'd planned to ask her in the morning anyway, but now would suit just as well.

She fell silent. "The biggest betrayal of my life. Yeah, it sounds overdramatic, but I trusted when I shouldn't have."

Not knowing what to say, he waited.

"I've always understood technology, how it worked, how to manipulate it. When E.A.F. asked me to help bring down a corrupt organization, well, the challenge was too tempting." Her laughter lacked warmth. "Foolish me. I was arrested, tried, found guilty, then banned from doing anything computer-related. Pierce got me a welding job on Demeter Station as a favor to my brother. I was halfway through my time served when E.A.F. announced that my sentence was extended for unknown reasons." She sniffed, sending a crushing weight through Cylo's chest. *Is she...crying?* "Then I got kidnapped. Which made things a thousand times worse," she blubbered. "E.A.F. thinks I ran away, which will add decades to my punishment when they catch me."

He bolted, entering her room without bothering to chime. She was curled on her side, facing the bulkhead between them, her fingers splayed across its Maloidian steel like she longed to touch him. He climbed onto the bed behind her and gathered her against him, letting her cry.

"Ensa, you have me now," he whispered. "We will fight your justice system on your behalf." He pressed his lips to her temple. "And if that fails, I will kidnap you permanently."

She sniffled then giggled. "Thanks, I think." She rolled over and snuggled into his embrace, then jerked back. "Cylo... Please tell me you're not naked?"

Her caress across his collarbone made him shiver. "I am. Does my nudity bother you?"

"No," she rasped. When she pressed her lips where her fingers had been, he stiffened his arms, bringing her closer.

"Ensa." He squeezed his eyes shut. "We cannot."

"Why not?"

"Qaff believes my DNA might worsen your—"

"I don't sleep with a man without protection," she mumbled, feathering her lips across his skin again.

Anger rushed to cloud his vision. "Why would you need protection when sleeping? Do your males harm you when you are most vulnerable?"

Her lips relaxed into a smile when he was far from joyful. Any male who'd hurt her would feel the wrath of an Etterian operative with his virak of poisons at his disposal.

"No, protection means a condom, a way to prevent pregnancy."

Condom? Images flooded his mind, explaining its purpose. He froze, his thoughts reeling even as darkness consumed him. "You stop the creation of damu?" Appalled, he wanted to shove her away from him but couldn't bring himself to do so. "How can your species do this? Damu are precious, to be cherished."

"Because I don't want to be giving birth every nine months. We haven't colonized enough planets to handle that big of a population."

He sat up, bringing her with him. "Explain. Every nine months? How is that possible when our females are only fertile once a year?"

She gasped. "Cylo, sweetheart, we're fertile every month."

"Ah." He cupped her cheek to run his thumb across her bottom lip. "I see." His fingers trembled when he activated his O.D.I.. "Qaff, what about human condoms?"

The male groaned. "Cannot thwart the strength of Etterian sperm, so no. Just kisses." The comm ended with a mumbled, "Maker, save me from—"

Cylo laughed at his grumpy battle-bond, but his humor faded when he gazed at her face. "A pity."

"Tell me about it," she said and slumped, resting her temple against his chest. "Just hold me."

"Anytime." Pulling her down with him, he tucked her head under his chin while running his hand up and down her tunic-covered back. Desperation drove him to slide under her garment to touch her skin, but he dared not.

Time dragged by. His thoughts drifted to what she'd been through and how best to save her.

Her breathing deepened, and yet, sleep eluded him. In the darkness of her room, her outline was clear to him. When her head fell back, he took the opportunity to study every delicate feature from her pointy chin, narrow jawline, tipped nose, and pale blonde eyebrows. Why weren't they different colors like her hair? He ran a thumb over one, finding its silkiness fascinating.

Her lips parted on a gasp, then her hair changed, the colors fading until the shade from his vision appeared. He froze. How... How had she done that?

Without waking her, he shifted until he could reach his O.D.I. "Qaff?" he whispered.

"Enough," the male hissed.

"To Wren's quarters now."

The door swished open a minute later. "What?" Qaff demanded, venturing in. Stilling at the sight of her hair, he raised his med-gun and ran it over her. "How..." He cleared his throat. "I will study the results." Waving his med-gun at Cylo's nudity, he said, "No mating."

"So you have said," Cylo grumbled. When the door shut, he resumed stroking her back, lest they'd disturbed her. He doubted they had with how low they spoke, but any intense emotion he or Qaff experienced might have.

He dozed off, somehow at peace with her in his arms. When she began to stir hours later, so did he, relishing this moment. Waking with a woman was a new experience for him.

She moaned, nuzzled her nose along his neck, then leaned back to meet his gaze. "Morning." She pulled away before he could respond, clambering over him amid a flash of smooth thighs and blonde hair.

"Ensa, you have changed."

She faced him then diverted her gaze as if his nudity *did* bother her. He smiled, liking that she found him distracting. Repeatedly snatching his focus from her bare legs to her toes took discipline. His was fast dwindling.

"Stop that," she said, offering him her back.

"Stop what? Looking at you?" He sat up while the bulkheads flickered. "Opacity: mirror."

She gasped, stumbled forward, and stared at herself. "One: wow. That your walls are interactive—"

"They change colors, too," he said, content to admire her animated face in her reflection.

She cleared her throat. "To be tested later. Two: what happened to my hair? The dye cost me a fortune." Feathering her fingers through her locks mesmerized him.

"You were dreaming," he said, resting an elbow on his knee.

She gaped at him. "I did this?" she squeaked.

He laughed. "Yes."

She headed to the door. "I've got to tell Qaff—"

"Did already." Cylo stood and stretched, slowing each movement under her fascinated gaze.

Her cheeks darkened. "You're gorgeous."

Appearance didn't matter to an Etterian, but her admiration of his physical form swelled his chest with unexpected heat. "As are you," he managed. He gestured to her tunic. "Perhaps you should dress before leaving your quarters?"

"You, too." She chuckled and veered toward the replicator. "Meet you in the med bay?"

He headed to the door and peered over his shoulder, catching her ogling his backside. "Agreed."

She whipped away, pretending to order garments.

He chuckled, pleased at how he flustered her.

"I feel that," she called as her door closed behind him.

Chapter Sixteen

"Your markers are stabilizing," Qaff said, his finger an inch above his tablet like Wren had caught him mid-task. "I have communicated with the lima kuu—"

"Who?" She scowled.

"Our great teachers."

"Wonderful," she said on an exhale. "Why not show everyone what an oddity I am?" She bit her lip. Qaff was doing his best to help her. He didn't need her pissy attitude. Sexually frustrated was more like it. "Sorry," she muttered.

"You would call them our medical experts," Cylo said, running his fingers through her now-blonde hair.

"Oh," she said, dipping her head. "So, if the changes are slowing, what does this mean?" She pointed at her hair. "My eyes are undecided on what color they should be, and I'm still purple."

"You could wake up tomorrow your original self." Qaff shrugged. "I cannot foresee what will happen."

"Are you saying I'll be able to control my physical attributes, like make my hair pink?" Her scalp tingled in anticipation. She snorted. *What an awesome superpower.* "How long until we reach Issneen?"

"Eight days or so," Cylo said.

"Shit. That long?" She glanced at him, wondering how she would fill her time. A sexathon was off the menu. *Argh.* Losing herself in orgasms would've been distracting. Who was she kidding? With Cylo it would be mind-blowing.

"Let us eat our morning meal," Cylo said, drawing her out of her thoughts.

"Breakfast," she said, "as in break your fast." But despite the irritation buzzing through her, she headed to the rehydrate. Today, she'd do the works: bacon, eggs, syrup-drizzled waffles, coffee.

Sitting at the table while Cylo tucked into a sauce-drenched rump steak, she stared at her plate. Keeping herself fed would help her recovery. She knew that but just couldn't start on the mountain of food she'd ordered. With coffee in hand, she sipped and waited for hunger to strike.

When he arched a brow at her, she chose a strip of bacon and bit it. She sucked in a sharp breath through her nostrils, lowered her cup, and picked up the fork. A mouthful of everything followed.

"Smells intriguing," he said when she shoveled in another bite of sweet-and-golden waffle.

"I could never afford this on Demeter. All my tokens went to coffee and noodles." She grinned and swirled the fork at her half-empty plate. Not that she'd mention splice, but yeah, that had taken a chunk of her earnings, too. That was behind her, and she'd keep it that way. Thankfully, Pierce hadn't mentioned it.

She narrowed her eyes on Cylo, trying to sense what mood he was in. Nothing was reaching her. Maybe she'd lost the ability when she'd re-dyed her hair? A girl could hope. "Why can't I pick up on your emotions?"

"I am eating. Should I be feeling something?" He cradled a metal cup filled with what smelled like lemon juice.

"No, I suppose not." She frowned at her plate, lowered the fork, and took up her cold coffee.

"I have Olin investigating your situation."

"Huh?" she asked. "Qaff's doing a great—"

"E.A.F.'s involvement in your past."

"Oh," she said, lowering her cup. "Wish him the best. I couldn't find anything to save my ass."

"If you are a Dar Eth, Etteria will fight for you." Cylo leaned in to catch her gaze. "Regardless, I will ensure you are freed."

"It's sweet of you to try." She smiled, strangely grateful for his conviction crossing the table to bathe her in confidence.

"Sweet?" He snapped his mouth shut, then grimaced. "It is honorable."

"Yeah, it's that, too." She scooped up her plate and carried it to the disposal unit.

He joined her, his chest brushing across her back. "Want to speak to Olin?"

She spun, almost smashing into him. "You think he would've found something already?"

Cylo shrugged. "We will not know unless we ask."

He gestured to the bridge and led the way, thank the Lord. It gave her the opportunity to admire his ass in his tight uniform and blessed her with a few seconds to catch her breath. That he would champion her was something she hadn't expected. He couldn't do the impossible, but just his support… Well… She blinked to stop the tears from forming.

For once, Fyca wasn't at the console. The only man on the bridge looked up from a table to the side.

"I have discovered nothing yet other than a short vid of a male in military uniform visiting your housing unit," he said, confirming his identity as Olin.

"What?" she squeaked, hurrying across to him. "Evidence? E.A.F. claimed that my all-night coding, poor eating habits, and lack of Vitamin D convinced me that he was real." On the table, a hologram formed of the general who'd broken into her home. It wasn't footage of her living room and therefore their conversations, but it did show his comings and goings. She squealed and danced on the spot, too happy to contain her joy. "This just might work. Please," she gripped Olin's forearm, "don't stop looking. The more we have, the better. If we can get the charges against me dropped, I'll be able to see my family without spending time in a cell."

"Agreed," Olin said and glanced at her hand.

She snatched it back and almost curtsied like a peasant asking forgiveness from her liege. Fyca and Brenda returned then, giving her a chance to escape any more embarrassment.

"Thanks again, Olin," she said and marched off, heading for the common. There, over another coffee, she'd consider what she could do to stay entertained. She was tempted to ask Qaff to knock her out in the med-E.D. Time flew by when she slept like she'd done on the Yithian ship.

Ignoring Cylo trailing her, she veered toward the med bay. "Tell me, is there a way to make me sleep?"

Qaff snapped his head up. "I beg your pardon, milady?"

"I hate boredom, Qaff. What am I going to do for eight days?"

He chuckled, his eyes wide in disbelief. "So, you want me to sedate you?"

"Is it possible?" she asked, gripping the edge of the bed at the center of the med bay.

"No." Cylo glowered. "That is not acceptable."

"Find something to do," Qaff said, glancing between Cylo and her then at his tablet.

She threw her hands into the air. "What? Eat? Drink?" She gripped her hips and mumbled, "Have you seen the size of my ass?" No way could she eat her way through this.

They blinked at her. Confusion rolled off Qaff, but anger flowed from Cylo. She glanced between them. They couldn't have heard her, right?

"We have gathered all of what Earth finds entertaining." Cylo gestured to the display vid.

"You have music, movies?" She beamed. "Why didn't you say so?"

Cylo pursed his lips, his nostrils flaring. "What did you do before the Yithians stole you?"

"I tended my bonsai, read novels, made jewelry." She laughed. "Tormented Pierce with space jumps that ended up getting me kidnapped."

"Bonsai," both men repeated, followed by flickering eyelids.

Qaff smiled. "Ah, those we cannot replicate since they are living plants."

She threw out her hands. "What just happened? Why did your eyelashes flutter?"

"That occurs when the O.D.I. instructs us on the meaning of a new word or subject we are unfamiliar with," Cylo said.

"It can do that?" She waved her forearm. "What else does it do?"

"It carries language protocols and synchronizes your Earthian comms to the ship. It also serves as a locator beacon and a communicator." Qaff offered his back while he moved from screen to screen. "A few Dar Eths have relocated their...tokens?"

'Wow,' she mouthed. "Mine already has that, but the language protocols intrigue me. Please...just in case, load Yithian and Maloidian."

Cylo scowled. "You believe we cannot protect you?"

"Of course not," she said, squeezing his upper arm then releasing him when his muscles twitched beneath her touch. She barely resisted shaking her tingling fingers. "I've seen you in action, remember. But it's better to be prepared than to be taken by surprise."

He cupped her cheek, his touch sending a frisson of heat through her. "You speak the truth." Sliding his hand down her neck, along her collarbone to her forearm, he activated her O.D.I. and shuffled through the options.

Despite her blood buzzing from his caress, she gaped; her focus zeroed in on what he chose. Why hadn't she stumbled upon these hidden functions? In honesty, she hadn't thought the device held more functionality than the bare minimum. And the E.A.F. considered her dangerous? Shit, had he said locator? She stiffened. Had Pierce known about this? Was that his around-the-clock Turner duty? And did that mean E.A.F. could find her?

"Can you disable the locator?" she asked, her voice husky.

"Why?" Cylo snapped his gaze up but didn't release her forearm.

"What if E.A.F. track me to Issneen?" She closed her eyes to draw in calming breaths, then glanced at Qaff. "I...don't want to go to prison, but I don't want to cause an incident either. What if I'm the catalyst for a war?" She scoffed. "Never mind, I'm not Helen of Troy. Still, how many will be inconvenienced when E.A.F.'s battleships are orbiting Etteria?"

"You do not grasp how important you are to our people." Qaff flicked through charts, his voice low as if he was lost in thought. "Our king would deny E.A.F. permission to land, even if it starts a war, all on the chance you become a Dar Eth and save a male."

"Oh," she said, her mind reeling. Male or female, Cylo had said. Etteria was *that* desperate? She hadn't realized that when she'd read the digi-mags articles on Etterians and their agenda.

"I have restricted your locator to the ship, for now," Qaff said, not glancing at her.

Relief hit her, and she offered the man a grateful smile. She couldn't say he was rude when he was far from it, but not looking at her was starting to worry her.

"Understand me?" Cylo hissed.

Gasping, she faced him, her mouth falling open. "Are we speaking Yithian?" To her ears, the sibilant sounds were too familiar. "Am I?"

He chuckled. "Yes. Come, I have a lump of gold you can have."

She frowned, unable to register what he'd said. "Did you say gold?"

"I mined it on my last drone run. Perhaps the replicator can create the tools you need?" When he headed to the passage leading to the barracks, she followed.

"You want me to make a piece of jewelry?" she asked, double-stepping to keep up with him.

"I know nothing about such things. Choose a project that is time-consuming." He entered his room and picked up a chunk of gold just lying there on his table.

"Do you know how much this is worth?" she stuttered when he caught her hand and placed the lump on her palm.

He shrugged. "If it will keep you busy."

She clutched the gold to her chest. His generosity astounded her. Maybe she could make something for him? A thick bracelet? A necklace? Would he wear it? "Thank you, Cylo. I cannot say how much this means to me."

"No gratitude is needed." He met her gaze, conveying how this meant nothing to him: no regret, dismay, or obligation reached her. "Now, what else do you need to do this?"

"Tools," she whispered, shock strangling her throat.

He nodded. "As expected. My knife-making has its own requirements."

"Knife—" She bit her lip, once more tripping after him. Drone-mining and blade-smithing? What else did this man do in his spare time besides rescue kidnapped women?

He led her through the common to a door on the side. The empty bay had high ceilings, and black crates clung to the metallic walls as if magnetized. A shiver at the cooler temp didn't distract her when he veered toward a workbench mounted at the rear of the bay. Beside it was a low counter with a replicator.

He activated it. "Order what you need."

She blinked at the menu, unsure how to phrase the tools in Etterian terms. Would they know what nylon-tipped pliers were? He waited, patient, so she typed in what she was looking for, all while clutching the gold to her chest. A pile of tools formed, in better quality than the second-hand tools she'd managed to scrounge on Demeter.

"I...think that's it," she said.

"Good." He touched the ridged corner of a metal panel. It slid open to reveal an empty cube-shaped closet. "Here is where you can store these." He pointed at the bench. "That is where you can work." He caught her free hand and urged her to stand in front of a flat circle on the grated floor. "Touch here..." He pressed a thumb-sized ridge on the bench's bull-nosed edging.

A bar stool rose out of the floor. It stopped just short of reaching her butt.

“Release the button when it is at the correct height for you.”

With a trembling hand, she placed the lump on the rubberized workbench. She faced him, slipped her arms around his waist, and pressed her cheek to his chest. “Thank you.”

He crushed her to him without harming her. “It is honorable to make you happy.”

She shook her head. “You are the only one who thinks like that, Cylo.” She pulled back and turned away to hide her tears.

He grasped her chin and forced her to meet his gaze. “I did not do this to upset you, ensa.”

He gazed into her eyes. Time slowed, and her breathing became labored. A slight smirk curled his lip moments before he caught hers in a sweet kiss. Her heartbeat thundered in her ears as she melted against him, unable to resist the lure of his warm and solid chest. The strength of his arms he trapped her within only seemed to add to the sense of security engulfing her.

“I’m not sad,” she managed when he broke the kiss. “These are tears of joy.” She chuckled, flicking a swipe across her cheek.

He frowned and released her. “You speak truth?”

“Yeah, women cry for all sorts of reasons.” She looped her arm through his and almost dragged him toward the common. “Come, I’m thirsty.” Because if this man was alone with her a second longer, she just might succumb to this attraction between them. And to hell with the consequences.

“But...” He let her lead him away.

She rested her temple on his bicep, hiding a smile. No man she’d ever known could compare to him.

Chapter Seventeen

"Cylo, the system has logged a disturbance in Lady Wren's quarters." Fyca's voice from Cylo's O.D.I. jerked him awake.

He leapt to his feet then hesitated, sweeping a glance down his naked body. After the last time she'd reacted to his nudity, perhaps a garment would be wise? A part of him wanted to dismiss the need to please her, especially when she was in danger.

With a grunt, he succumbed. A quick order from the replicator filled his hands with a pair of sleep pants in a thin, gray fabric. He yanked them on then raced to her room. Once again, he barged in, especially since he'd wasted time covering himself.

A shiver traveled down his spine and tightened his muscles as if he prepared for battle.

Wren wasn't there.

"Fyca, track her O.D.I."

"Done. She is...above me."

Relief washed over Cylo while he hurried to the viewing deck. When he peeked through the hatch, a bundled Wren lay on the floor. She whimpered.

"Ensa?" Was she ill? Had her condition worsened?

"Make it stop. The dreams... I can't—"

Each of her sobs pierced his heart with a sharp stab. He kneeled beside her, burrowed into the blankets, and slipped underneath to pull her against his chest. "I am here, Wren."

She moaned, snuggling deeper into his embrace. Not wanting to add to her sensory overload, he struggled to control his reactions to her sweet-scented softness and rein in his thoughts and desires.

"Dreams?" He ran his hand up and down her back, hoping to soothe her.

"Everyone's on board." Her whisper would have been lost had he not been Etterian.

"It is worsening?" As he'd feared. He crushed her against him, helplessness driving him to do something. Anything "Come, ensa, Qaff should retest you." He pressed a kiss to her temple—all he'd allow himself. "I will ask him to let you sleep in the med-E.D."

She raised her head, hope casting warmth across her pale purple face. "You promise?"

He frowned. The shadows under her eyes hadn't been there over dinner. She'd been lively, her gaze admiring. When had her condition deteriorated? And she'd begged to be sedated. Had she used the excuse of boredom to hide something more alarming?

He gritted his teeth. Her continued suffering was *his* fault. *Fool.* "Why did you not tell me?"

"At first, I was myself in my room. Then thoughts and feelings trickled through. It was tolerable, but during the night..." She swallowed hard. "The brain relaxes, opening a world of imagination. There are no inhibitions."

Nudging her away from him, he gestured to the ladder. "Let us head to medical." While she scrambled from under the mountain of blankets, he tapped his O.D.I. "Qaff, to medical."

"On my way," the male said, his voice thick with exhaustion.

Cylo descended after her. She waited for him in the passage. Her breath hitched when he faced her.

"What is it?" he asked, inching closer to grasp her elbow.

"Um...your pajamas..." Her cheeks burned a dark purple. She marched off, abandoning him.

He scowled at his sleep pants. "What is wrong with them?"

Since she wasn't there to assuage his confusion, he chased after her, in time to catch her climbing onto the med-E.D. bed. Her tiny toes and feet led his focus up sculpted calves and smooth-looking thighs. Qaff typed on the device's console, forming the dome. She squeaked when she began to float.

"Sleep well," he said without glancing up.

Cylo leaned a hip on the side of the bed, near enough to splay his fingers across the dome if she needed him. "How long until we know?"

"No idea." Qaff arched a brow at him. "Her exhaustion levels are high. I will awaken her after she has had eight hours of sleep."

"Eight?" Cylo growled.

"Humans require between six and ten hours of sleep to be fully functional. It varies from person to person, though." Qaff faced the wall of display vids. "I shall share my findings when I send them to the lima kuu."

Dismissed, Cylo marched to the comm—too stimulated to be at peace. To find rest now would be impossible. "Fyca, return to your Dar Eth. I will cover your shift."

The male beamed. "My thanks, Cylo." He leapt out of the chair and left.

With Wren sedated, Cylo released the control he had on his thoughts and freed his longing. If only he could— Do what? Kissing her would encourage the need to claim her. With her new...talent, she had to have a clear idea of what he felt for her. He didn't know whether she fantasized about him. If she was meant to be another male's Dar Eth, she wouldn't appreciate any interest but her Eth's. She *had* said, however, that she reacted to him like no other male she'd met before.

He gazed unseeingly at the passing stars, trying to unravel this dilemma. His future had always been clear, his thoughts and emotions in line with his goals. Now, he was at odds.

His O.D.I. dinged, sending a ripple of energy up his forearm. He drew in a slow breath and activated the message he was sure was from Qaff. The results were alarming. The DNA markers had slowed on her appearance, some still shifting, others remaining fixed. As to her empathetic or borderline telepathic abilities, they glowed yellow on the scans as if they raced toward an end Qaff was hesitant to specify.

Cylo opened a comm to another male who might be able to help.

"Operative Cylo, how may I assist?" Adviser Kanzo filled the comm's display vids with his bare chest and gray sleep pants.

Cylo winced at having disturbed the adviser's rest. "My apologies, I—"

Kanzo glanced down, a frown forming. "You seem agitated. Medic Qaff has communicated Lady Wren's latest results. Her abilities are...expanding."

"I would have said declining," Cylo muttered.

"Indeed. Into a realm Etterians are not familiar with. Hence why we turned to the Durn for assistance so many centuries ago. Our lima kuu have departed on a scimitar. They will meet you halfway."

Cylo slumped, relief swift to strike. "My thanks. Do they yet know what can be done to heal her?" His voice hitched. He stiffened, swallowing to hide his...vulnerability.

"I spoke with them yesterday. They have some ideas, but after this new information, I suspect they are eager to reach you before..."

At Kanzo's hesitation, every muscle in Cylo's body tightened. "Yes?"

"She is beyond our skills to aid."

"Alodon's balls." Cylo ran a trembling hand over his face. He'd prefer her purple and someone else's Dar Eth than dead.

"Qaff indicated that she cannot find rest which triggered a retest. Perhaps—" A smile burst across Kanzo's features. "When will she awaken from the med-E.D.?"

Hope hitched Cylo's breath. "In five hours."

"I shall comm then." Kanzo's image flickered to black.

"Maker. The male could have at least hinted at what made him smile." Cylo gripped the edge of the console and studied the kaleidoscope of colors—all good. Five hours? What could Kanzo accomplish in that time?

Cylo pushed out of the chair to pace the comm. Worrying about Kanzo's cryptic promise wouldn't shorten the hours. Only action could rid him of this...helplessness. He marched to the common, pulled a greatsword off the bulkhead, and moved through the strike-and-defense techniques all Etterian warriors were taught. The domed med-E.D. lurked at his peripherals, urging him to look. He did, only when he changed stances. She was a lure, disrupting his focus. Drenched in sweat a while later, he clicked the greatsword into its brackets and headed to the replicator for a towel. With it looped around his neck, he ordered a chilled container of water and strolled to medical. The lights had been dimmed. Qaff had no doubt headed to bed.

Wren's skin was a paler purple. Perhaps she was close to returning to her normal? Though, his mind might have been toying with him, a hope on his part.

"How is she?" Hiossu asked, coming to stand beside Cylo.

"Still changing." He didn't glance at the Maloidian when Wren was a far prettier sight.

"Olin says the *Nahatyr* is en route. He, Qaff, and I will rendezvous with the *Phoenix*. Your lima kuu will continue the journey with you on the *Kevol* to Issneen."

Cylo swallowed a growl at receiving the news from an...outsider. "Why was I not informed?"

"Qaff chose not to, citing your obvious distraction." Hiossu offered a kind smile Cylo didn't need or appreciate. "A male on board would have had to act as ambassador. Since you rescued her, it is logical you assumed the responsibility."

"Indeed." Cylo almost snorted at that untruth.

"I shall await her awakening. Why do you not seek your rest?" Hiossu's suggestion made Cylo step back to meet the male's gaze.

"I am expecting a comm from Adviser Kanzo." Cylo folded his arms across his sweat-drenched chest and hid a grimace. "Perhaps a quick cleanse?"

Hiossu bowed his head and headed toward the rehydrator. Cylo fled, determined not to take too much time. As he endured the air dryer minutes later, he wondered if Kanzo knew whether women had an issue with sleep pants? Since he was an Eth, his Dar Eth would have mentioned a...distaste for such attire.

Cylo ordered a fresh pair of gray sleep pants, wanting to test Wren's reaction. If need be, he'd ask her. When he strode into the common, Hiossu nursed a glass of Jucot wine.

"Odd choice of garments," he said between licking his lips.

Cylo chose not to respond. Instead, he settled on the flip-down bed and activated his tablet. A message from Kanzo confirmed what Hiossu had said. Three lima kuu were on board the scimitar *Nahatyr*. Still, what plagued him was why Kanzo planned to comm in two hours, especially after he'd transmitted the changed plan. That Etterians were going above and beyond to save his Wren... No, not his. Not yet. He gazed at her, her features at rest and serene. Her white-gold hair floated around her face. Her long tunic hid her until mid-thigh.

"Does she look less purple to you, Hiossu?" Cylo glanced at the table only to realize the common was empty. How had he not heard the male leave?

Scowling, he leapt off the bed and returned to the comm since he'd sent Fyca to bed. Seated in front of the console, he closed his eyes. For an operative, two hours of shallow sleep was more than enough.

TOO MANY IMAGES SLAMMED into Wren's mind the moment she surfaced. Shards of agony lanced through her skull. She winced and squirmed, trying to sink to the bed. When all she did was roll over midair and bare her cotton-covered ass, she cursed. *Not again.*

"Need assistance?" Cylo smirked, standing there in his low-riding yoga pants.

The man had an Adonis belt that rivaled any she'd ever seen. *Damn*. She couldn't help but stare. And drool, a little. She snorted. A lot. And her throat had dried up. Anything she attempted to say now would come out way too husky. Sure, she'd love nothing more than to do the horizontal with Mr. Stunner, when he just stood there, looking like he'd materialized out of a men's digi-mag. But he couldn't.

Her cheeks warmed. Her nethers tingled. *Argh*.

"Please," she managed.

He circled the bed and tapped the console. Down she floated, landing face first on the bed. *Shit*. If the med-E.D. was going to become her haven, she'd better master the descent.

"How do you feel?" he asked.

She peeked at him through the veil of her hair, then narrowed her eyes, trying to sense what he was feeling. Nothing reached her. If she didn't have a splitting headache from everyone else's thoughts and dreams, she'd have hoped those horrible chemicals had finally worked out of her system. Did he no longer fantasize about her? The disappointment hit her like an ice-cold shower. She shivered, sadness dropping her gaze. Slithering off the bed, she cast him a wan smile, with the full intention of heading to her room.

"There has been a change in plans," he said, striding after her.

"Oh?" she asked over her shoulder without glancing at him.

"The lima kuu will not wait for us to reach Issneen."

She froze and faced him. He halted mid-stride but not fast enough. Her temple bounced off his chest. He looped an arm around her and spun them. No doubt she'd caught him by surprise when she'd stopped like that. But she couldn't bring herself to be remorseful when his cologne teased her nose and the sheer warmth of him made her want to rest her cheek on his bare pec.

In that second, time stood still. She was but a woman in her lover's arms. His presence surrounded her in safety, in the surety that she was desired.

She shook her head, trying to focus. "Were the latest results that bad?"

He shrugged. "You are stabilizing."

She smiled. "That's good, right?"

"On your appearance only."

"Shit," she muttered. "I'm purple forever?"

"Those markers haven't settled yet, but the activity around them has slowed."

"Phew." She slumped.

That meant she still had a chance. Maybe if she concentrated hard, she could compel her DNA to return to normal? She almost rolled her eyes at that bit of nonsense. At least the medical experts meeting them halfway cut the remaining time to four days. Now to start her dismal day. But with Cylo on her six?

"I'm going to shower." She paused and beamed at him. "Or do you plan on watching me?"

His cheeks darkened when he ran his gaze over her bare legs. "No, but hurry. Adviser Kanzo will be comming you soon."

"Why?" She frowned. "Never mind, I suppose it's important. I won't be long." She let the door shut on his face. What would she have done had he said yes, that he'd like nothing more than to ogle her naked body?

Nothing, probably. What a fool she was.

Christmas carols were the only way she could drown out intrusions. She blared them out while hurrying, not wanting to be caught...um...unprepared for whoever this Kanzo was. An adviser wanting to speak to her did sound ambassadorial. She stared at her jeans. Were those too informal? Could she afford to offend an Etterian diplomat by being underdressed? She drew in a long inhale. This was all bullshit.

She stomped to the replicator and ordered tailored pants and a button-up shirt. White made her hair look washed out, and with her lilac skin, she didn't know what other color would suit her. So black it was. She slipped into a matching bra and panties, then the smartest outfit she'd worn since her court appearance. At the memory, she cursed again, finding she'd been doing that more and more after what she'd been through. Pierce and Dallas wouldn't believe she had a hidden 'miner' vocabulary. Her mother more so.

Black flip-flops completed the outfit since Kanzo wouldn't see her feet. She hoped.

Her stomach gurgled, so she left for the common. She'd carried her coffee and a grilled cheese sandwich to the table by the time Cylo strode toward her, once again in his uniform. Grateful that he wasn't in those yoga pants, she thwarted a sigh of relief with a sip of coffee.

His gaze settled on the 'V' of her neckline where she'd left a few buttons undone. He didn't comment, nor did any emotional reaction reach her. She bit into her grilled cheese to hide a moan of disappointment.

He sat opposite her, a plate of steak and a glass of juice his breakfast. Was that all they ate? Because they didn't have a choice or out of preference? With the rehydrator's menu being so extensive, she had to assume it was the latter. He ate his meal in silence, his focus on her. She chewed slowly, her mother's admonishments to be ladylike ringing in her ears.

"You appear paler..." He stroked the knuckles of her hand gripping the coffee.

"Oh?" She lowered the mug to study her skin. "Yeah, I do." She grinned at him. "Any day now, I'll be my usual self."

"And your eyes flicker between gray and green."

"So Qaff was right." Which meant the bad stuff still driving the experts to reach her had to be horrific.

"Adviser Kanzo for you, Cylo," Fyca said.

She dropped the sandwich, wiped her hands on a napkin, then rose, taking the coffee with her.

"I like what you are wearing," Cylo said, his voice hoarse.

She peered at herself. "Thought something a little more formal might be in order. Just in case."

He grunted and led the way.

The man filling the screens on the bridge, or as Etterians called it, 'the comm,' was handsome. Then again, despite them all being bronze-skinned and black-haired, she couldn't say she'd seen an ugly man.

Fyca left them alone.

"Adviser Kanzo, this is Lady Wren." Cylo gestured to her.

She hesitated, wondering if she should be curtseying. Hysteria bubbled laughter in her chest which she hastily tamped down. "Hello, Adviser Kanzo." His neon-blue eyes told her he had a Dar Eth, but the woman could be Etterian or human. Not that either mattered.

"Good morning, Wren. Please, I'd like to introduce Iddan."

Cylo's instant grin told her this was a good thing.

A man with navy-blue skin and white hair and eyes stepped into view. "Hello, Wren. I am Iddan, a Durn. Kanzo tells me you have developed the ability to sense others' emotions and thoughts?"

She nodded.

"Unless you learn how to block them, you will slowly sink into madness." His grimace hinted at having endured the insanity assaulting her now. "It is simple but requires a strength of will to maintain. Imagine a door. Use detail. Make it out of any material or markings that you can relate to a specific person."

She blinked at him. "Um, I can't sense anything from Cylo. I'd need someone to test—"

"Fyca, return to the comm," Cylo said to his O.D.I.

The pilot hurried in and slid into the seat.

She stared at him then summoned an image of a white door with a massive crossbar as a handle. Across the top, she wrote his name, digging her finger into the paint as if it was still fresh.

"Once you have the door in mind, open it," Iddan said.

She obeyed and cried out, falling to a knee when memories, thoughts, and desires crashed into her. Cylo roared something at Iddan while lifting her to her feet.

"Close the door," the Durn said, his voice calm.

She slammed it. The ringing of a fireproof metal door reverberated through her skull. She gasped. No longer did Fyca's thoughts torment her. "How is this possible?" she whispered, raising her gaze to Cylo's.

"The mind is a powerful tool. We have yet to fully understand how humans compare to the many species we have studied." Iddan offered a sweet smile. "Comm me if you need further guidance."

Tears slipped free. She flicked them aside while beaming at him. "Thank you so much."

"You are on a scimitar, yes? I would suggest you relocate to the viewing deck or, if the scimitar has the stock, thicken the bulkheads around your quarters. When you sleep, your control weakens."

"We do not, unfortunately," Cylo said, running his hand down her arm to lace their fingers. "The use of the viewing deck is wise. My thanks, as well, Iddan and Adviser Kanzo."

She held out her free hand. "Um, Iddan, wouldn't it be easier to lock myself behind a door?"

Cylo's hand twitched, drawing her gaze to his long fingers. She smothered a shiver at the phantom sensation of his touch along her inner thigh.

Iddan laughed. "Indeed. I had not thought of that. It would be simpler than creating a door for every person you meet. But do know that should you open that door, you will be hit with a massive sensory overload."

"Fair enough," she said, quickly picturing a submarine-like door, old, with rusted metal brackets and a brass plaque embossed with her name. She 'walked' through and closed the door behind her. Silence engulfed her, leaving only her thoughts and feelings. But the door threatened to open, like the hinges or lock were broken. She shoved her full weight against it, begging it to stay shut. Several attempts followed until, sweat-drenched, she stepped back.

She returned to reality with a jolt.

The screen showed the passing stars. Iddan hadn't bid her goodbye or anything. But she was so grateful that she spun and threw herself at Cylo. He caught her against his body, allowing her to cry like a toddler. When her sobs turned into sniffles and her eyelids threatened to seal, she pulled back and let herself rest her temple on his chest.

"Sorry," she muttered. "When did you learn to do this?"

"Do what?" he asked, still rubbing her from her shoulder blades to her lower spine.

"Imagine a door to enclose me."

He chuckled. "I did not. I have been using my willpower to control my reactions and thoughts."

She forced a chuckle and shifted away from him. "That's amazing."

"I am glad not to have to do so anymore." He caught her chin and raised her face for a perusal. With swipes of his thumb, he swept aside her tears. His touch was so gentle that flutters consumed her core. "What is wrong with my sleep pants?"

His question stunned her, leaving her reeling. "Your...pajamas?" Heat burned her cheeks. Memories flashed of his carved chest, his narrow waist, and Adonis belt. Not to mention the way the silk had clung to his thighs... She cleared her throat, not sure what to say.

"Yes. Why do you react like this?" He angled his head. "Your breathing and heartbeat are erratic. Your face is flushed, your eyes wide."

She coughed. "No reason," she rasped.

He scowled. "Why do you deceive me?"

Anger rolled off him. That didn't bother her. What did have her leaping to grasp his biceps were the sour notes of pain. "Cylo, um, you look...good."

He stiffened, then a smile bloomed, dimpling a cheek. "Ah, now I see. You like how I look as much I like the look of you?"

She nodded and left him, not wanting to go into how this attraction couldn't lead anywhere.

"Wren," he called, trailing her.

She faced him. "You said there can be nothing between us."

"Yes, I did." He toyed with a strand of her hair. "For now." He lowered his hand. "If thick bulkheads are all you need, spend most of your awake time in the shuttle bay. That way, you need not expend all your energy controlling your door."

She sucked in a shuddering breath at his thoughtfulness. "Thank you."

What she wanted to do was close the distance and press her lips to his. But to do so would lead to her wanting more, craving him. Instead, she spun on a heel and headed to the shuttle bay. Iddan had been correct in his suggestion. Hiding in the viewing deck had brought her some relief. She'd make it her bedroom when she was too tired to think or dream.

For now, getting her mind off Cylo was her core focus. And failing that, she'd have to decide: to toss caution to the wind or turn her back on him for good.

Chapter Eighteen

Days passed as Wren hammered and twisted the gold into thin ribbons. Cylo tried not to disrupt her, so he came and went, checking in on her. Sometimes, like now, he'd sort through his correspondence on his tablet, using a crate as his perch. The regular tap-tap-tap of her tools soothed him.

"I can sense you," Wren said, snatching Cylo from his reading.

Since she'd taken up his advice, spending her days in the shuttle bay, she'd stopped using her door. Or so she'd told him one afternoon over what she'd called 'tea.' That decision had meant he needed to be on his guard again. If it meant she didn't suffer, he'd gladly bear the pain and discomfort.

"I was wondering where you were," Lady Violet said, offering a smile as she ventured deeper into the bay.

Wren whipped up her head, her face strained. "Cylo was kind to help keep me sane." Her expression softened, and she tossed a wink at him.

Not that he knew what it meant, but the aches it summoned made him squirm. Her cheeks darkened to a soft purple, her skin having almost lost that hue completely.

Lady Violet flicked aside a gray curl. "Durok mentioned the chemicals had an adverse effect on you. I was worried—"

"Or curious?" Wren smirked.

"That, too." Lady Violet chuckled. 'After all, how many lilac-skinned women do I know who are also jewelry-makers?"

Cylo almost snorted at Lady Violet's hope of seeing what Wren was working on. Every time he'd tried to peek, she'd swept a cloth over the workbench. When she'd first done so, it had stung—the pain hitting him in the chest like the slap of a dagger's blade. She'd clasped his forearm, peered into his eyes, and said, "It's a surprise. I'm not hiding it to hurt you."

Which meant he had to be patient.

As an operative, doing so was something he could endure. And in the meantime, he could master controlling his emotions. She didn't need to know how many hours he'd spent remembering the way her black garment had clung to her body. Or how he'd longed to press a kiss to the underside of her knee. After he banished those memories, he found himself admiring the curve of her cheek or how she chewed on her bottom lip when she was in deep concentration. Her mutterings were amusing though he doubted she knew she was doing it.

His O.D.I. buzzed. He dragged his gaze away. The *Nahatyr* was less than a day away. Joy warred with sadness; his time with Wren was ending. Worse, he was nowhere closer to finding out if she could be his Dar Eth.

"You're so talented," Lady Violet was saying.

"More like a reason to keep my mind and fingers busy."

"True." On a sigh, Lady Violet's shoulders slumped. "When Durok's on shift, I'm bored as hell."

"Oh?" Wren faced her. "What did you do before this...adventure?"

Lady Violet gasped. "I...never thought that was possible."

Wren grinned. "Look at this. Cylo ordered all my tools from the replicator."

"You can do that?" Lady Violet threw back her head and laughed. "Please, excuse me." She hurried out of the bay, calling, "Durok, honey."

Wren chuckled and continued to tap-tap-tap.

The way her hair tumbled down to hide her face fascinated Cylo. He drew in a shuddering breath and willed himself to focus on his tablet and the research he'd found on ancient Hatimaye techniques.

"Cylo?" Her rasping voice so near snapped his chin up. She stood beside him. How had she done so without him hearing her approach?

He frowned. "What is it, ensa?"

She pinched the tablet and slid it out of his hands, placing it on the crate beside him. A smile formed as she ran her hand up his chest armor. At the collar, she dug her fingers between the fabric and his skin, drawing a hiss from him. With a yank, she pulled him toward her.

Her mouth across his caught him off guard. The taste of her hit him like a hammer to his solar plexus. He grasped her at the elbows and drew her closer, then glided his hands up to her shoulders. Warm skin filled his palms, and her scent enticed him to sink into her.

She slipped her tongue in to meet his. A groan escaped him. His heart thundered against the barrier of his ribs. She broke away but didn't leave him. Instead, she brushed her wet lips down his neck.

"Maker," he whispered as a shudder raced through his taut body. His eyes burned. Squeezing them shut only summoned sensual images of her, things he dreamed of doing to her...with her.

She moaned and climbed onto his lap to settle her backside across his malehood while facing him. Madness had him in its grip, and he looped an arm around her waist to crush her against him.

"Kisses only," she mumbled, her hot breath fanning his skin. "I want them, as many as you can spare." She rose onto her knees on either side of his hips. Cupping his cheeks, she peered into his eyes. "So beautiful, Cylo." Then she placed a kiss on each eyelid, her lips so soft, sweet, that he wouldn't have been able to stop her had he wanted to.

"Minus susa..." He splayed his fingers between her shoulder blades and pressed her to him, wanting to experience her unbound breasts against his bare chest. Images flashed, so real, he could almost believe they were memories: a puckered nipple, the weight of a breast, the silkiness of her skin, and the salty tang of sweat clinging to her cleavage.

"Have dinner with me tonight," she said while kissing her way along his jaw.

He chuckled. "I eat the evening meal with you every night."

"No." She leaned back to gaze at him. "Like a date."

"Date?" The O.D.I. hurried to inform him, sharing images of a fruit or a couple in candlelight. As in romantic? "Yes," he growled.

Her smile crawled across her plump lips. He stared into her eyes, mesmerized by the steel gray so reminiscent of polished Maloidian. He touched her cheek to hold her still.

"Ensa, your eyes... What color were they?"

She angled her head to nuzzle his palm, sparking a mini explosion in his core. "Brown-green, why?"

"They are gray."

She froze, her enticing mouth gaped, then she asked, "Is that bad?"

He chuckled. “Good that they are no longer changing. Good that they are a remarkable steel-gray.”

“Bad that I’m still purple.” She rested her temple on his chin, shifting out of his touch to do so.

“Perhaps that genetic marker has not stabilized.” *Maker, please let that be so.* Normalcy would make her happy. He didn’t care what color she ended up being. As long as he could call her his.

She clambered off him, sliding her body across parts of him that would forever remember the brief frisson of heat she’d summoned. “I’ll get Qaff to check. Dinner, tonight. Dress...” She ran her gaze over his armor. “Nice.”

He stared after her disappearing back, the air in the shuttle bay a little colder without her presence. What had she meant by ‘nice?’ He only wore his sleep pants or armor. Was the latter not— Ah, yes, the man in the O.D.I. image had worn strange garments: a white tunic, deep-gray coat, over pants like her blue leggings. He’d browse the human section of the replicator for something suitable.

Excitement sparked to life in his chest. A date with the woman he couldn’t help and couldn’t resist. Why she’d kissed him he’d ask her this evening. They’d managed to keep things...platonic these past few days.

It helped that she’d moved into the viewing deck, as Iddan had advised. No longer was she next door to his quarters—the temptation alone had almost killed him. The suggestion for her to sleep above the comm had eradicated the shadows under her eyes.

Her well-being mattered—had since he’d met her. Maker, if he was being honest, before he’d left the *Gladio* for Yithia. Then it hadn’t been her specifically, but now...

He sucked in a steady breath, willing his arousal to calm. She had such a hold on him. It had to be the Ethera.

Around his thoughts went. He slumped then forced himself to straighten. Patience.

When he strode through the common, only Qaff was there, seated at the table with a plate of kreso before him. Cylo headed to the replicator, intent on ordering what was needed for this ‘date.’ He flipped through the options under human garments. The blue leggings were easy to find... Jeans was what they were called. Next was the tunic—a long-sleeved button-up *shirt* with a collar. He grunted and ordered it in his size.

“What are you doing?” Qaff asked, sliding his empty plate into the waste disposal.

"I have a date with Wren this evening. She told me to dress...better." He flicked a dismissive hand at himself.

Qaff chuckled. "You could wear your ceremonial armor."

Cylo blinked then laughed. "My normal armor with a cloak?"

Qaff rubbed his chin. "True. What else do you need?" He squeezed beside Cylo to browse the jackets on offer. "Whoa, why do they have so many?" He scrolled through. "I like this one. It looks similar to what the O.D.I. showed me, and it is almost as long as a cloak."

Cylo selected the overcoat in deep blue but chose the dark gray option. "My thanks," he said, with the garments stacked in his hands.

"Where is your date going to happen?" Qaff swept out an arm, encompassing the common and medical.

Cylo grimaced. Here meant no privacy. "We are meeting in the common, but perhaps, somewhere else would be preferable. I shall research."

"Wise," he said and left Cylo to his own devices.

Taking control of this date might be a good idea. Especially after her kiss. He didn't want to share her or suffer through distractions. He dumped the garments onto his bed and sank onto a chair to activate his O.D.I. A quick search revealed too many choices. A picnic offered the best privacy. Except, the viewing deck wasn't available. Which left the shuttle bay.

He hummed. Could he make that work? Perhaps many blankets to soften the floor? He deactivated the security cams, not wanting them to be recorded.

And what about food? He scrambled, hurrying through a cleanse. While he air-dried, he ordered the blankets and packed a basket, of all things, with roast chicken sandwiches, potato salad, strawberries, and a bottle of champagne. None of which he knew he'd like the taste of, but that didn't matter. Although, the sandwiches did smell good.

Pulling on the leggings was a struggle. They were tighter than he was used to. The shirt's fasteners took a moment to figure out. The shoes in the O.D.I. images appeared too constrictive, so he hadn't ordered them. He was thinking twice about the leggings, too, but at least he could wear his boots. He eyed the overcoat with dubiousness.

Never would he have thought he'd be in this position when Malo had tasked him to save the women. Would he sacrifice this inconvenience for having never met Wren? No.

He grunted and slipped into the overcoat, liking how snug but not uncomfortable it was across his shoulders.

"Opacity: mirror," he commanded the nearest bulkhead.

The male before him wasn't himself and did resemble the O.D.I.'s example except for his braid draped down his chest. He flipped it behind him then hoisted the basket. The true test would be how Wren reacted.

She was waiting for him in the common, wearing a black V-necked robe that gathered at her waist and split, flashing her knee whenever she moved. His step faltered as he swept his gaze over her. *Maker, she is beautiful.*

She did the same, scanning him in a slow, sensual way that darkened her cheeks. The musky scent of her arousal tickled his nose. He beamed then smothered his grin. That she found him attractive bolstered his confidence in this ridiculous outfit.

"A picnic?" She arched a brow at the basket.

"I like this garment on you," he said, a sudden awkwardness tying his tongue.

"I know," she rasped.

His breath hitched, and he met her gaze, allowing himself to sink into her steel-gray eyes. 'Is this wise?" he asked. "A date leads to...more."

"I don't care about the consequences. I'm tired of fighting this." She crossed to him on impossibly high footwear that enhanced the curve of her calves. When she was close enough, she rested her hand on his chest, sliding it inside the overcoat. The heat of her palm sent a quiver of warmth through him. The shirt's fabric was so thin, her touch burned his skin as if he was naked.

His stomach knotted. To hell with the meal. He wanted her...beneath him.

He swallowed hard. Her recklessness meant he needed to be stronger for them both. "Shall we?" He gestured to the shuttle bay's door then tucked the blankets under his arm.

While she led the way, he stayed back, eager to admire the dress clinging to her backside.

"Come, ensa," she said, tossing a smile over her shoulder.

He groaned and trailed her through the door, turning to ensure it locked behind them. Between her work area and his perch, he flicked out the blankets, then placed the picnic basket in the center. She sat and bent a knee to undo her footwear. He crouched beside the other one to assist, unable to resist stroking her ankle to her toes. Even there, her skin was silky smooth. Setting the footwear aside, he chose not to release her; the temptation to run his palm along her calves was too unbearable. He pushed the hem of her garment up with a sweep of his thumb. His goal was clear in his mind, and when he spotted the prize, he dipped to press a kiss to the underside of her knee.

She trembled beneath his touch, and the rich fragrance of her desire filled the air between them. He met her gaze, content to admire the flush on her cheeks, her parted lips, the desperate need in her eyes that mirrored his own.

"Why did you kiss me earlier?" he asked, caressing her where he'd just moments ago kissed her.

"I couldn't bear it anymore."

"Bear what?" He glanced at his fingers trailing circles across her skin.

"Your desire, the imagery, what you longed to do to me."

He lifted his chin and smirked. "So my control failed?"

"Yes," she said, throwing her head back when he nudged her legs apart with his knuckles.

Her garment pooled across the juncture of her thighs, exposing her black undergarment so transparent, she could have skipped wearing it. His breath hitched, and in a daze, he ran his hands up so that he could rub her sex through the sheer fabric.

"Oh," she gasped, her eyes squeezed shut.

He paused to remove the coat, tossing it aside. In that split second, he committed to pleasing her. What the training vids on human mating had shown him was that a male didn't need to pursue his own gratification. In fact, he had to ignore his needs to ensure she remained well. His malehood twinged in protest.

He drew in a deep inhale, savoring her scent. His mouth watered, his tongue recalling the taste of her. This wasn't what he'd had in mind when she'd asked for a date. But now, with her leaning back on her elbows, her glorious legs bare, his hands at her sex, he wanted to be nowhere else. He lay on his side next to her and stroked along her jaw to guide her mouth to his.

"Just kisses," he whispered against her lips.

Meeting his gaze, she pouted. "Stupid DNA."

He chuckled. "Indeed." While he nipped her bottom lip, he trailed a pattern from her knee to her sex, drawing moans and pants from her. "Just touches." Through the fabric, he stroked his thumb up and down her seam, her cries urging him on. She whimpered when he slipped between her undergarment and her skin.

A growl lodged in his throat at her need coating his finger. Her breathing became shorter, raspier the longer he tormented her. Her cheeks darkened, her lips parted, and she keened.

Maker. His chest swelled, and his malehood pulsed with such longing...

He pulled away, shuffled until he could spread her thighs with his shoulders, and settled with her backside in his palms.

"Cylo," she said, pushing herself up. "You do that, then I get to do that."

He stilled, his mind filling with images of her mouth on his malehood. "Do not threaten me, ensa." He curled his fingers around the thin straps of her undergarment. With sharp tugs, it peeled away.

This moment... He studied the pale-gold dusting of hair over her sex. So beautiful. He brushed the tip of his nose across the softness, then, with a peek at her, he licked her.

His nostrils flared, and the urge to feast on her stiffened every muscle in his body.

Every muscle.

Chapter Nineteen

Wren had hoped she'd find herself on her back, but not this soon. Not that she was complaining. Lying there so exposed reminded her of her alien smut and her longing for a male with a forked tongue. Oh, the way Cylo swirled his...was next level. Every sweep had her on the cusp of orgasming, then he'd change, almost driving her to demand he hurry up. His smirk when he met her gaze told her he knew what he was doing to her.

Just touches. She hummed. Oh, yes, they could be teenagers without doing the act. Still, the way her body twanged, she wanted him thrusting into her, filling the hollow ache inside her.

"Hungry?" he asked, his breath huffing across her sensitive nub.

"Starving," she said, lifting her hips without an ounce of shame.

"Good." He chuckled, sending a vibration through her sex just as he sucked on her...hard.

Joy exploded through her, shuddering her limbs and stealing her moans. Her knees tingled, goose bumps shot across her body, and heat pooled in her core amid spasms. They crashed over her in consistent ripples with no end in sight. She widened her eyes and cried out again, trembling against him.

He shifted onto his haunches, his lips glossy, and his gaze admiring. "Ensa, I could do this forever."

"Cylo," she whispered, tears at the back of her eyes. She wanted to cry at the profound emotions he invoked in her.

He frowned, concern floating toward her. "Did I hurt you?"

"Oh, no, never," she said, scrambling to sit up. "It was amazing."

His smile was gorgeous as it formed. "I am pleased." His focus shifted between her face and her exposed sex. He yearned to fuck her; that much she could pick up.

"Your turn," she said, rising to push him back with a hand splayed across his chest.

"It is not—"

"Hush," she said. "You agreed."

"I did not," he said and caught her hand with his and trapped it in place. The heated muscle of his pec warmed her palm.

"You did." She licked her lips, eager to explore that impressive bulge in his jeans.

He opened his mouth to argue with her when she stroked his cock. A shudder shook his body, and the sweetest moan escaped him.

"Let me attend to your chore," she said, prepared to beg if needed.

When he hesitated, she hurried to undo the button of his jeans. The sheer size of him peeled the zip open. She inched it farther down, her focus on the head peeking out.

Flicking aside his shirt, she worked his jeans out of the way until his erection stood center-stage.

"Oh, my," she whispered. Tiny nodules ran along the sides, and a ridge near the head called to her to rub its silkiness.

When she obeyed the instinct, he groaned, his flat stomach flinching.

Smirking at him as he'd done at her, she asked him to spread his legs with the nudge of her knees on his inner thighs. He obeyed, his breathing ragged.

"Do you need a safe word?" she asked, trailing a finger over the head of his cock, then across the ridge.

"Safe?" he asked, his voice hoarse.

"If you want me to stop."

When he blinked at her, she shrugged and ran her tongue over his length. He growled, his body taut. Since he didn't pull away, she saw it as approval. Sucking him into her mouth became addictive in an instant. The hot, hard, smooth feel of him competed with the smoky sweetness of his pre-cum. Lust compelled her to shuffle closer. She cupped the base to take him deeper, lost in how he tasted, how he reacted with muted moans, how he tried to control his hip thrusts.

"Ensa," he rasped.

Loving that endearment and his deeper voice, she moaned while bringing her hands in to play. She glided them up and down the length of him, then paused to rub circles at the base or on the ridge.

"I cannot control—" His breath hitched when she swiped her tongue across the head of his cock.

A series of grunts accompanied jets of honey sliding down her throat. She snuck a peek at him while maintaining a steady rhythm of suck and stroke. He'd arched his body, his braid pooling under him. *Wow.* Her eyes burned, reminding her to blink.

She broke away when he opened his eyes, no doubt to ask her to let go. Falling onto her ass, she folded her legs beneath her and smiled at him. He said nothing, just stared at her. A wealth of his emotions washed over her: affection, desire, contentment, and sadness.

They resonated with her since she, too, wished they could explore what this was between them. "Shall we eat?" she asked, glancing away.

Expecting him to bring the basket closer, she didn't anticipate an Etterian man sprawling her onto her back, his arm looped around her waist. She gasped and met his gaze inches from hers.

"Thank you for insisting." His eyes swirled that dark-to-neon blue, and a potent emotion she'd liken to love tickled the edge of her senses.

Her heart twanged with yearning, that he could love her, that he would choose her despite her purpleness. He stole a sweet, slow kiss then pulled back to set the basket between them. As he unpacked, she wondered why he didn't cover his still-erect cock. It painted the term 'eye-candy' in a new light.

"How do you open this?" he asked, his voice filled with frustration.

She dragged her gaze from his pelvis and took the champagne bottle from him. Unwinding the agraffe, she worked the cork up until it popped out. She handed the bottle to him so she could dig in her cleavage where she'd hidden his gift. While he poured, she held out the bracelet.

"I made this for you." The heat from her skin had warmed the gold, but in her hand, all she saw were her mistakes: tool marks, not enough burnishing, where she hadn't hammered the metal thin enough.

He froze, split his focus between her face and the bracelet, then after a minute, he set the bottle aside. "For me?"

With her hand extended, the ambience was becoming awkward until he slipped it off her fingers.

"What is it?"

"Here." She unlatched the clasp then wrapped it around his wrist. Against his bronze skin, the gold shimmered. "It's a bracelet. I don't know if you can wear it with your uniform, but I made it for you anyway."

He stroked it, his touch reverent. "It is magnificent. Your skill is breathtaking."

She swallowed a scoff and let his compliment bathe her with joy. To him, she was a jeweler. "I wanted to thank you for everything you've done for me."

He studied her, his gaze caressing her face. Again, 'beautiful' reached her across the narrow space between them. He offered her a flute of champagne then shook his wrist, the bracelet catching the light.

She sipped and smacked her lips at what tasted like expensive champagne. "How did you know what food to pack?"

"O.D.I." He grinned. "This does smell intriguing." He waved a sandwich before handing it to her. "I trust I have chosen well?"

"You have." She didn't have the heart to tell him that he could've picked anything as a meal. There wasn't just one way to prepare a picnic.

He bit into the sandwich and hummed. "This is good."

She gathered two strawberries, one in her palm, the other between her fingers. The rehydrator was amazing, capturing the texture, the tiny seeds, the tart aroma. She held it to her nose then took a bite. A groan slipped free. The last time she'd had a real, honest-to-goodness, Ganymede-grown strawberry was the night of her debutante party. So long ago when she was a different and naive Wren.

"Better than a fulfillment?" he asked, his focus on her mouth, his breathing harsh.

"Fulfillment? Do you mean orgasm?" She held the other strawberry for him to taste.

His lips brushed her fingers when he obeyed her. While he chewed, his attention remained fixed on her.

"Well?" She arched a brow.

"It is not better than your mouth on my malehood."

Heat exploded across her cheeks at his unexpected words. "Yes...I suppose you're right."

He took her flute, sipped from it, then set it aside. Then he crawled to her, forcing her to sprawl beneath him. "Maker, Wren, I do adore your mouth." His gaze flicked to her eyes. "I adore everything about you."

She swallowed hard. "Same," she managed as he swooped in for a kiss.

He plucked at her lips with his, then conquered her with his tongue. Despite the residual orgasmic tremors still thrumming her sex, she ached for him. She wrapped her arms around his neck and met him in battle. If he could feel a bit of what he invoked in her, she'd be happy.

Just kisses. And touches. Cylo willed his thoughts to focus on the now and not on what he dreamed of doing. It would take no effort on his part to peel off these pants, to tear off her garment, and thrust into her—the scent of her fulfillment snagged his attention over and over until he couldn't recall the taste of the tickling beverage or the pink fruit.

He pinned her to the blankets, intent on kissing her until he could no more or until sleep swept them away. Tomorrow, she would no longer be his alone. Her lips were as soft as hahyt petals, the tiny creases around her mouth mesmerizing. He traced one with his fingertip. Maker, what was this he was experiencing, this overwhelming warmth, need to protect her, and to cherish everything about her?

She smiled, and his heart skipped its beat. He tried not to frown at his irrational reaction to her.

"What's the matter?" she asked.

"I do not want to lose you," he said, the inevitable hitting him like a battle-bond's punch to the gut.

"Well, we're friends, right?" Her cheeks brightened. "More than that."

"Indeed." He shifted to ease his painful arousal.

"When we get to Issneen, you're not leaving me there, are you?" Her eyes widened.

"No," he said, conviction tightening his throat. "I shall remain at your side until your Eth claims you."

"Or you find your Dar Eth," she whispered, lowering her gaze.

"Oh, ensa, when you meet him, you will not want me around."

She angled her head. "What are the signs? How will I know?"

When she nudged his chest, he drew back so she could sit up.

"He will fall to a knee, enduring an unbearable pain. His eye color will change to ice blue." He brushed aside a curl then buried his fingers into her hair. "His allegiance will forever alter toward you. Not even the king can separate you."

"Sounds romantic and scary." She brought her knees up then wrapped her arms around them. "What happens to me?"

"The same if you were Etterian. For humans, I have heard you will become addicted to your Eth."

She grimaced. "Not sure I like that. I'm quite partial to my independence."

He shrugged though he was far from nonchalant. "You become his world. It is just that you, too, should change."

"I suppose. Marriage is different for humans. It's a partnership."

"As it is for us, ensa, but there is no separation. The soul-mate bond, the Ethera, will not allow it."

She stilled. "What if you die?"

"You will be free to love another. If you, as a human, leave me or die, as you say, I cannot do anything but follow you."

A tear slipped free, shimmering as it traveled over her cheek. "So you are doomed if you don't find her and doomed if you do."

He lifted her onto his lap, ignoring her yelp of protest. "A Dar Eth is a gift, bringing with her joy, light, and life." He pressed a kiss to her temple while cuddling her close. If he had a choice, she would be his.

"I'd choose you in a heartbeat."

He jerked back, having not realized he'd spoken aloud.

"Since you didn't kneel for me, I'm not her." She scrambled onto her knees, straddled him, and rubbed her sex along his exposed length in the process.

He shut his eyes to better savor the feel of her.

She cupped his cheeks, compelling him to look at her. "I tell you what. Let's give your Ethera a deadline."

"Deadline?" His O.D.I. hurried to update him. He laughed. "You cannot issue such a limitation on something ethereal."

She raised her chin in defiance. "I have free will."

If only the Ethera worked that way, but he was open to the idea of it. "Very well. What do you have in mind?"

"Would you take me if I stayed purple?" She held his gaze while nibbling on her bottom lip.

"Of course." An easy question to answer. "Your skin color does not change who you are."

She beamed. "Let's give your medical experts a chance to fix me. But even if they don't, we hook up...say, a month from today."

"Is that enough time for them?" *Maker, I'll give them a week and no more.*

"It should be." She traced his bottom lip with her thumb. "Since we're not jeopardizing your void, we're abstaining for my sake."

He poked the blackness in his soul and should have marveled at its retreating mass. But with Wren, he'd stopped questioning the miracle that she was.

"Sex is just...sex, but I want you, Cylo." Her cheeks darkened, and she dipped her chin, hiding her expressions. Doing so forced him to guess what she was feeling.

"What do you sense from me?" He held her gaze and released his meager control.

Her mouth parted on a gasp.

"Good. Now you know. And when the time is right, I expect you to be as vulnerable with me." He snatched a kiss, then another, sprawling her onto her back to dust her cheeks and eyelids with the barest of caresses. She giggled and squirmed, her fingers digging into his shoulders.

"My apologies, Cylo, the *Nahatyr* is two hours away." Fyca's whisper through the O.D.I. must have been audible to Wren; his intrusion weakened her smile.

"How is that possible?" Cylo asked while brushing hair off her face.

"Durok increased our propulsion, and since the *Nahatyr* was already at max speed, it closed the distance between us sooner." Fyca cleared his throat and added, "The lima kuu will be within porting distance in an hour."

"My thanks," Cylo said, sadness crushing his chest in a vise grip.

"What is it?" she asked.

He touched his temple to hers. "We have run out of time, thamani."

"No." She shoved at him until he leaned back. Her face was pale, her eyes wide. "They're here?"

"Almost." He sank onto his backside and stared at their uneaten picnic. "I can no longer be selfish." He offered her a tentative smile but couldn't manage to keep it in place. The light glinted off her gift. He caught her hand and pressed a kiss to her palm. "Thank you."

She leaped to her feet. "If you abandon me, Cylo, I promise you, I will be such a pain in your ass—"

He chuckled. "I look forward to the experience."

She blinked at him then huffed. "Where I go, you go."

"Truly?" He smirked and ran his gaze over the 'V' of her garment, accentuated by her ragged breathing. "Cleanse with me, sleep beside me, dine with me?"

She stomped her foot. "If you get off this ship, I'm coming with you."

"Fair enough, minus cesu." He rose to his full height and gathered her against him.

She rested her chin on his chest while looping her arms around his waist. "Thank you." She sighed and pulled away. "Let's clean this up and head to bed." She glanced at him and grinned. "Separate beds."

"For now." He dropped a kiss on the crown of her head and started to gather the discarded food items. The black sliver of her undergarment caught his attention. He tucked it into a pocket, hoping she didn't notice.

"And maybe you need to..." Her cheeks glowed. "...Cover all that." She gestured to his undone pants.

He threw back his head and laughed.

Chapter Twenty

"Can't sleep?" Wren asked Qaff as she headed for the rehydrator in the common.

Cylo had said something about changing into his armor. He'd cast a glance at her wrinkled dress. His gaze had lingered on her cleavage, his desire bathing her in renewed joy. The man had game. Damn, if her body didn't tingle in anticipation. Especially with his memories hitting her. A dreamier version of her sprawled beneath him had indeed been beautiful. She blushed at how he saw her.

"Not with the lima kuu about to port." Qaff's voice snatched her from her thoughts. "They will have many questions before I leave."

"Where are you going?" She sank onto the bench in front of him.

"I will travel with the *Nahatyr* to Yithia. Olin, myself, and Hiossu will aid where we can."

She coughed, choking on a sip of coffee. "Hiossu, too?"

"His suggestion." Qaff stared at her cup. "What is that? It smells interesting."

"Coffee. Let me get you a cup." She ordered for him and slid it onto the table. "I chose it sweet and creamy for you, but how you prefer it is for you to discover on your own." Again, she sat opposite him. "Tell me, Qaff, why isn't Cylo my Eth?"

He hummed between slurps, the cup's rim almost resting on his lip. "As I told Cylo, the Ethera triggers when the Eth sees all of the Dar Eth, but you are purple."

"So, I have to be my normal me?" She slapped the table. Cylo could've been ravaging her already if it wasn't for those stupid scientists.

"Yes, or permanently this color. Until the markers stabilize, I suppose." Qaff smacked his lips after another sip.

She raised her forearm to eye level and glared at it, willing her skin to change.

"What are you doing?" he asked, a smile curling one side of his mouth.

She slumped, giving up on the futile attempt. "If a dream undyed my hair..." She caught a curl and held it an inch from her nose, briefly considering trying to make it pink. "These great teachers—what can I expect?"

"Questions, tests, and—"

"Like a lab rat?" She curled her fingers into fists. If the lure of normalcy wasn't dangled before her, she'd almost resent them, Qaff, Hiossu, and his crazy uncle. Well, the latter could rot in whatever their hell was.

Wait, as Qaff had told Cylo? She grinned. So Cylo asked him, too? A shiver shot down the nape of her neck, sending a ripple of delicious goose bumps outward.

Qaff angled his head and inhaled, flaring his nostrils. Anger hardened his features. "Your scent is..." *...Like Cylo's. Did they— No. He knows the risks.*

She jerked back, then sniffed herself. Did the smell of 'sex' cling to her? Her cheeks flushed, and she bolted, abandoning her half-empty cup. "Off to shower."

She made it to the barracks without encountering anyone. Except, when the door opened to the passage, Cylo stood there, barring her from reaching her room. His eyebrow shooting up said she'd surprised him. Her heart stuttered, and hot need pooled in her core.

He caught her wrist and yanked her against him, then with a sidestep, he had her pinned to the wall. He rested his hand next to her ear and leaned in, surrounding her with his spicy cologne.

"I was thinking of you," he whispered, his breath fanning her chin and lips.

"Oh?" she asked, unable to vocalize anything more...complicated.

He hummed. "Where are you heading?"

"Qaff says I smell—"

"Like me?" Cylo rubbed his nose along her cheek, sending a spark of heat down her neck.

"Yeah." She grasped his hip, digging her fingers into the firm flesh she found there. "Thought I better change before—"

"Want me to watch?" He feathered his lips across hers, stealing her breath.

"When we can fuck, that's—"

He crushed her to the wall and kissed her, claiming her with that skillful tongue of his. Her knees threatened to buckle. Thankfully, he held her up with his bulk. She slipped her hands up his armored chest and around his neck. This plastered her to his body. She moaned then tilted her head to deepen the kiss.

He tastes so good.

She hooked her leg around his hip, trying to rub where she ached across his hard bulge that was digging into her belly. It wasn't enough. Before she could climb him like a crane strut, he broke the kiss.

Blinking at him, she struggled to gather her thoughts through the emotions pouring off him and—

Amusement hit her first. Hiossu strolled past them without saying a word.

Shit. She stole a peck from Cylo, then slipped around him, dragging her nails across his abs. "See you in a bit."

Inside her room, she slumped against the closed door, sucking in deep breaths to calm herself. When she could trust her knees, she staggered to the shower. That man was lethal. Untying the wrap dress reminded her that she was sans panties.

"Oh, you hussy," she said, then giggled.

She unclipped her bra and dropped it to the floor. Adding another metaphorical padlock to her door, she raised her face as the spray activated. The hot water drenched her, and along with the divine orgasm he'd wrung out of her, energy thrummed through her. She didn't dally, not when the next stage of this insane adventure would kick off soon.

Jeans, a T-shirt in deep purple, and flip-flops had her feeling herself again.

"Opacity: mirror," she said. In the reflection, her hair shimmered as she ran a brush through it. In all honesty, her old rainbow-colored hair against her lilac skin would have made for a wild image.

Whatever was in the water did amazing things to her hair and skin. She missed the sharp flavor of toothpaste, but her teeth were clean just from a gargle. She'd tried to order perfume or deodorant from the rehydrator with no success. Her eyebrows knitted into a frown. Cylo had said he could smell her arousal. Did that mean they had heightened olfactory receptors?

She gasped, and her cheeks brightened. If Cylo could smell her, then so could every man onboard. "Just great," she muttered, tossing herself a glare. "Damn Etterians need to come with warnings."

"Ensa?" Cylo's voice via her O.D.I. made her drop the brush. While she scrambled for it, he said, "The lima kuu are here."

She squeaked, tossed the brush onto the bed, and bolted out the door. Her fingers trembled, so she curled them into fists and tucked them under her arms. Here she was, running toward her doom or salvation. She peeked around the wall at the three older men gathered in the med bay. Nerves had her breathing like an asthmatic splice user.

"Wren?" Cylo appeared before her, his brow arched like a raven's wing in flight.

"Oh, hi," she whispered, peering around him.

"What is the matter?" His concern pouring over her made her square her shoulders.

I'm scared. But she didn't speak those words.

A soft smile curled his sinful mouth. He offered her his palm. "Come."

She stared at his hand then took it. His touch calmed her staccato heartbeat. At last, she could draw in a deep breath. He led her across the common. As they approached, the three experts alongside Qaff fell silent and waited for her to reach them.

"Lady Wren, allow me to introduce—"

"Maker, she is exquisite."

"Thank you," she said, smiling at them, not sure who had spoken.

They glanced at each other.

One man said, "We have not done anything yet that needs your gratitude."

"Oh," she flicked a dismissive hand, "for the compliment."

"Ensa, no one spoke," Cylo whispered.

Her world tilted. She tightened her grip, needing his touch more than ever. "I heard someone clear as day..." Her cheeks flushed cold then hot. "Qaff, earlier... Did you say, 'He knows the risks?'"

He leaned back then circled the medics to stand between her and the med-E.D. "I thought it." He swiveled and hurried to the mounted display vids, tapping them in a frenzy. "On the bed, please."

She didn't budge, her mind reeling. If she'd *heard* his thoughts, then her door wasn't strong enough for whatever the hell was happening to her. Worse, she'd surpassed empathy. She cupped Cylo's hand and brought it to her lips for a kiss. Closing her eyes as she savored the scent of his skin, she willed herself not to cry. And yet, the sting of tears was so forceful, a lump lodged in her throat.

Breaking away, she kicked off her shoes and splayed her hands on the bed, planning on hoisting herself onto it.

Up she went, crushed against Cylo's chest when he scooped her into his arms. "I am here, ensa."

Unable to trust her voice, she pressed her temple to his shoulder and held on. He lowered her onto the bed she was fast coming to hate. Every time she was in the stupid machine, more bad news awaited her. When he stepped back, the dome formed. Thankfully, only Cylo stood beside her. The others gathered around Qaff.

"Do I have to sleep?" she asked.

Qaff poked his head up. "Yes."

"Shit," she muttered, moments before her eyelids grew heavy, and that warm buzz consumed her mind.

CYLO SHIFTED HIS ATTENTION between the lima kuu and Wren. "Am I understanding this? That she is reading thoughts now?"

"If they are tied to strong emotion," Medic Ariez said, flicking through charts.

"Lady Eight's markers are slowing. They used to switch every nanosecond." Medic Zive frowned. "I would say the changes are almost complete."

"Indeed," Qaff said. "A minute between."

"She may remain this skin color." Medic Yelur said, casting a glance at Cylo. "Your Dar Eth is something unknown, Operative Cylo. I assume that is acceptable?"

Cylo winced, the pain through his heart almost crippling him. "She is not mine, but yes, she is more than acceptable."

Yelur harrumphed.

Medic Zive snapped, "I am concerned about her psychology. Telepathy is a powerful tool, and a dangerous one in the wrong hands."

Cylo scowled. Zive spoke the truth, but to imply Wren could be a spy?

"Can you help her?" he demanded, holding Zive's gaze. "Or is she just an oddity you wish to study?" His tone dripped venom.

"Unknown implies we *must* study her," Zive said, not backing down. "As to whether we can help her, that is an unknown, too."

The urge to deactivate the med-E.D. and whisk Wren to safety gripped Cylo. He gritted his teeth, fighting the urge. His males wouldn't harm her, not on purpose.

"Let the med-E.D. re-analyze her." Yelur grasped Cylo's shoulder. "The more information we have, the better we can help her.

"That the Maloidians are intent on this path is most alarming," Ariez said when he glanced at Qaff. "Have you compared her compatibility with Maloidians' and Yithians' DNA?"

Qaff stilled then sent his fingers across the console keys. "Doing so now."

Cylo held his breath. He forced himself to release it and the tension forming a knot in his gut.

"Whatever your findings, they must never know." Yelur swept his gaze across those gathered.

Cylo grimaced. "Whether successful or not, they will continue with these experiments. Qaff, once you have informed us, you are free to depart on the *Nahatyr*."

The males Cylo had started this mission with had almost all left him. If it wasn't for the Ethera, Durok, too, would no longer be on board. Not that Cylo blamed them. Only he was committed to Wren's welfare.

"Operative?" Ariez arched a brow.

Cylo yanked himself out of his thoughts. "Yes?"

"I was saying how remarkable your female is."

He pursed his lips, not wanting to remind the older male once again that she wasn't his. Instead, he asked, "In what way?"

"Consider all she has endured, and yet, she greeted us with a smile. A lesser being would despise us for our inability to end these abductions. King Xeus was most adamant I inform you that henceforth, Etteria will have a zero-tolerance approach."

Cylo grinned at that bit of good news. "Kill them on sight?"

"With proof of their G.C. violations, yes."

Cylo bowed his head. "Of course." Even though he had every intention of firing first. Diplomacy had done nothing to thwart these kidnappings. As Hiossu had said, females had died...that the Maloidian knew of.

"Oh," Qaff gasped, flicked a glance at Zive before their O.D.I.s buzzed.

"This does not bode well," Yelur muttered, reading off his wrist. "Restrict this information to us five. We will convey these findings to the medical council in person. For now, let us find a way to stabilize Lady Eight's markers."

"Agreed," Zive said. "Pity we do not have her DNA prior to this..." He curled his lip. "Incident."

"We do." Qaff paused amid clearing the counter. "Olin discovered it in the historical data on Lady Wren."

Ariez beamed. "With that, we should be able to create a—"

"Do not say cure," Zive growled. "What has set cannot be undone."

"But you *can* help her?" Cylo asked.

Qaff frowned. "Another concoction might do more harm than good."

"She is still vulnerable to influence. Have you mated her yet?" Zive met Cylo's gaze and held it.

"For the last time, I am not her Eth," Cylo gritted out.

Zive stared at him for too long. "An injection of Etterian DNA might be reckless, but if you lay with her, her body's natural ability to assimilate sperm may ease the shock of—"

"No," Cylo roared. "I shall not mate her to appease your curiosity and definitely not if it will endanger her further."

He shook with so much fury, he could barely control himself. A large part of him wanted nothing more than to sink into the pleasure between her thighs. Thankfully, the sane side of his soul held him accountable.

"Build her DNA as it is documented. If injecting it into her does not change the outcome, then find a male with void to spare." Zive stormed past Cylo.

"Find a male?" he whispered, his heart thundering in his ears. A roar started in the pit of his stomach, and only his clenched jaw stopped it from escaping.

"Start the DNA replication, Qaff. I shall work alongside you." Ariez settled beside him. "Then leave. The *Nahatyr* is eager to depart for Yithia."

"Already begun," Qaff said and shoved the tablet at Ariez. He bowed and disappeared into his quarters.

Cylo gazed at Wren's serene face, his chest swelling even as his fury dwindled. Yes, he'd be the male to lay with her...should it be required. It wouldn't be a hardship.

He almost snorted at that. On their date, they'd come damn close.

And yet, Qaff had said not to. Who did Cylo listen to?

That she was compatible with Yithians and Maloidians meant the xemi had succeeded. If they learned of this, they wouldn't know which scientist and his concoction had worked. This knowledge would only encourage further trials. Zive was correct to insist this discovery remained sealed.

"Are you done?" Cylo gestured to Wren still asleep.

"Indeed." Ariez tapped the med-E.D.'s console.

The dome retracted while lowering her to the bed. She moaned and stretched, her every movement sensual.

"Ask her," Zive muttered between sips of giyua. "Let her decide her fate."

"Do not dare," Cylo muttered.

She stiffened, glanced at them, then sat up. "And?"

"We will re-introduce your original DNA to perhaps..." Zive winced. "I cannot deceive. They managed the impossible, milady."

Cylo grabbed the male by the arm, glaring him into silence.

"No, let him finish." She shifted to the edge of the bed. "Are you saying whatever they did to me worked? That humans can now have sex with these...sharks?"

"Not humans... You." Cylo released Zive and settled nearer to her in case she needed him.

"And you're hoping my old DNA will do what?" She swung her legs off the side, her focus fixed on Zive.

"Stabilize the last markers," Zive said, pulling himself free.

"But?" She pinched her brow.

Zive's stern expression softened for a moment. "My concern is your compatibility with Etterians. That has been weakened."

She frowned. "What? So you want to throw your DNA into the melting pot that is my body?" She muttered a few curses. "Qaff insisted that Cylo and I didn't—" Her cheeks darkened. "Regardless, DNA transfer via penetration isn't a thing."

Ariez offered a weak smile. "It is when yours is vulnerable to Etterian sperm. It is why Princess Oriana and Prince Enyl glow."

Wren squeaked, her eyes wide. "In what way?"

"Like bioluminescence," Ariez said, shifting his focus between her and the tablet. "Something in the protein bonds and enzymes impacts Earthian physiology. Princess Oriana also has a mutated gene tied to her red coloring. And since they are paired, the prince shares this phenomenon.

Zive squared his shoulders. "We assumed Cylo was your Eth, but if he does not suit, we will find another—"

"I'm not about to fuck a stranger," she snapped.

Zive stiffened, his expression once more stoic. "An injection of pure Etterian DNA might worsen your condition. We were hoping your body's natural—"

"No." She pushed herself off the bed. "Don't you have a say?" She scowled at Cylo.

"I, too, rejected the idea." *No matter how tempted I am.*

Pain scrunched her brow, then she grinned, her joy slicing through. "I would never say no to you."

She must have read his thoughts. His breath caught at her new skill *and* that she'd choose him... Let him have her even if it was only once. He swallowed hard. A glance across the common confirmed they had an audience. So he met and held her gaze, not sure how this telepathy thing worked. *Finish what we started at the picnic?*

"Yes." Her answer set his senses ablaze.

Having a somewhat telepathic discussion with her was mind-blowing.

"Unless your void can't." She stroked the collar of his armor; the heat of her fingers seared him.

It has not expanded, remember?

"Then you have nothing to lose." She beamed.

Not true. He covered her hand with his, trapping her fingers. *I cannot lose you,* ensa.

"You're stuck with me. We made a deal." She tugged her hand free, caught his, and laced their fingers. "Come, Cylo."

"Now?" He peeked at Ariez and Zive, who, despite listening to them, flicked through something on the tablet.

"Return here afterward." Zive didn't glance up.

"And I will ensure we are en route to Issneen as soon as possible." Ariez strode to the comm.

Cylo faced Yelur, half expecting a final comment from him, too. The lima kuu peered into Cylo's eyes before crossing medical to the display vids.

"Ensa." Cylo hesitated and drew her close. "This is reckless." He released a shuddering breath.

"I could die tomorrow, an hour from now, next week... I do know I want this...you."

"You are not dying," he growled.

She scoffed. "You'd swear I was leading you to the gallows."

"Gallows?" His O.D.I. hurried to educate him. He grimaced at the imagery. "You did this to your people?"

"We are a brutal species."

"And no, you are not leading me to such a death. Never think that." He pressed a kiss to her palm, his fingers trembling. *To mate her today couldn't compare to having her for an eternity.*

"I feel the same." A tear slipped free and glimmered as it forged a path down her cheek.

He ushered her to his quarters, swiveled on a heel, and took her to the viewing deck instead. There, only *his* thoughts and emotions would bombard her. The smoothness of her hand in his, her ragged breathing, the smile that threatened to form on her plump lips—everything registered and hit him in the chest.

He climbed the ladder first then pulled her up and through the hatch. After sealing it, he faced her but managed only a step when she removed her top garment.

A chill shot into his core, pulsing out liquid heat.

Maker, is this truly happening?

Chapter Twenty-One

At Cylo's thoughts, Wren froze. Okay, removing her shirt might have been too eager, but she didn't give a damn. At last, she was about to get horizontal with the one man who made her blood sizzle. But when he just stood there, gazing at her, shyness struck like her first day at school.

She angled her head as if doing so would sharpen her new ability to pick up his thoughts. But nothing more reached her as if he was stunned into silence. She cleared her throat and faced him. What was the rush? If this was one and done, she should take it slow, savor each moment. He kissed like a connoisseur, his tongue was beyond talented, and he already knew how to make her see stars, galaxies, and supernovas. Well, maybe there was room for more.

"Come here," he said, pointing to his booted feet. *Please.*

Although she loved his commanding tone, the imp in her didn't budge. She grinned. "And if I do not?"

Alodon's balls, I love that she challenges me, but not now... "Ensa, I want you. If I move from this spot, I fear what control I have might shatter."

Her eyes widened even as her heart froze then burst into an explosion of activity. That he was honest with her, had verbally revealed how he felt, that alone propelled her toward him.

"Here?" she whispered, not two feet from him.

His features hardened, and a pulse ticked at the base of his jaw.

She inched closer until she was a foot away.

"Minus cesu, what am I going to do with you?" He wrapped his fingers around her upper arms and yanked her against him, plastering her to his taut body.

The warmth of him hit her first, then the velvety texture of his skin registered. She clung to his biceps, loving the strength and play of muscles beneath her fingertips. He nuzzled her neck, drawing in deep breaths between nips that sent shivers outward. Liquid heat trickled to her toes and weakened her knees.

Maker, I dreamed of this. "It is my wish to undress you," he said, his breath puffing across her goose-bumped flesh.

She opened her mouth to agree to anything, but with a sharp tug, her bra fell away. He spread his fingers across her back, his breathing rougher.

"Your skin is so soft," he mumbled. *I ache to taste every inch of you.*

Communicating with her telepathically added a whole new level of intimacy to this moment. She feathered kisses where she could reach, hating that his armor prevented her from truly enjoying being plastered against him. "I hope I get to undress you, too."

He leaned back and thumped his chest. His armor parted, granting her a sliver of bronzed skin, not a hair in sight. The urge to press her lips there squashed any lingering shyness. The taste of him made her sigh—hot, scented, and all male. When she licked him, he thrust her away from him.

Thamani.

With a hand holding her back, he slipped out of his armor, letting it fall. Her gaze locked on his taut nipples, darker than his skin tone. She tried to wrap her lips around each bud, but he wouldn't let her.

She stamped her foot and glared at him.

His attention wasn't on her face but lower. *So beautiful.*

From where his outstretched hand touched her, he stroked down until a breast filled his palm. Her breath caught, and her head fell back as she relished his reverent touch. When he rubbed a thumb over a nipple, pleasure shot outward. She hummed in approval.

Must taste.

Movement disturbed her pleasure, but she couldn't bring herself to peek. Something hot and wet latched onto a nipple. She looked then, finding him on his knees and his mouth on her. He wrapped his arm around her ass, keeping her in place. From one breast to the other, he bathed her in worship.

Addicting.

She sank her fingers into his hair and held on, knowing he'd keep her standing.

Garments. Off. Now. Despite his thoughts warning her, when he pulled back, she almost went with him, but his grip on her hip kept her upright.

He glided his hands down one leg until he reached her foot. Off went her flip-flop. She kicked off the other, not wanting to waste a second on something so simple.

My thanks. He chuckled as he stroked up her other leg to hook his fingers in the waistband of her jeans. With a jerk, the button popped off. Another yank had the zipper sliding down.

Control yourself. Soon. He ran his fingers along the waistband while dusting kisses across her belly. Every inch he exposed when he removed her pants was blessed with a kiss. Every inch but the part of her that wept for him.

I am stronger than this. He paused, buried his face between her legs, and inhaled. Then continued until she could step out of her jeans and underwear. Naked before him, she waited, half expecting him to stand. He lunged, taking her from vertical to sprawled on the floor in the blink of an eye.

She barely had time to gasp. He abandoned her to rip off his boots and pants, giving her a glimpse of his gorgeous body before he lay on top of her. She pouted at the lost opportunity. What was visible while he kept himself off her in a permanent push-up did little to assuage her disappointment. Her view was filled with broad shoulders into bulging pecs and biceps, his ripped abs next—the stuff of fantasies.

"What is it, ensa?" he asked, his gaze snagging hers. *Is she anxious?*

"Nothing like that. You get to look, but I don't?"

He laughed. "We have time...later." He lowered himself until he pressed her into the blankets.

She sighed, appeased for now. With her arms around him, as best she could, she peered into his lovely eyes flickering between navy and neon blue. She could drown in the mini light show happening in his irises.

"Your eyes," she whispered. "Is that normal?"

He hesitated mid-descend, his lips a breath from hers. "What color are they?"

"They swirl between dark and bright blue." She cupped his face. "They're beautiful."

His smile was slow, on a sensuous crawl across his sinful mouth. "As are you, thamani." He kissed her then with languid sweeps of his tongue. *I could kiss her for an eternity.*

She melted, her limbs weak and warm even as a knot constricted in her core. It throbbed, ached, demanded. She writhed, desperate to have all of him touching her while hoping to find some relief for the craving building within her.

He broke the kiss and caught her gaze. With a deep inhale, his eyelashes fluttered shut. *Maker.* "Your scent is intoxicating." He growled when she hooked her legs around his hips, forcing him closer.

At that victory, especially when his erection pressed into her and pinged sweet need through her, a smile formed. She loved how she could rattle him and how open his reactions were.

"We have now, later, tonight." She winced at her eloquence. "Fuck me again and again."

Alodon's balls. He trembled, his breathing ragged, but he, at least, caught her beneath her knee and lifted her leg. That she barely registered when his hard cock rubbed along her folds.

She whimpered when he paused. Panic gripped her, that he might stop, and she tightened her arms. "Please." She licked her lips. "Cy..."

Instead of plunging in, he kissed her again, enchanting her with his tongue. She succumbed, letting him lead her. There was no other choice. She couldn't force him to hurry.

When he broke away, he held his cheek to hers. "I like that: Cy."

"Oh," she managed, her heartbeat in her ears, her voice raspy.

All thoughts of teasing him with his new nickname shot out of her mind when he inched into her, stretching her to accommodate his girth. Every nerve tingled in pleasure, and the sensations he invoked were indescribable. She bit her lip and savored this moment. What she wanted was to be fucked and hard. But this... This was good.

When he was fully seated, his breath caught. *Oh, Maker.* He jerked back to meet her gaze, his eyes warming as he stared at her. *My Wren.*

Tears burned at the back of her eyes, and her heart swelled.

"I am keeping you," he whispered, but she wasn't sure she heard him correctly.

She opened her mouth to ask, needing to know they were more than lovers. But he withdrew and thrust into her, clouding her mind. Her core zinged, and that desperate craving rose and crashed over her. All she could do was enjoy the sensations, the emotions, culminating in an overwhelming state of awareness.

Something circled her soul, like ribbons of bright energy. A wealth of warmth came with it, spreading from her chest to lower. His eyes widened, he stilled, and gave her a sweet kiss. A cheek caress preceded another deep thrust. She couldn't focus on both, and him finally fucking her was more demanding. The tension built, her core tightened, and to hell with breathing. She clung to him, let him take her to the pinnacle.

With a cry, she tumbled off the edge, arching into him when an orgasm slammed into her. No emotions other than her own bombarded her, and for that precious moment, she was just Wren, a woman in love.

Thamani.

My ensa ra ensa.

His thoughts trickled in as the ecstasy faded. He dusted kisses over her cheeks and threaded his arms under her to crush her against him. She tucked her face into the curve of his neck and took a long inhale, loving the heated scent of him. Fuck. She was a goner. And yet, none of his emotions hit her.

His endearments didn't necessarily mean he loved her back.

You are quiet.

She hummed. "Sorry. Just enjoying this."

His chuckle rumbled through her. *As am I.* He leaned back a little and kissed her. "My apologies on not giving you a fulfillment *before* finding my own," he said, his breath fanning her lips.

"I came," she hurried to say.

I know. He kissed her again. *It was magnificent.*

Heat scorched her cheeks when she had nothing to be ashamed of or proud of. He'd wrung the orgasm from her.

I do not want to withdraw. "Am I too heavy?"

She squeezed him, not wanting him to move. "Stay where you are... Please, Cy."

He caught her lips for another sweet kiss. *Keep calling me that.*

She grinned. "I will. How long do you think it will take my body to work through your DNA?"

What she wanted to ask was if this transfusion would need multiple sessions. Already, a familiar craving had taken up residence in her core. She relished the feel of him still buried in her.

"I cannot say."

She snuck a peek at his almost-neon eyes. "Do you think multiple sessions would help?"

"Many..."

"Fuckings?"

He growled. *That word from your mouth drives me mad with need.*

"Oh?" She pursed her lips.

"Do not dare," he warned though laugh lines crinkled around his eyes.

"I fucking love it when you fuck me and make me scream your fucking name."

Minus cesu. His grin was wicked. *You did not make a sound. Perhaps I need to try harder.*

"Fuck me from behind." The idea and imagery of it had fire exploding outward. As if he hadn't just plundered her, she ached for another round.

He pulled back and out. Cool air sent a frisson of goose bumps over her skin, but she watched him and waited.

"I have seen educational footage on this." He rested on his haunches, granting her an unparalleled view of his body. The only thing he wore was her bracelet.

Muscled thighs, carved in stone, flowed into narrow hips with a rigid cock eager for a licking. An Adonis belt flanked his abs.

Wow. She mouthed the words. *Just wow.*

He didn't move but gazed at her, patience draped across his shoulders, affection in his eyes. She flipped onto her hands and knees like a good girl and arched her back. A glance showed him staring at her, but this time, desire darkened his features.

"Exquisite." He ran his hand down her back and over a butt cheek.

A purr lodged in her throat. Since when had she become so brazen? He stroked a finger along her sex, summoning a whimper. The urge to pinch her thighs together took ahold of her, but she resisted. The growing ache was potent, demanding, addictive, and she wanted more. No, *expected* more.

You are wet for me. This pleases me. He grabbed her by the hips and rubbed his length along her seam.

She mauled the blankets beneath her while wiggling her ass. If he didn't—

He thrust into her, drawing a long moan out of her.

Too deep. Too much. But if he stopped, she'd kill him.

He hissed. *I have never felt like this, ensa.* Then, without another word, he pistoned in and out of her with amazing force and stamina. She cried out, her senses overwhelmed like she was about to explode. He touched every inch of her, hitting her G-spot with accuracy.

Surges of pleasure washed over her. She lost count of the peaks, one after the other. He didn't give her a chance to breathe between orgasms. She mewled and whimpered while begging him not to stop.

Until he did, roaring his release.

He collapsed over her, wrapped an arm around her waist, and flipped them, landing on the floor with her back curled against his chest. All without hurting her. He nuzzled her hair aside and pressed his lips to her neck.

She shivered but didn't pull away. Instead, she layered her arms over his and trapped them to her. His ragged breathing matched hers.

None of his thoughts reached her. No emotions, too.

And in the quiet of the viewing deck, she lay there, stunned yet content. "Incredible," she managed when she could speak.

More than that. He tightened his arms, melding her to him.

She supposed she had to head to the med bay for another assessment. The thought made her want to snuggle into his arms and not move. She understood their concern that she was losing compatibility with Etterians. And not being able to be with Cy compelled her more than desire did. She wanted to be his, not some green alien's or silver shark's. If anyone had asked her at the beginning of this adventure, she'd have said she wanted nothing to do with any aliens. But of the three, she preferred Cy. She valued his competence, strength, sweetness, and kindness. She liked how he grounded her and accepted her despite her worsening symptoms.

She loved how he protected her, no matter what happened, and even from his own men. He slipped out of her, allowing her to roll over within the circle of his embrace. He let her, widening the space to allow her to do what she wanted. Which was to kiss him.

Again, he let her, meeting her tongue with his own skilled assault. She glided her arms over his chest to slip around his neck and deepened the kiss.

I could die now.

She jerked back and met his gaze. No, he had to live until he found his Dar Eth. That thought doused the renewed spark of desire that had started to unfold in her stomach.

"I'm hungry," she said, sliding out of his arms. "Come. Let's eat and have your lima kuu test me again."

He hesitated. "Do you think your body has—"

"I don't know, but it won't hurt to check."

He cupped her cheek, brushing his thumb across her bottom lip. *I do not want to share you. I want to remain here...in our own world.*

She grinned. "You like sending me your thoughts?"

His breath shuddered out of him. *I like the intimacy of it.*

"So do I." And she stood before the tears slipped free.

Action and distraction would keep her sane and her broken heart together. Because, no matter what the med-E.D. said, she couldn't keep him.

Chapter Twenty-Two

"This is most interesting," Ariez said when Cylo led Wren into medical. The older male was looking at them and not at the console like usual. "Come. Let me assess you. I am hoping to see changes." He grinned, softening his features. "It is rare to have such an intriguing patient."

"I do try." Wren chuckled when Cylo lifted her onto the bed.

His chest swelled, and because he couldn't resist the temptation, he stole a quick kiss.

"What do you expect to find?" he asked while gazing into her beautiful eyes.

"Nothing, for it is too soon. But..." Ariez tapped the console, summoning the dome. As it formed, it broke Cylo and Wren apart. "It would be amazing if something did happen." As she drifted off to sleep, Ariez sidled closer. "The med-E.D. should assess you, as well."

Cylo bowed his head in thanks. "Please. She mentioned my eye color fluctuating." He exhaled, slow and controlled, exhaustion pounding at him. She, at least, got dome-induced naps, for which he was grateful. He didn't like the shadows under her eyes. "I am hoping it is the work of the Ethera, but I need to be certain."

"I understand." Ariez flipped through holographics options. Lights pulsed over Wren. "We know so little about the Ethera. The Durn created it, yet it acts as if it has a mind of its own."

"Or like it is programmed along certain parameters. When it strikes, the pain is said to be excruciating." Zive strolled into medical. "All the Eths have fallen to their knees, yet...you have not."

Cylo grimaced. Wren was his regardless of whether the Ethera agreed or not.

"Medic Qaff noted that your void is shrinking. If it continues to do so, more so after the mating, then it shows the Ethera is adjusting the parameters to suit the situation," Zive continued.

"Indeed." Ariez beamed. "You make a remarkable pairing. One for the annals."

Cylo scowled, not giving a damn about the archives. His future with Wren was unknown in the eyes of Etterian law. He'd take her and flee if Etteria tried to stop him from claiming her.

"Cylo to comm," Fyca called, his voice reverberating through medical and the common.

Cylo patted the dome in farewell, his bracelet gleaming in the lighting, then hurried to Fyca's side. "What is it?" He nodded at Lady Brenda in greeting.

"I am picking up an odd reading. It is almost as if we are being followed, yet there is no ship." Fyca zoomed out and across the display vids, showing endless space.

"A malfunction?" Cylo frowned.

"At first, I thought it residual signatures from the *Nahatyr's* departure. But..." Fyca glanced at his Dar Eth then met Cylo's gaze. "My instincts say otherwise."

"We are but a few days from Etteria and at full fusion pulse. Who would dare to attack us? And at that speed, is that even possible?" Cylo stiffened. "I had heard on the buzz—"

"Stealth?" Fyca ran his fingers across the console, flickering the forevids from light spectrums to sound sensitivity. "Nothing."

"Send an alert on a secure channel to all nearby battleships." Cylo waited for Fyca to do so. "Then open comms on this...illusion."

"But—"

"We shall revert to Etterian arrogance." Cylo grinned.

Fyca chuckled and hit a button.

"Maloidian, I am not in the mood. Kindly state the reason for this pathetic attempt at subterfuge." Cylo put enough boredom and disrespect in his tone to anger the most bombastic of commanders. The Maloidian bit was a hunch. Best case, he was speaking to nothing. Worst case, an unknown species with phenomenal military might was on their backside.

With three humans on board, he didn't like the latter. As good a pilot as Fyca was, they wouldn't fare well against untested firepower.

Silence reigned. Cylo willed his heartbeat to calm, but that knot in his stomach didn't ease.

"Scimitar *Kevol*, this is battleship *Vindar*, Supreme Commander Kyah here. Do you require assistance?"

"Share the comm," Cylo whispered, wanting whoever was out there to know they were not alone. "An escort to Etteria would be appreciated." He grimaced. Asking for such made him appear weak, scared, when he was far from it. Had there been no females on board, he would have challenged the illusion. "Fire up the chokaar, Fyca," he muttered. "Let us be cautious yet prepared."

"Indeed," Supreme Commander Kyah said. "We have been tracking you since the *Nahatyr* left."

Cylo nodded at Fyca who shared the findings on the anomaly with Kyah.

The supreme commander continued, "Battleship *Ntima* is also en route and will meet you at the halfway point."

"My thanks, Supreme Commander." Cylo squared his shoulders, clasped his hands behind his back, and glared into the forevids. "Maloidian, I grow impatient. You have two seconds before I start firing the chokaar in a grid pattern—"

"Oh, like Battleship?" Lady Brenda giggled. "I loved that game as a kid."

"Teach me that this night," Fyca said, spinning in his seat to smile at his Dar Eth.

"It is I, Ambassador Barro, on my way to meet with King Xeus. Do not fire. My apologies for the delayed response. The ship has new functionality we are not familiar with."

Cylo kept his features stoic. The odds of an ambassador receiving an advanced ship without a trained pilot were laughable. But since he'd revealed himself, Cylo wouldn't call him a liar.

"Should I send my data officer to assist?" He had to offer even though Olin was no longer on board. If Etteria could gain stealth tech, any future covert operations would have a higher success rate.

"That would require we both slow our ships," Barro said.

"Yes," Cylo confirmed. This would delay their arrival, but he was hoping for no more than an hour. The knot in his stomach hardened. He couldn't shake the thought that this was a trap.

"Very well."

Cylo glanced at Fyca. "Pilot, all systems halt." This was reckless, but what choice did he have? He'd rather learn what he was dealing with than run to Issneen like a coward. "Ambassador, please share your location and prepare to be boarded."

Fyca ended the comm. "We do not have a kuta."

"I am aware," Cylo said, flooding his tone with strained patience.

Fyca pushed on. "And with Olin not on board—"

"I will go." Cylo arched a brow like him going was ever in doubt.

"Alone?" Fyca scowled.

"No." Zive pushed off the doorframe and ventured deeper into the comm. "I have data analysis experience, and as an Eth, your life is not expendable. I insist you remain with Lady Wren."

Cylo glared. "For the last time—"

"Your eye color fluctuates even when you are not emotional." Zive gave him a pointed look. "On the slim chance the Ethera is working, we will act as if it has chosen you."

"I have to agree with Medic Zive," Fyca said.

"I do not need your approval," Cylo snapped. "My mission, my scimitar, my decision."

"We have no idea what awaits us." Zive folded his arms across his chest.

"I am trained for this." Cylo wasn't about to back down. Not only was it his right, but endangering anyone else wasn't an option for him.

"You wish to steal this knowledge," Zive growled. "That is dishonorable."

"In your world, yes. In mine, if it is for the good of Etteria—"

"Informing King Xeus of this discovery would allow him to barter for it. There is no need to act dishonorably. Which is why I will go." Zive crossed the comm and stopped an inch from Cylo, shoving his face into his. "I pull rank as a lima kuu."

Cylo bristled. "Alodon's balls, this is not—"

"Enough," Yelur said, his calm voice slicing through the tension. "I will go with Zive. You," he pointed at Cylo, "will come, too, but you will not take lead. Guard the door and our backs."

"*That* you have been trained for," Zive finished with a firm nod.

"I have the location," Fyca said, making the forevids zoom into a strip of shimmering stars. A bay door opened, serving as a beacon of light. "Target confirmed."

Cylo scowled at the elder males. "Suit up."

He marched off, stomping his displeasure like a damu. Grimacing at his behavior, he paused, drew in a shuddering breath, and proceeded to stride to his quarters. There, he summoned a spacesuit from the replicator and peeled it on, trapping his braid down his body to an ankle. He pocketed daggers then strapped a blaster to his thigh. With a new helmet tucked under his arm, he returned to the common.

Wren was in stasis with Ariez vigilantly monitoring her. She was safe, for now.

Cylo squeezed Ariez's shoulder. "I leave her in your care. Do not let any harm befall her." The knot spread from Cylo's stomach to his chest and wrenched hard. Why did it feel like he was abandoning her? "Trap," he muttered. "Durok?" he said into his O.D.I. "Guard the females."

"On my way," the male gruffed.

Cylo waited with his gaze on Wren. His heart swelled, wishing he could kiss her lips, bury his face in the curve of her neck, and inhale her scent. For now, she was safest within the dome. Durok strode toward him, his greatsword in hand. Behind him, his Dar Eth followed. She clutched a blaster to her chest, her chin raised with determination.

"What's going on?" she asked, her gaze switching between Ariez, Cylo, and Wren.

"We are boosting across to a Maloidian ship." Cylo gripped Durok's shoulder. "Expect the worst."

"Understood," he said.

Zive and Yelur waited at the shuttle bay's door. When they slipped into the bay, Cylo followed. The door sealed as the bay door opened, the shield still in place. They flipped their visors over their faces when the lights flashed to green, indicating a loss of pressure, life support, and gravity. The endlessness of space was between them and the lit square of the other ship.

Zive went first, launching himself out. He would reach there eventually. With a tap of his heels, his boot boosters activated and propelled him faster. Yelur was on his tail. Cylo stepped out and used the side of the *Kevol* to push off. He hit his heels at the same time and shot forward, veering around Yelur to land on what looked like nothing but was firm beneath his feet. The thrill of an impending battle summoned a grin.

"I go first." He bowed his head at Zive drawing near. "As your guard."

Zive pursed his lips but gestured to the door where a Maloidian male stood near the edge. Cylo strolled onto the floor, Zive and Yelur trailing him. Heat hit him like a thick blanket. He grimaced and adjusted his suit. Then, flicking the visor back, he bowed his head in greeting. The Maloidian hurried aside, his smile too welcoming. It did nothing to loosen the knot of tension in Cylo's gut.

"Greetings, Etterians. I am Ambassador Barro. Thank you for coming to my aid." He clasped his hands in front of him.

"I am Cylo. Data Officers Zive and Yelur." He fell in behind Zive, his hands at his sides and close to the blaster.

A cursory glance around the ship showed nothing new: the same old design with emphasis on comfort. Instead of a common was a seating area of sorts with soft-looking cushions and discarded beverages littering a too-low circular table. A Maloidian female lounged on one. She ran her gaze over Cylo, her scent intensifying. She liked Etterian males, so it seemed.

"This way." Barro swept his arm out. "The comm is—"

"I know the way," Zive said, slipping around the male. "Cylo, wait here."

Gritting his teeth, he assumed the expected position, focusing on the female. While he appeared obedient, he sharpened his hearing, picking up the gentle footfalls of another female. For an ambassador to travel with so few in his entourage was unusual.

What is out of place? Look for the details.

He started with his senses—that of smell: the sweet muskiness of Maloidians, the tart aroma of jucot wine, and the metallic tang of ozone and steel. He'd already tested his hearing, listening in as Yelur and Zive grumbled to each other while soothing the ambassador's ego. Which left taste and sight. There was no way he'd lick the bulkhead. He smothered a grin. Wren would find that funny if he did so.

The display vids showed scenes from Argaxx—dark skies with lilac lighting and deep caverns. Something was amiss. It all seemed idyllic like the ambassador was on a cruise with his lovers.

Cylo stiffened. Their bodies were well defined with sculpted muscles and restrained strength.

Serratu Kayarra. Two of them.

He activated his O.D.I. and messaged Fyca. This made no sense. Why would an ambassador feel the need to have assassins guard him?

"Is that jucot wine?" Cylo summoned a smile, crossing to the nearest female.

She unfolded her legs and inched to the edge of the seat. "Yes," she said, her eyes narrowing in what she must have thought was seductive. She smirked while offering him a glass.

He brushed her fingers when he accepted, then made a show of sipping. Used to giyua, the wine was too sweet around the bitterness of sjari leaves, but he hummed in approval. Smacking his lips for added effect, he kept his gaze on her and his focus on the surroundings.

"Name's Cylo," he rasped, dropping into the nearest seat.

"Eysso," she said, running her hand along her thigh to her knee. Doing so swept aside her garment and exposed her muscled leg, confirming his suspicions. He couldn't help but compare her to Wren and find the Maloidian lacking.

"Been to Issneen before?" he asked, taking the smallest of sips.

"It is my first time. I heard it is beautiful." She stretched and, in doing so, closed the distance between them until their thighs almost touched.

He wanted her to make the move. Anything else could be misconstrued. He leaned back, adding an air of nonchalance, despite the odd, muted burn in his chest.

When she touched his knee, bile rose to choke him. He swallowed a gag and his shock. Never had he reacted to a female like this, no matter her species. Nausea churned, and the pain intensified the longer she was near him. Something drove him to get away from her, as fast as he could. But he dared not react when she'd take it as rejection.

He layered his hand over hers, registering the coolness of her skin. She sighed. Maloidians liked warmth, craved it.

A pearlescent shimmer rippled over the ship. Through the shielded door to the expansive space, the thin line of Maloidian steel became visible. Zive hadn't lied when he'd said he had some data-analysis knowledge. Since it didn't sound like their business was done, Cylo smiled at the female.

"Am I your first Etterian?" he asked, setting the glass aside. Little doses of sjari caused a high. Too much killed; then again, too much of anything was lethal.

"Yes." She huffed out a laugh. "Is it that obvious?"

He lowered his voice to rasp, "If we had more time..."

He'd do nothing, but she didn't know that.

Her eyes widened, the solid black warming. Her scent intensified. Oh, she liked the implication, or was it his tone? He'd test the latter on Wren.

Just imagining her reaction hardened him like he hadn't twice had his fill an hour ago. He drew in a shuddering breath, his fingers twitching with the need to touch purple skin. Not wanting to reveal his secrets or weakness, he willed his body to still.

"Are you alone?" he asked, running his nose up her neck. He didn't breathe, not trusting himself not to gag. Her scent wasn't unpleasant, but it was missing something and was far too potent. Added to the nausea roiling in his gut from the poisoned wine, he had to be even more vigilant.

His inability to 'play' a role couldn't be the work of the Ethera, could it? If so, how had the other Eths suffered through this when encountering females not their Dar Eths? Perhaps their lighter eye color had deterred advances though would a Maloidian behave according to Etterian expectations?

Neither would a human bound to their internal compasses and barely adhering to the rules laid down by their law or government. Which meant every one of Wren's reactions was all her.

His chest swelled. She chose to be with him, not succumbing because of an ancient bond beyond her control. He was addicted to her, obsessed almost.

The second Serratu Kayarra sank onto the seat beside him, sighing with happiness—no doubt from the body heat he exuded. Such a weakness could be exploited. He threw his arm around her shoulders and tugged her into the curve of his body. She moaned and burrowed into him, splaying her fingers across his chest without hesitation.

They were too easy to manipulate—

He growled. "Put the dagger back."

She chuckled, waved his most recent creation at him, then slid it into its sheath.

He leapt up and away from them, running his hands over his body. "Eysso." He opened his palm, waiting.

She shrugged and placed the dagger into his hand.

He narrowed his eyes at them but gave them a smirk as if he found their actions amusing. "At this rate, laying with either of you might have been the death of me."

"Perhaps," the second female said, her tentacles swaying in a peaceful rhythm despite the heat in her gaze. She was enjoying toying with him.

A muted grunt snapped his gaze in the comm's direction.

He stiffened then scowled when both females hugged his sides.

"We have orders to kill him, Korre," Eysso said in Maloidian. "Pity."

Mm, so this wasn't an impromptu call for aid? Barro had planned this. But why?

"I say we keep him in our quarters." Korre stroked his chest, her gaze fixed on the path her fingers took.

Again, nausea squeezed a knot in his stomach. He swallowed past the lump and feigned a struggle to shake them off.

"We could tell Barro we tossed him out an airlock."

Eysso ran her fingers along his jawline. She hummed. "I like the way you think."

At another of his daggers leaving its sheath, Cylo gritted out in Maloidian, "I do not." He shrugged them aside and with ease. When he reached for his blaster, he met a foot extended so beautifully by Korre.

She lowered it with as much grace.

He smirked. "Very well. No weapons." He infused his expression and stance with as much arrogance as required—as taught by Malo.

"I look forward to drugging you into submission." Eysso lunged, her kicks and punches blurring.

He responded, meeting each of her blows with his left hand. "I am not impressed." He arched a brow at her. "Perhaps Korre will fare better?"

Eysso grunted when Korre shoved her aside for a flurry of punches. Her dark cheeks, warm eyes, and pursed lips said she was enjoying herself. Her knee thrust upward had him leaping back, forcing him to bring his other hand in to play. The bones of a knee hitting his inner thigh muscles could take him to the floor. At the least.

She pulled back, her breathing ragged.

"So, if I am at your mercy, what will you do to me?" He tapped his chest armor and allowed it to fall away.

Their gazes fixed on his exposed chest, distracting them. Yes, he'd stripped away a layer of protection, but an operative didn't need it.

"Oh," Eysso gasped.

Thumps from the comm reminded him that no matter how entertaining, he needed to end this. He attacked Eysso, looping his arm around her throat and pinning her back to his chest. As she struggled to free herself, he tightened his hold. Korre struck, but he simply kept Eysso between them, letting her take the brunt of every glancing blow.

Eysso stopped wiggling just as Korre's high kick knocked her out of his arms. She collapsed to the floor. Korre didn't wait but dived at him.

He laughed while ducking and side-stepping her efforts. Stings registered where their nails had connected with the skin on his arms and chest. The scent of his blood twitched his nose, and he huffed, unable to help being impressed. But they hadn't wanted to kill him—a foolish decision on their part.

Movement caught his gaze. Zive stood in the doorway, a blaster trained on Korre. He had an arm thrown over Yelur, propping up the injured male.

"Fire," Cylo whispered.

Too late, Korre faced Zive and fell to the floor with a gasp. Eysso lay still, her eyes wide. Zive shot her, too.

"Help," Zive muttered. "Yelur's a heavy bastard. Or draw your weapon. I want no more surprises."

Cylo shrugged on his armor and unstrapped his blaster. "What happened?"

"We have been deceived. That male is not Barro."

"When claiming so put us at ease. We were the fools," Cylo said. "Well played."

"Normally, I would suggest we return to the *Kevol*..." Zive's eyes narrowed. "But I am angry."

"Indeed. What do you intend to do?" Cylo waved his blaster at the two females. "I assume this fake Barro is dead?"

"Correct. Comm Supreme Commander Kyah. Have him send males." Zive propped Yelur against a bulkhead and withdrew his med-gun. "We will remain here until they arrive, then meet up with you and Lady Wren on Issneen." Zive nudged his head at Cylo's O.D.I.

Pursing his lips, he tapped it and raised his wrist to his mouth. "Supreme Commander Kyah, we require assistance at this location."

"We are already en route," the supreme commander said. "The situation did not sit well with me, so I sent a kuta. ETA ten minutes."

"My thanks." Cylo glanced at Zive. "Want me to wait?" He tried not to shuffle on his feet, not needing to reveal his eagerness to return to Wren. But he suspected pulling on his helmet had done that.

The elder medic ushered Yelur to the seat Cylo had occupied not five minutes ago. He rose and faced Cylo. "No, it is not necessary."

"Go. We shall steer this ship to Issneen." Yelur clutched his side, a fine sheen of sweat on his brow.

"These two are Serratu Kayarra. Be careful." Cylo checked his sheaths again before rolling the females over until every one of his daggers had been returned to him. He stunned them again for good measure then strapped his blaster in place.

"Comm if you need me." He bowed his head, knocked his heels, and launched through the shield toward the *Kevol.*

As interludes went, this one had been interesting. What happened in the comm to change Zive's opinion on stealing? By taking the ship to Issneen, he was delivering stealth technology to Etteria. Cylo had chosen not to mention this.

The male's eyes had swirled from dark to light blue, so angry was he, and not knowing the state of his void, he was capable of anything.

As Cylo aimed for the *Kevol's* shuttle bay, a kuta barreled toward him. Beyond that was the looming shadow of the battleship *Vindar.* He hit the button on the inside of the door as he glided into the bay, sealing it behind him.

"And?" Ariez asked when Cylo strode into the common, tugging off his helmet.

Wren sat up and swung her legs off the side of the bed. She tossed him a smile. He'd never seen a more beautiful sight. A deep inhale filled his lungs with her scent, and that knot of nausea in his stomach faded.

"It was a trap. I suggest you comm Zive for the details. He did not share much with me." Cylo set the helmet beside her, caught her hand, and pressed a kiss to her palm. "They remain on the ship." He glanced at Ariez. "Be cautious. Zive's void..." He didn't know how to say it.

"I understand,' Ariez said, turning away.

"You, me, a cleanse, and bed," Cylo whispered, scooping Wren off the bed.

"I've just slept," she said, resting her fingers on his bicep.

He hummed, peace descending on his chaotic thoughts. *I am exhausted, ensa, but I need to hold you. If you give me an hour, I should be able to—*

She cupped his cheek. "You can hold me for as long as you want to."

He tugged her by the hand toward his quarters, pausing when the door shut behind them to comm Fyca. "Get us to Issneen as fast as you can."

"Acknowledged," the male said.

Cylo kept his focus on Wren until the comm ended. With a tap at his chest, his armor slid off. He unsheathed his daggers one by one, setting them on the table. Her gaze wasn't on his small arsenal but on him, on every inch he exposed. He smiled at her open fascination when he removed his boots and pants.

You are fully clothed. He gestured to her.

"If I undress—"

Oh, I think I can spare you a little extra attention. He grinned.

She returned it. "I'd like that." Under his vigilance, off went her garments until only his woman stood before him.

"Exquisite," he rasped, testing out his huskier voice.

Her cheeks darkened, and her staccato heartbeat echoed in his ears. He threw back his head and laughed. As he'd realized, he was addicted to her.

He held out his hand, and she took it, letting him lead her into the spray. Water drenched them in seconds, but he cradled her close, savoring her silky skin over a hip, the sweet indent at the base of her spine, the way her hair clung to his fingers when he glided his hand to the nape of her neck.

He swept his lips over hers, but a compulsion drove him to linger, to inhale her breath in some insane attempt to capture her soul, to merge it with his. Foolish, he knew, but holding her wasn't enough. Despite his weariness, he pinned her to the wall, spreading her thighs to take the width of his hips. His malehood rubbed against her wet heat.

She whimpered but didn't pull away. Instead, she looped her arms around his neck, angled her head, and deepened the kiss. Her tongue served only to intensify this craving to fully consume her. Everywhere her body touched his, he burned for her.

"Thamani," he hummed when he leaned back to lose himself in her gray eyes.

"And all these scratch marks?" she asked, arching a brow.

Of no importance. He grinned, inching his Fuyra-hard malehood into her soft channel.

She gasped, and her eyes widened then narrowed when she groaned. Her legs tightening around his backside sank him deeper. He growled, pressed his temple to hers, and withdrew.

A thrust merged their ragged breathing. And as he brought her to her fulfillment, the skitter of joy to the head of his malehood drove him on, but what mattered more was the synchronization of their heartbeats.

He stole a kiss, then chanted 'ensa ra ensa' when ecstasy exploded across his body, stiffening every muscle, heightening each sense. She was his, and when they reached Issneen, he'd ensure all knew it.

Chapter Twenty-Three

Issneen wasn't quite what Wren had expected. Who was she kidding? The planet had thrown her a curveball: pink skies, red oceans, gray soil, peppered with a variety of blue fauna and trees. The air was richer, too. She sucked in great breaths while twirling with arms outstretched in a pool of glorious sunlight.

Cy smiled at her, his beauty stuttering her heartbeat. As it always did. Ariez had said the DNA implantation had been successful, making her equally compatible with all three species—that she didn't need any more 'deposits.' But she hadn't been able to keep her hands to herself. The boundary had been crossed. And if one afternoon had such an impact on her unstable genetics, many sessions with Cy wouldn't hurt.

He hadn't once suggested they stop. Even now, he touched her in some way when near enough. There was just something about his hand at her lower back that shot a thrill through her.

The shuttle the Etterians had sent to bring them to Issneen was behind her, the solidness of the ramp beneath her feet. Before her lay an intricate garden, with floral-lined walkways. She sniffed, picking up a saltiness she couldn't place. A susurration teased her ears. Based on her preferred literature, both scents hinted at a beach nearby. She couldn't be sure, having never been to one.

She glanced at Cy. "Is there a—"

He would dare... Cy narrowed his eyes in a glare that implied death was forthcoming. She swung her gaze ahead, catching sight of a blue-skinned man with white hair flowing around his shoulders. On his arm clung a blonde woman.

"Who are they?" she asked, keeping her voice low.

"Zucis," Cy hissed then pinched his lips, looped an arm around her, and drew her into the curve of his body.

The blue man did look familiar. She studied him, then grinned, trying to pull away from Cy. He held firm. At the base of his jaw, a pulse ticked.

"It's Iddan," she said.

"We shall see," Cy said. *Stay close to me, ensa.*

Ariez stopped beside them. "Why do we delay? I have secured quarters for Lady Wren within the medical building."

"We wait." Cy's tone was hard.

"Lady Wren, a pleasure to meet you. Is that correct, *ohara*?" The blue man smiled at the woman, his gaze lingering on her face in what Wren could only term 'adoringly.'

"It is. Hi." The blonde beamed. "I'm Cyndi; this is Iddan...my man."

"Male," he said, but his intimate smile implied it was an ongoing game between them.

"I'm Wren, and this is Cylo...*my* man." Wren leaned her temple on Cy's chest.

I like the way you claim me as yours. He tightened his arm, and the featherlight caress of his lips across her hair registered, then he shifted his hand to her hip, allowing her some breathing room.

"Yours?" Cyndi frowned. "But his eyes..." She shrugged. "Never mind. Who knows how the Ethera works?"

"You are human, yes?" Iddan asked, arching a pale brow. "My dhutya says purple skin is not normal."

"He means me, his true mate." Cyndi blushed. "It's such a pretty lilac. When Iddan mentioned what had happened to you, I couldn't believe it."

"Went through hell to get it." Wren chuckled, waving her arm in front of her. "One star: wouldn't recommend."

Iddan patted Cyndi's hand resting on his forearm. "Medic Ariez says your door is failing?"

Wren swallowed and forced a smile. "I've been strengthening it every time it fails."

And your telepathy? Iddan met her gaze.

She squirmed, not liking any voice but Cy's in her mind. "Fewer incidences, though—not many emotional events occurring. Etterians are pretty stable." So true. She'd picked up a little fear and random thoughts before Yelur and Zive had left the ship, but she'd lumped it under dream thoughts since she'd been in the med-E.D. at the time.

How could she explain to Iddan that Cy communicated with her often, but only what he wanted her to know? He'd once revealed he used control to spare her from his thoughts and emotions. And only when he was adoring her body had he revealed hints of what he felt. Except for that one time he'd dropped everything and shown her how much she meant to him. That flood of intense warmth wasn't describable, yet her blood had sung, high on hope.

"This is good," Iddan said. "When we heard you were on your way, Cyndi insisted on being your 'welcome committee?'" He frowned. "An unusual concept."

"Indeed," Cy said. "You may visit when Wren is settled. For now—"

"Excellent," Ariez said, marching ahead. "I will share her location." He bowed his head at Iddan then nudged his chin at Cy.

Wren flushed at their rudeness. It wasn't as if she hadn't been probed and prodded enough already. "Do come for coffee. And I appreciate the welcome."

Cy closed his fingers around her elbow and ushered her after Ariez.

"What's the rush?" she hissed.

We do not keep the king waiting.

"What?" she squeaked, glancing at her flip-flops, leggings, and baggy T-shirt. She raised a hand to her hair, no doubt a mess from the breeze.

You are beautiful, thamani. He caught her fingers and brought them to his lips for a kiss, all while leading her down white stone pathways to giant doors in the distance. She didn't even get a chance to stop and smell the pretty white flowers.

"Still, Cy, a king..." She squared her shoulders and drew in a hurried breath. He couldn't be worse than facing the judge who'd held her future in his hands. Although, that hadn't gone in her favor.

You were taken, harmed, still suffer... King Xeus is a concerned male.

"Can't Ariez just show him my medical results?" She harrumphed. "Fine. I'll meet your king—"

And queen.

"Shit," she muttered, a shiver running through her when those massive doors swung open with barely a whisper. Marbled flooring, high ceilings, colorful banners hanging down pillars made this more real...intimidating.

Cy chuckled. *You are adorable.*

"I'm glad you find this amusing." The urge to shake him off and stomp ahead gripped her, but she didn't want that to be the king's first impression of her. Instead, she curled her arm around Cy's and held on, letting him lead and shield her.

She didn't know what she expected, but it wasn't an empty room. A dais said this was a throne room, but there was no furniture except stone-benched alcoves. No gilded throne, either. A little disappointing.

Her footsteps echoed, forcing her to glance at Cy's booted feet. Why didn't he make a sound? Despite wincing, she didn't try to soften her tread—an impossibility when her flip-flops went thwack-thwack. The idiot could have warned her. She tossed him a glare.

"Lady Wren, a pleasure," a man said, striding through a hidden door behind the dais.

She pasted on a polite smile.

Cy nudged her forward, tossing her at the wolf's feet. "Adviser Kanzo, I present Lady Wren Turner."

"Remarkable," Kanzo said, holding out his hand for a shake.

She took it. He released her after two pumps and stepped back, showing no curiosity beyond— His eyes were ice blue. Ah, yes, an Eth.

Breathe. Cy placed his hand at her lower back.

"Yes! She's here," a woman squealed, skipping toward them. The brightest smile spread her cheeks, and a waterfall of curls cascaded around her with every movement. In leggings and a T-shirt in dark blue, she put Wren at ease. Even her slippers squeaked on the polished stone floor. "Hi, hi, I'm Macy. So sorry about those hideous sharks and squidheads messing with your life. Hubs is dealing with them, don't you worry."

"Thanks?" Wren managed. She got the comparison between sharks and Yithians, but squidheads... Did she mean Maloidians? And who was Hubs?

"Zoo, you coming?" And off jogged the woman, disappearing through the door Kanzo had just taken.

Wren glanced at Cy. "Who—"

Queen Macera and King Xeus.

"She's the queen? Why didn't you say she's human?" *Wow, talk about a whammy.* Imagine finding your soul mate, only to learn it made you royalty? Wren smothered a chuckle. *Nope, no way.* She wouldn't give up Cy for anything, not even ruling a planet.

And out strolled a giant of an Etterian, bulging with muscles while oozing authority. He caught Macy in his arms and carried her toward them.

"Behave," he mumbled. "Welcome, Lady Wren. Well done, Operative Cylo. The lima kuu have recommended you for a commendation."

Cy frowned. *Why?*

This was the moment Wren wished her fancy knew mind-reading skills went both ways. She'd have loved to say something sassy about getting a badge for bedding her. Instead, she smirked at him and wiggled her brows. The poor man wouldn't know what she meant, but she couldn't help teasing him.

"My thanks, my king." He bowed his head at Xeus.

"You may return to your duties. With Malo distracted, Etteria needs you on Earth."

No. Fear squeezed her throat and allowed her nothing but a gasp.

"My duty is here...beside Wren." Cy looped an arm around her waist and drew her close. She leaned into him for good measure. No way was she letting the king take away her man.

Xeus stiffened. "She is not your Dar Eth."

"Not yet," Kanzo said, slicing his gaze between them. "You do understand that Ariez has secured quarters...where you cannot be unless injured."

"You speak truth, Adviser Kanzo." Ariez clasped his hands behind his back, appearing patient when he was far from it. "The Ethera has yet to strike, but it has had an influence on Cylo's void. We are studying the effects."

Cy smiled. "Then I should be in medical, as well." He had such hope in his voice even as he dug his fingers into her hip to keep her near.

"The barracks are near enough," Ariez said. "Now, if we may start our assessments..." He swept out an arm, gesturing to a door to the side.

Cy's grip tightened. *No, it is too soon.*

She curled against him, nuzzling her nose into his armor-encased chest. "For a month, remember?"

A week.

She angled her head back to meet his gaze. "Even better." With a kiss to his chin, she pulled out of his arms. "Come find me."

He took a step as if to follow her.

"Cylo, a word," King Xeus said.

Ariez marched through the narrow door, assuming she was on his six. She touched the frame and tossed a glance over her shoulder at Cy, his gaze fixed on her. Ice slithered down her spine and settled in her bones. She couldn't shake the thought that this was goodbye.

When she dragged her gaze away, Ariez was far away, his long legs taking him almost out of line of sight. She broke into a jog, tearing after him.

"It will be good for him to be away from you. A test, so to speak." Ariez glanced at her when she fell into step beside him, her breathing a little ragged.

Oh, well, that makes sense. "Why? What are you hoping will happen?"

"The Ethera does not like separation. If it is at work here, you will both suffer." He grinned. "Fascinating."

She couldn't help but laugh at the adorable man. "The way you're enjoying this, I'm going to assume you only like me because I'm a puzzle."

He laughed. "And entertaining."

"Fair enough."

She couldn't complain about such a test when the last one had been to have sex with Cy. Would he have gotten around to it if Ariez hadn't demanded it? She tried not to think about it because, in truth, it no longer mattered. They were lovers, and if she was honest with herself, she loved him. As she trailed Ariez, she prayed being apart worked. Even now, something tightened in her chest and squeezed, hindering her breathing. Or was that her unfit body?

She smiled.

Either way, time would tell.

Chapter Twenty-Four

Cylo's gaze lingered on the shut door. Rage gritted his teeth and shot fire along his veins. He should have anticipated not being allowed to stay with her. Malo taught them to consider all scenarios. Needles skittered over his skin, driving him to follow.

"The Ethera is such an unknown. Do you believe she is yours?"

At Xeus's question, Cylo focused on his king. "I do. My body has been reacting as if I knelt. My eye color only needs to change."

Xeus crowded Cylo to stare into his eyes. "Indeed. Then I will grant you the time. Every pairing is precious."

"And she's been through so much." Macy offered a sweet smile. "Ava says we shouldn't cause any more upheaval. It's obvious Wren likes you, Cylo."

Like? He almost scoffed at the weak word. What flowed through him—heart, body, soul—was more potent.

"I agree. You did well, Operative, collecting a Durn, rescuing the women, with two pairings happening on board the *Kevol,* and possibly for yourself, too... I am most pleased."

Cylo thumped his chest. Thanking his king again lacked sincerity, for him. But a gesture of honor from one warrior to another, Xeus would appreciate.

And he did, giving Cylo a grin. "Now, Kanzo will issue you quarters close to Lady Wren. Let us hope the Ethera is merely delayed."

Cylo bowed his head, but instead of leaving, he hesitated. "Any news about the Maloidian stealth ship?"

"Ambassador Barro was found imprisoned in a utility closet. He is well and grateful for the rescue. We have informed Alllero..." Xeus pursed his lips. "For now, we house the ambassador and his aide as guests."

"Aide?" Cylo frowned. "I met two Serratu Kayarra on board."

"Warning noted." Kanzo typed on his O.D.I. "Adding security."

Good. Cylo had one more question. "And the stealth tech—"

"Is not ours...yet." Kanzo smiled. "Its use would be most helpful."

"My thanks." Cylo bowed his head and strode in the same direction Wren had gone.

As he hurried after them, hoping to catch up, his O.D.I. buzzed with the number of his quarters and that of Wren's. He laughed, so grateful for Kanzo's efficiency. He stopped at his quarters first, planning to disarm himself before...

Come find me, she said.

Already, he missed her. The muted pain uncoiling in his core was bearable. Yet, he wasn't a fool. It would worsen the longer he went without seeing her.

The quarters in the barracks was easy to find, on the ground floor, and by the entrance. He need only take the passage, exit the building, stroll along the walkway, and enter the medical building. All medical suites and equipment were in a large common area. Around the main room was a wide corridor with quarters leading off it. Each floor above housed medics and lima kuu. Which meant Wren was nearby.

Ensa? He shut his eyes and waited.

Silence met his mental call.

None of the med-E.D.s were in use. No medic assisted an injured male. He focused his hearing and picked up muffled conversation. Searching the building would be a waste of time, but he did so, locating the door to the corridor. Along it he ran, scanning the numbers beside the door, then halted in front of her door. He grinned and palmed the panel. The chime announced his request to enter, but no movement or voice showed the room was occupied.

Maybe Ariez had already taken her for tests. Cylo would be at peace as long as he knew where she was.

Frustrated, he tapped his O.D.I. "Ariez, where are you?"

"In my quarters," snapped the older male.

"And Wren?" Cylo swallowed, his voice too hoarse as panic set in.

"Secure."

"No." Cylo curled his fingers into a fist. "I need—"

"Time away from her. I understand."

"Do not make me find you," Cylo roared. "It will not go well for you."

"Threats? And under an hour apart?" Ariez hummed. "Interesting."

"We are not test subjects." Cylo gritted his teeth. "Very well," he said to Ariez and disconnected the comm. "*Ensa*?" He brought his wrist closer. His O.D.I. buzzed, failing to connect. "Where is she?" he yelled at the bulkheads. He bit his lip, on the verge of begging. His void pulsed in warning. He was an operative; he could endure.

But he didn't *want* to.

He stormed off, returning to his quarters. There had to be a way. He had her location, but he suspected Ariez had moved her somewhere else. The medic couldn't keep her locked up and undergoing pointless tests, not without putting her to sleep or notifying Kanzo. Cylo squared his shoulders. He wasn't about to run to the adviser with complaints. For all he knew, Ariez would only keep her hidden for a few hours, and Cylo didn't want to look like a fool or, worse, weak. He sank into a comfy and stared out the glass panels at the garden outside. So picturesque but its beauty didn't matter. Not without Wren beside him. He raised his chin to the ceiling, his jaw clenched, his muscles tense. His fingers toyed with the bracelet she'd made for him, the only proof he had that she existed.

He'd rest now because if he didn't hear from Ariez or Wren by evening meal, he'd come up with a plan. Darkness suited him for what he might need to do.

Issneen, the Royal City of Etteria
Days Later

"Operations Commander Malo et Daro," Cylo said into the display vid. It flickered, but no face appeared. Was everything going to go wrong this day? "Data officer on duty?"

"He is not taking any comms," a male said.

Cylo grunted. "Elite Warrior Garix et Orix." An image appeared of Garix eating what looked like a stick of meat. "Why can I not reach Malo?"

The giant of an Etterian grinned. "This mission has been incredible, Cylo. Malo found his Dar Eth."

Joy exploded like a supernova and twinged fresh agony in Cylo's darkening soul. "Truth?" he managed, rubbing his chest to ease the ache.

"Why do you seek him?" Garix asked, bringing his face closer to his O.D.I.

"To inform him that I cannot yet return to the *Gladio.*" Cylo grimaced.

Which he should've done days ago since arriving in Issneen, but he'd been busy, searching for his Wren. So far, none of the quarters in the medical building housed her. No one had seen her either. And Ariez had stopped taking his comms. A glance at the wall of display vids showed nothing. So many sec cams wasted. It was that or watch the entrance himself, but he'd approached this as a mission, unable to guard all the doors in and out of the building. A sensor at her supposed room had revealed no movement or heat signatures. He hadn't picked up her scent on his scouting trips, best done at night when the building wasn't so busy.

"His Dar Eth just came out in a revealing garment while he was on the comm with Prince Enyl."

A memory of Wren in her dress bolted across Cylo's mind. A crushing weight squeezed his chest, and he struggled to breathe. "Inform him of my status," he said when he realized he'd yet to answer.

"Very well." Garix's image faded to black.

Breaking into the data analysis office hadn't helped, other than to give Cylo full access to everything. He'd simply changed his designation to security which he'd used to enter Wren's supposed quarters. She hadn't been there. Nothing was out of place, and her scent hadn't lingered.

A sweeping glance at his room reminded Cylo how near yet far from Wren he was. He sank into the comfy and stared unseeingly at the vids. Was this his life now? So devoid of color? The loss of her had grown almost too heavy to bear. He poked his void and scowled at its expanding mass, returning to its oppressiveness prior to Iphara. That wasn't a good sign.

When he tried to sleep during the day, thoughts of her plagued him: her smile, charm, sweet scent, soft lips... Which was why he was awake at dawn after yet another futile search. He raised his wrist to eye level and stroked the bracelet she'd given him.

If he could just hear her voice one more time...

Prepared to beg Kanzo for help, he lunged for the door, desperate to hold her. His body shook with the compulsion. But where was she?

Throwing himself against the bulkhead, he slid down it until he was on his haunches. He activated his O.D.I. "Medic-on-duty, do you have time to assess me?"

If the male did, Cylo might catch a glimpse of Wren in a med-E.D. Hope blossomed like the birthing of a star when it was stupid to expect anything.

"Of course, warrior. How may I assist?"

"Review Medic Qaff's findings for Operative Cylo et Endylo." He deactivated the comm and scowled at his workbench where mangled strips of metal were his attempts at blade smithing—each one a failure.

What was he going to do? Dying on a battlefield on Gikaet was no longer possible, not with King Xeus forming an alliance with the Gika. Rebels were fighting the changes to the status quo, so there was a slim chance he could find a way. His fingers twitched with the urge to hold his greatsword. He could traverse the underground passages to hunt down the Gika.

A dismal future awaited him, but the thought of leaving Etteria... No, never holding Wren again drove a red-hot poker through his heart. He couldn't force himself to abandon her. One week, they'd agreed. It had been three days. Time stretched before him like a desert without a spark of life.

"Head to medical," the medic said via the O.D.I.

Cylo sprinted but skidded to a halt when he entered. The medic waited beside a med-E.D.—the only one soon to be in use.

"Is it always this quiet?" Cylo asked, throwing himself onto the bed.

"Yes, but the proving grounds is in two days." The medic grinned.

Cylo grunted, willing to test his mettle against many males with the anger saturating the marrow of his bones. The dome closed, and blessed sleep gripped him.

He jerked awake what felt like seconds later, swinging his legs off the side as the dome retracted. A sweep of his gaze across the room showed no Wren.

"I am sorry for your loss," the medic said.

This snapped Cylo's focus to the male. "For?"

"Your Dar Eth." The male bowed his head, then tapped the med-E.D.'s console. "Your void is voracious, devouring every ounce of joy and light left in your soul. It will not be long now. Perhaps on the proving grounds you may find a worthy death."

Cylo growled, "Forward these findings to Medic Ariez."

"I will do so, but I cannot guarantee that he will read them. He is tasked with an unusual patient."

Cylo tried not to stiffen, to reveal his interest. "Oh?"

"I do not know who she is, but he visits her every morning."

"My thanks for the assessment," Cylo said, keeping his tone cold while fire burned in his belly.

Morning? He'd thought too many males came and went for— He gritted his teeth. *Fool.* Ariez used the crowds to mask his comings and goings. Before he 'strolled' off, Cylo glanced over his shoulder at the young medic. "Tell me, which entrance does he use? I do not wish to run into his cheery self."

The male smiled. "Not to worry. He takes the path behind the building."

Cylo made it outside before he sprinted to the rear of medical, diving over bushes, around trees, across the gravel path to throw himself behind a hedge of anahla flowers. West of this location was Xeus's court and the Pools of Crustiiu. He swallowed a curse, castigating himself for not asking the male in which direction Ariez headed. Excitement had tangled his tongue at finally learning something he could work with; he hadn't wanted to chance raising the medic's suspicions. One word from him would put Ariez on the defensive.

East were the markets, individual quarters, and the tidal pool. Beyond Xeus's court was the canteen, a new building he didn't know the purpose of, and the proving grounds. If he had to hide someone, east was more logical. The magnus sun climbed and set, with no sign of Ariez. Cylo had long sought shelter from the heat within the shadows of the hedge. A male squatting for hours would draw attention, so he hid himself, twisting his body to do so. With his gaze fixed on the door, he swirled each foot to keep the blood flowing. At any moment, he might need to move, and a numb limb wouldn't help.

He blinked when Ariez walked through the door, disappearing inside. Cylo froze, swinging his gaze west. He scrambled up, mangling the bushes in the process. Anahla scattered their petals in protest. The sweet scent encouraged him to draw in a deep inhale. Grinning, he took the path toward the proving grounds. He peered ahead, trying to assess where Wren could be hidden. The path split to the right, disappearing into the caves with the heated pools of Crustiiu. He hesitated. Having bathed here once or twice, he couldn't recall if the caves extended beyond the common areas.

The suns were setting, and he had until tomorrow morning to investigate. If he found nothing, he'd trail Ariez. But impatience made his fingers twitch. He refused to endure another sleepless night without her.

Steam rose like ghostly fingers. The damp heat dewed his skin with sweat. Lighting mimicked flickering torchlight, adding warmth to the dark gray interior. In the natural pools, the colorless water bubbled. The carnivorous omeika's existence tainted their oceans red. No color meant it was safe to bathe. Yet, no bathers were in sight. No muted conversations teased his ears. Through cavern after cavern, he moved, taking moments to confirm any private pools weren't in use. He reached the final pool. Nothing.

He swiveled on a boot heel to head back when a stray breeze cooled his brow. How unusual. Excitement sparked, and the Ethera leapt to life. He grinned. She was near. But where? A hidden door, perhaps? He raised his nose to sniff, picking up the salty tang of the ocean and the aroma of...coffee?

A giggle from behind him had disappointment slumping his shoulders. He couldn't search now, not without someone noting his presence. But he could wait here... He stripped, tossing off his armor and kicking his boots aside. An extended soak would do well to mask his intentions while he studied every nook.

He hissed at the heat but sank into its depths anyway. Sprawling his arms along the rocky edge, he sniffed the air before shifting to another spot. Once he'd determined from where the breeze came, he crossed to the opposite side to study the wall.

The couple turned amorous, so he lowered his hearing. When they didn't intrude, he climbed out of the pool to run his hands over the rock, from the entrance to the corner where the scents were the strongest. And yet, there was no entrance. No secret doorway. He glanced at the hole in the cave's ceiling. The suns had set, and the night had progressed during his distraction.

Grabbing a wrap, he yanked it on and waited a second for it to activate and conform to his body. He stood in place and assessed whether he could reach. As low as the ceiling was, he wouldn't be able to touch it...unless... He hurried to the corner and ran, using a well-placed foot on the wall to leap and catch the edges of the gap. Hanging by one hand, he glanced down and grinned. *Alodon's balls, now that was fun.* He pulled himself through, ignoring the cool air drying the hot droplets on his legs.

Donning his uniform might have been wise. He shrugged and faced north, following his nose.

Chapter Twenty-Five

Cylo summoned the shadows to surround him—a futile attempt to hide a white-wrapped Etterian male sneaking across the top of the Crustiiu caves. Certainty compelled him onward; desperation demanded he didn't give up. Up ahead was a crevice—a dark scar across the gray rock. His bare feet made not slipping easier, but his boots would have spared him from the sharper edges. None of his discomfort mattered. He enhanced his hearing, listening for approaching footsteps or voices.

Peering through the crack, the shape of another pool was visible in the unnatural torchlight. He gazed south to the entrance of the caves, a little farther than expected. A step at a time, he circled the crevice, catching glimpses of what lay beneath: just a pool, a wall, and a door. He gripped the edge of the crack and lowered himself through, dangling in silence as he assessed the space. A sniff fired joy along his veins to settle in his heart.

Wren's scent...

He dropped and landed in a crouch. Beside him, the water bubbled, and heat warmed him. Nothing else stirred. He faced the door and placed his palm on the sec panel, expecting it to open. If it didn't, he was quite prepared to break into the data analysis office again.

The door whispered as it glided aside. He didn't hesitate, slipping past before it shut. Her scent hit him then—full-bodied, sweet, and tainted sour. He found himself sliding into her room, not sure how he got there other than to acknowledge it had been swift. Her muted sighs said she slept.

After all this time, he was content to gaze upon her in the dim lighting. She lay on her side, her hands clasped and tucked under her cheek. Over her hip draped a blanket, and from under it, peeked a bare leg. A tight, sleeveless tunic clung to the top half of her and emphasized the curves of her body. He peeled off the wrap and let it slither to the floor. When he lifted the corner of the blanket, he almost moaned at the tiny white strip covering her sex. She didn't stir when he climbed in beside her, not even when he curled an arm around her. Only as he tugged her against his body did she whimper.

"Cy," she mumbled, rubbing her nose across his forearm.

The vise around his chest eased, and for the first time in three days, he could breathe without pain lashing him. Her scent filled his senses; the warmth of her skin against his coated his soul with peace. He'd found her.

Did you miss me, ensa?

She hummed and pressed a kiss to his arm across her chest.

A craving so fierce almost made him flip her onto her back to claim her mouth. But he'd dreamt of this reunion, needed to go slow to cherish every second. The Ethera made demands he wholeheartedly agreed with.

"Wren," he rasped, yanking her closer until she layered his front. He cupped a breast, massaging it as he kissed her neck.

"What took you so long?" she asked, twisting to meet his gaze.

He wasn't about to share how much he'd suffered—what he'd done to find her. "We said a week."

She growled. That sound from her slammed need into him and hardened his malehood to its full length. It throbbed in anticipation. He ran his hand over the softness of her belly to the silken curls between her thighs.

Her moan made his fingers tremble as he stroked her. With a tug, he tore the one side of her undergarment for better access. She didn't complain but instead spread her thighs for him. It wasn't enough, the slickness of her need, her body filling his arms... He doubted it would ever appease this longing to consume her, to have her be a part of him.

"Cy," she cried out, trembling when her fulfillment struck. The muskiness of her arousal made his nostrils flare.

He shifted her onto her back, tore the other side of her undergarment, and hoisted her leg up to his hip as he settled between her thighs. She wiggled and peeled off her tunic, granting a full view of her breasts.

Maker. All thoughts fled as he slid into her; the glide of her wet heat over his malehood was heaven, bliss, a divine blessing. She lifted her other leg and hooked it around his hip, sinking him deeper.

Arching his back, he groaned, savoring the sparks of fire and joy she inspired.

"Three days was too long," she said, wrapping her arms around his shoulders and pulling him down. "Now fuck me, Cy." She stole a kiss then met his gaze. "Show me you missed me."

He growled, not needing encouragement. With each withdrawal and plunge, he chased ecstasy, hers and his. When a flood of liquid warmth drenched him, his core spasmed, and a spark raced to the head of his malehood. He roared, unable to halt the cascading pleasure and not wanting to.

Still buried in her as the tremors continued, he gazed into her gray eyes and smiled.

I...love you, thamani.

She gasped, her eyes widened, then softened, and a tear slipped free. "What did you say?"

I do not care that you are not my Dar Eth. He slanted his mouth over hers, desperate to taste her, to duel with her, to have her claim him. *I cannot let you leave me. Not again.*

"I love you, too." She stroked his jaw, her beautiful eyes glistening with unshed tears. "I have for a while."

He grinned. *Good. Ready for more?*

Before she could answer, he inched his way out of her, only to inch his way back, slow, steady, igniting every nerve, each sense, while he savored her breathless moans, her tiny gasps, the stillness when she was on the cusp of a fulfillment.

What followed was something he planned to repeat, more so than the mere act of mating. For in these unhurried moments, he met her, who she was, and fell in love again.

EVERY NIGHT, CYLO SNUCK into Wren's quarters. He'd asked her to hide his presence in case Ariez separated them again, but he was a fool because his scent lingered. Ariez would have known the moment he entered Wren's quarters after their reunion. Still, something as unexpected as fear governed Cylo's actions. The rock walls weakened signals until she was unreachable. Which meant she could sleep at night without disturbances other than Cylo's nightly visits.

He couldn't communicate with her, leaving him with no way to know she was safe. So the moment the quiet settled, he headed there.

She'd taken to sleeping naked—a fact he appreciated. Already, his malehood hardened in anticipation. And even though he'd had her twice a night, it was holding her that he looked forward to the most. He basked in her lyrical voice as she told him about her day, the findings, the setbacks. Only one marker had yet to stabilize. They were in limbo as Eth and Dar Eth.

Like before, his void had shrunk. Although, he had yet to be reassessed. As long as he stayed with her, nothing mattered. He leaned against the bulkhead, gazing upon her while she dozed. He'd drawn many fulfillments from her in the last hour, and for that reason alone, he allowed her to sleep. Soon, he'd join her.

Into the silence came the muted hiss of her door opening. He froze, then peeked through her bedroom door. A glance told him everything.

A female in black darted across the common, her steps delicate. The delicate footfalls told him not-human. Her small frame said Maloidian as did the sweet organic musk of her scent. He waited until she neared.

She didn't.

He couldn't peek again without revealing his presence. The familiar tap of a blaster button had him diving into the doorway. The sting of a stun registered when he hit the floor, jarring his shoulder. His right arm had numbed.

He lunged after the fleeing female. She was fast, slipping out before he could reach her. Outside, he fought his shock that anyone would dare to attack on their home ground. He allowed anger to propel him after her. She took him through a maze of rocky pathways until she breached the royal gardens. He didn't bother to mark where he was or how to return. Catching her was imperative.

She sprinted ahead; so did he. And at last, he tackled her to the ground, the momentum sliding them across the gravel.

He used his weight to pin her when he had only his left arm. “Who sent you?” he demanded. “Who?” he roared when she didn’t answer. He flipped her over but kept her in place. Knocking back her hood revealed the pale-yellow features of Korre.

She smirked. “Hello, Cylo.” Her gaze dipped to his naked form.

“Why Wren?” he asked. “Speak or die.” He wrapped his fingers around her throat and squeezed, backing up the threat.

She laughed. “You will not kill me.” She touched her lips then his, spreading a familiar bitterness. The tingle on the tip of his tongue confirmed her choice of poison.

He scoffed. “The venom of the Foutas frog cannot harm an operative.”

Her eyes widened, and fear darkened her cheeks. “I cannot tell you. Exile is certain death.”

“Why Wren? Can you share that?”

She glanced to the side. “If you vow to kill me...” She met his gaze. “I have failed twice. It is unacceptable for—”

“A Serratu Kayarra.” He leaned back, granting her a little breathing room. “Very well. What do you know?” Such a question triggered his O.D.I. to begin recording.

“The Earthian carries evidence of Maloidian attempts to destroy...Etteria.”

“You speak of Iphara.”

“Yes. Chemicals injected into weak females to create sexual compatibility. But this is a side effect. The true goal is to create biological weapons no Eth would suspect.”

“Part of this plan we are aware of. It has been documented and thwarted. How would Wren be a weapon? How can she be triggered? And what could a small female do to us?” He frowned at this not making sense. “What of the other females? They carry the evidence, as well.”

“A Durn—”

“Alodon’s balls,” he hissed. *And I delivered him to the battleship.* Ice drenched him, but he stayed in place. “Who sent you?”

She pinched her lips. “Barro. Now do as you promised.”

He cupped her cheeks, pressed a kiss to her temple, and snapped her neck. Angling his head, he listened for her heartbeat. When nothing reached his ears, he leapt to his feet and commed Kanzo. He shared what he’d learnt.

“Maker,” Kanzo gasped. “Guard Lady Wren. I will have Barro questioned while I reach out to Supreme Commander Kyah and Jokta.”

"Keep me informed, if you can, Adviser." Cylo returned to Wren, not bothering with the maze. He took the direct route—through the hole, across the top, and into the crevice. A quick dip in the pool removed the sweat coating his body and any lingering Foutas venom on his lips and tongue.

Dripping wet, he entered her quarters, expecting to find her awake. The silence deafened him. He bolted for her bedroom.

She hadn't moved, and the burn mark on her thigh said it all. He'd taken the brunt of the stun but not all of it. White blinded his vision as panic tore through him. His O.D.I. wouldn't work here. And he wasn't leaving her, not again. He faced the display vid in the common room. "Warrior-on-duty," he said. "Send Medic Ariez to Lady Wren now. She has been wounded."

"Acknowledged."

Cylo returned to her side and gathered her in his arms, taking the time to cover all but her thigh with the blanket. Her heartbeat calmed him as did her reedy breathing. She was alive, warm, and not bleeding. Three facts he used to bolster his unstable hope.

"What happened?" Ariez strode in, knelt beside the bed, and used his med-gun on her.

"A stun from a Maloidian," Cylo said.

"Set to too high a level for humans, by the look of it." Ariez scowled. "Stun her then what? She dies a natural death? Take her off-world?"

Instead of answering, Cylo played the recording.

"Alodon's hell," Ariez muttered. "The med-E.D. now."

Cylo didn't hesitate, leaping to his feet and taking Wren with him. He trailed Ariez, half-running while trying to keep his gait even and not jarring. She shivered in his arms, and he cradled her close. When they neared medical, Ariez hurried ahead. He activated the med-E.D. Only when Cylo lowered her onto the bed and stepped back did he realize she was naked.

"Will she live?" he had to ask, for once in his life needing assurances.

"What does the void say?" Ariez asked, moving between consoles.

Cylo almost scoffed at that. Every part of him knew she'd survive. His void had diminished to a pinpoint of black nothingness.

"It would consume you if she was dying," Ariez said.

Cylo's breath hitched. "Truth?" He blinked his vision clear, unable to grasp why everything was blurred.

Under his vigilance, her wound healed, new skin formed, and her lilac skin took on a healthy glow. Her curves, the flow of her hair, the softness of her bottom lip, the daintiness of her tiny toes were even more beautiful to him.

Pain lashed him, snatching his breath. A crushing weight around his chest froze his heart. Roaring consumed his ears, and the sweet flavor of her fulfillment exploded across his tongue. He remembered the first taste of her on the floor of the bay. The way she'd wrapped her lush lips around the head of his malehood.

His eyes burned, but he refused to look away from her suspended form. His knees weakened; his splayed fingers on the dome kept him upright. He pressed his temple to the dome. "I love you, Wren," he whispered. Visions...memories of her rolled across his mind.

"Step aside, Cylo. Let me wake her."

Ariez's voice came from afar. Cylo spared him a nod and shuffled back. The hiss of the dome retracting accompanied the gentle lowering of her body to the bed. She moaned, drifting up from the med-E.D.'s deep slumber. Ariez's footsteps retreated then returned. He offered her a garment, his gaze averted.

It was a ceremonial wrap...in Cylo's bloodline color.

Dazed, he admired the way the white silk draped her curves when she slipped it on.

"Do I want to know what happened?" she asked, holding out her hand to Cylo.

"A Maloidian operative snuck into your quarters and shot you with a blaster."

She gaped, smacked her mouth shut, then asked, "A spy?"

"Because of Iphara." Cylo closed the distance; her fingers touching him wasn't enough.

"Good news." Ariez flashed a smile. "This was your final assessment."

Wren frowned. "Why? Not that I'm unhappy about this."

"You have stabilized." Ariez faced the display vids, tapped charts, and streamed information. "Seems the stun was the final catalyst needed. Congratulations to the both of you."

She frowned. "Thanks?" She shuffled on her backside to reach the edge of the bed.

"Your quarters are ready." Ariez swiped his wrist across Cylo's. "I had the bulkheads and ceiling reinforced."

Cylo froze. "No more pools?"

"The rock's protection is no longer needed." Ariez waved a hand, dismissing them.

Cylo checked the location then lifted Wren into his arms. He carried her out of medical and south, closer to the ocean. His mind reeled over everything he'd learned. At least, there was no more talk of separating them. That was progress. That hell was finally over.

Outside her quarters, he lowered her feet to the ground, then palmed the panel. As he ushered her in, he asked, "Before I adore every inch of you, do you have any more questions?"

She laughed. "If I did, it can wait."

Maker, I love you.

"Oh?" She arched a brow as she slipped out of the wrap. "Cy," she rasped, cupping a cheek as she rose onto her toes to kiss him. "And I you."

He yanked her against him, looping his arm around her waist. Angling his head to deepen the kiss, he halted when she pressed a finger to his lips.

"What happened to the spy?"

Chapter Twenty-Six

Wren awoke to an empty bed. At first, she raised her head to listen. Nothing audible or mental reached her. Regardless, she followed her morning ritual of 'thickening' her door. She'd opened it when Ariez had shown her to her quarters in the medical building. The painful cacophony of thoughts not her own had crumpled her to the floor.

While curled into a ball, he'd carried her to the pools. As grateful as she'd been for the isolation, it meant she couldn't see or speak to Cy. Hot-tubbing, catching up on her reading, and watching movies between regular test trips had filled her days. As she'd assumed, regular doses of Cy's DNA had tipped the balance. Still, its introduction hadn't changed her compatibility with the... What had Macy called them? Sharks and squidheads?

Wren chuckled and stretched, working the kinks out of her back and relishing the ache in her nethers. The rumpled blankets snagged her gaze. Cy had thoroughly loved her, and yet, she wouldn't say no to another round.

A quick shower and a coffee were in her future. This was her wonderful life now. Padding barefoot and naked to the bathroom, she stepped into the cubicle and raised her face to the water's spray, wondering where Cy had gone.

A shadow darkened the corner of her eye. Squeaking, she spun then slumped at her man leaning his shoulder against the bathroom door's frame. He gazed at her, adoration in his expression. Sweat glistened on his skin. He tapped his chest and slipped out of his armor, piece by piece, until naked, he joined her.

I wanted to wake you.

She swirled her backside across his growing arousal.

Ensa, if only... He pressed a kiss to her neck while running his hands over her hips and belly. *Adviser Kanzo and Lady Ava are en route.*

She swiveled within his arms to press against his body. "Not even a quickie?"

His eyelids fluttered then he laughed. *Later. I vow.*

He wrapped his arms around her, gave her a tight hug, then left. With a wrap in hand, he waited for her. Standing there with the dryer blowing while he dripped onto the floor was the man of her dreams. She snorted. Not that she'd ever thought she'd find someone like him.

When he drew the wrap around her, he closed his arms for another hug. His breath fanned her ear at his whisper, "Thamani." He gathered her against him while they dried, then he ushered her out of the bathroom.

She snatched leggings and a T-shirt from the hidden closets, but her fingers brushed the white robe Ariez had ordered for her. Cy's stunned reaction had her thinking it was important to him. "I can wear this? Or is it for fucking?"

He growled, grabbed her hips, and yanked her to him. *It is a ceremonial robe in my bloodline color and worn to announce to all who you belong to...*

"Oh?" She met his gaze and wiggled her brows. "And to whom do I belong?"

"Wren," he rasped, crushing her against him.

His cologne, the heat of his body, his arms around her—she shut her eyes in sheer happiness.

"So anything in white?" she asked, stroking his jawline. At his hum, she patted his cheek and drew away. Under his attentive gaze, she wrangled on her bra and panties then slipped into the kimono-like garment. The door chimed as she toed on her flats.

He thumped his chest, locking his armor in place.

"We need to get you some casual clothes," she said, dancing past him.

Those blue pants from our date night? He trailed her then called for the door to open.

"Oh, yes," she mumbled, her cheeks warming. He'd looked so damn sexy in denims.

"Adviser Kanzo, Lady Ava, do come in," Cy said, gesturing to the white chairs.

"We're just stopping by for coffee," the black-haired woman said with a little wave. "I'm Ava, Etteria's only hairstylist."

"Well, that's good news," Wren said, fluffing her hair. She didn't need to brush or condition, not with the quality of their water and whatever they put in it. "Where are my manners? May I offer you a beverage? Coffee, Ava? Giyua, Kanzo?"

"Please," they said in unison then chuckled at each other.

Wren stared at them a little too long, trying to pick up any thoughts. Just a sense of well-being, of happiness. "Plain coffee or something fancier?"

"Not picky," Ava said, smiling.

"Cy?" Wren called on her way to the rehydrator.

Whatever you are having, thamani.

Once everyone held a mug, she sank into the chair beside Cy. "Why do I feel this is more than a morning coffee?"

"I wanted to meet you, of course." Ava cradled her cappuccino.

Kanzo smacked his lips after sipping his lemon juice. "And I have news." He put his mug onto the low table. "Ambassador Barro is behind Iphara and the attack last night. Xeus has yet to inform Queen Alllero considering her poor health. Same with regards to the ship Barro used."

"And while we have it?" Cy asked, downing his coffee with relish.

Kanzo grinned. "Etterians do not steal... Unlike operatives. Zive and Yelur mentioned your insistence that we learn what we can."

Cy shrugged, throwing his arm across the back of Wren's chair. He caressed where he touched her, drawing patterns with his fingers. "What would Malo do in this circumstance?"

"Indeed," Kanzo said. "Xeus has asked Prince Citus to visit the queen and ask her for the information."

Cy pursed his lips. "Diplomacy."

"Yes," Kanzo said. "Serratu Kayarra Korre has been prepped for transfer to the Caverns of Dooirin. She will be honored for her service."

Cy bowed his head.

"The Durn Zucis revealed his intentions, granting Jokta time to secure the women. According to the interrogation, he used this mission to flee the clutches of Yithia." Kanzo glanced at Wren. "The lima kuu are now searching for the marker Korre mentioned."

Wren frowned. "What? I thought all was well."

"Korre revealed the sexual compatibility was not the only goal." Cy caught her hand and shifted it to his thigh. "Some sort of trigger once the Ethera occurs."

"Like a time bomb?" Wren gasped.

"Something like that," he said.

"Well, that's not good. Does Ariez know?" Why had the man let her go with an all-clear? "And what does this thing do?"

"We do not know...yet." Kanzo grimaced.

That happy cloud she'd woken up with evaporated. She tried to reason with her sinking heart. Cy wasn't her Eth, so she couldn't kill him.

"Have you told the women?" she asked.

"Without his Dar Eth, the male is guaranteed death. We cannot say with certainty that she will kill him." Kanzo leaned forward. "As soon as we learn anything, I will inform you...two."

Whatever happens, we will face it together. Cy squeezed her hand.

"As to the issue Cylo asked me to investigate: Earth Armed Forces has requested your presence. I have set a time and date on Demeter Station. I do believe that was your home?"

Wren blinked. "I've violated so many of the stipulations that they'll want to arrest me."

"I would not agree to the meeting if that was the case. Olin's findings caused an uproar among your leaders." Kanzo smiled. "The *Kevol* has been assigned to you. Fyca and Durok will join you since both their Dar Eths wish to visit Earth. Where you go afterward is for you to decide."

She rubbed her temple. They'd just landed, and here she was heading into space again.

"The officer quarters have been reinforced as per Ariez's instructions, if that is your concern."

She met Kanzo's gaze, then glanced at Ava and Cy. "Sounds like you want me to go."

"I do," Cy said, bringing her hand to his lips. *I would like to meet your blood-bonds without you being detained.*

She forced a smile she was far from feeling. "You'd like my dad. My mom, though, she can be scary." She wasn't about to mention her brothers.

"Excellent." Kanzo grinned. "I will have additional officers' quarters built from the barracks for Fyca and Durok."

Ava laughed. "Like a pleasure cruise."

"Indeed." Kanzo set his empty mug on the table. "If you do not have questions, I would like to spend a little time with my wife."

Ava's cheeks bloomed. She set her cup down and rose, clinging to Kanzo's arm when he joined her. "Thank you for the coffee."

Wren and Cy escorted the couple to the door.

"I thought you said he wasn't her Eth?" Ava asked as they strolled off. "His eyes are neon. You can't get more Eth than that—" The door shut.

Cy froze then caught Wren's chin between his forefinger and thumb. "What color are my eyes?"

"A breathtaking turquoise." She pulled out of his grasp to kiss his palm before carrying the cups to the waste disposal. If what Ava said was true, that she was his Eth, Wren would have to walk away from Cy...to save him. She didn't have the strength to even think about it.

Cy sat, staring at nothing.

"What's your...void like?" she managed to ask, looping her arms around him from behind. She kissed his neck, trying to ignore her pounding heart.

"It is a beam of warm light where darkness once reigned." He leapt from the chair and circled it, catching her by her hips. "Do you not see, ensa ra ensa?" *You are forever mine and I yours.*

"We chose to stay together," she said, burrowing into his embrace.

"No, thamani." *Dar Eth.*

She jerked back but didn't get far. "I will kill you, Cy. No, please don't tell me the Ethera happened..."

He scooped her up and swung her, laughing as he did so. "You have saved me. Those three days without you were torture. I cannot bear a separation again. And if that means I die by your side, I will be a happy male." When he set her feet down, he met and held her gaze. *Where you go, I go...as your husband.*

She ignored the tear that slipped past her defenses. He was right. Who knew what tomorrow would bring? She wasn't going to be a chicken and not cherish every moment with him. "Where you go, I go, as your wife."

He chuckled. *Is that so?* He nudged his chin at their bedroom. *I do believe I promised you a quickie.*

Epilogue

Demeter Science Station

Year of 2254, October

WREN NEVER EXPECTED TO ever set foot on Demeter again. Approaching it had been surreal. Her beloved Pluto was unchanged in her absence. She snorted at that bit of silliness. The *Kevol* had docked in a prime spot. When she strolled down the ramp, she half expected the station head to be there to greet her.

Instead, Pierce stood there. His eyes were huge as he scanned the ship then settled on Durok and Fyca. When he spotted her, he glared at her.

"Wren, what have you done?" he hissed, grabbed her elbow, and pulled her aside.

She could only meet his gaze for a second.

Before he floated, his feet dangling.

Cy held him off the floor with a grip on his jaw. "Do not touch what is not yours."

Her chest swelled. Damn, how she loved this man. With Pierce's face mottling, she patted Cy's arm. "Relax, thamani. Pierce is like a blood-bond."

Cy dropped him. "The rule still applies." He scowled. "We are in the open." *I do not like it.*

Pierce straightened his jacket then rolled his jaw. "Explain. Now."

"Fine," she huffed. "Pierce, you remember Cylo, right?" She laced her fingers with Cy's and rested her cheek on his bare bicep. "Repeat after me... Husband."

"What?" Pierce scowled. "Your brothers are going to kill me."

"They can get over themselves." She flicked a dismissive wrist. "I'm not your problem or theirs anymore."

"She is mine." Cy beamed.

Pierce stilled then laughed. "That's right. I might not have the authority to say this, but welcome to the family, Cylo." He glanced over his shoulder. "I have stalled as much as I could, babe. E.A.F.'s here."

"I know." She squared her shoulders, not willing to admit how much Cy's presence comforted her. Kanzo had said all was sorted, but humans lied.

"Pony?" Dallas thundered toward her, his arms open wide. The six-foot-three man with his massive shoulders and barreled chest was a big ol' teddy bear. On him, though, his space boots looked small.

Another blood-bond? Cy shuffled forward, serving as a shield.

"Heard about your adventure. Wanna spill the deets over splice? You still owe me a night of drinking, if my memory serves."

"Those days are behind me." She smiled at Cy. "I have another addiction now."

He smirked. *If you keep looking at me like that...*

"You'll do what?" she whispered.

"Do not tease me, ensa," he rasped.

"Who's the hunk?" Dallas asked, offering his hand to Cylo.

He took it and pumped it twice. "Her husband."

"Shit." Dallas gaped then snapped his mouth shut. "That was quick. He knock you up?"

She laughed. "Cy, this is Dallas. And I hope so. Now, what's with the welcome?"

"Just preparing to fight them off." Dallas took a massive wrench from his pocket. She didn't want to know what else he was hiding and where.

"We shall see," she said, giving the man a sideways hug. "I have it on excellent authority that my criminal record is history."

A thump-thump of marching boots cut across the chaos of the crowds.

Pierce lunged to stand beside Cy just as a unit of eight men in full E.A.F. uniform escorted a suited man to stop before them.

With a weak voice, the poor man's gaze on Cylo, he said, "Turner, Wren, Identification number: 222510180522081-A, age twenty-nine, on parole for corporate espionage."

"Yes?" She squeezed Cy's arm and stepped forward.

"This is to inform you that due to the evidence provided by King Xeus et Pius of Etteria, Earth Armed Forces has dismissed your sentencing. Your record has been expunged and all technological rights returned to you."

She blinked at the court representative. Two months ago, she'd have been over the moon. Now, with Cy beside her, none of this mattered. Sure, her name had been restored, and yet, she couldn't say she was happy or sad about it. The supposed general who'd done this to her still roamed free.

"Thank you," she said.

"Furthermore, you will be recompensed for the damages done to your reputation and livelihood." He offered her a chip.

She accepted it on instinct.

He spun on his heel and, with his men, marched off. No apology, nothing.

Clicking the back of the chip, it read her thumbprint and illuminated a green number. The ludicrous amount did appease a little of her unhappiness.

Dallas whistled. "Guilty conscious, I'd say." He grinned. "Let's celebrate."

She laughed. "Sure. Coffee." She faced Cy. "If that is all right with you."

His expression softened. *Anything for you, thamani.*

Dallas huffed. "Fine."

With Cy by her side, they cut a swath through the gawking crowds. She'd say they marveled at him, so handsome and scary with that scowl. Yet, she couldn't dismiss her inner voice that said they stared at purple her. She tightened her door, keeping all but Cy from penetrating her thoughts. So far, so good.

Nothing had changed. Life went on, and Coffeeholics was exactly where it had always been. Cylo paused in the center and studied the coffee shop, leveling his ice-blue gaze on everyone and everything. Some people scurried out; others slithered in. As soon as a seat by the glass windows opened, she sank into it.

Beyond, the unending construction was the foreground to space.

Excitement had her bouncing her knee. Real coffee and the expensive kind. Though, she doubted it was better than the rehydrator.

"Two cappuccinos with whipped cream," she said to the server, then cupped Cy's thigh under the table. "We came all this way for what?"

Closure. He draped his arm across the back of her chair.

"True."

Pierce sliced glances between them. "I get you're purple now, but what's with the weird conversation?"

She shrugged. "Side effects." She wasn't going to go into it, especially when he'd demand she prove it.

"Well, I did let your brothers know you were coming home." He smiled at the waitress...again.

Wren wanted to ask if he'd bedded her yet, but Cy shifted closer.

She likes him. With a nudge of his fingers on her shoulder, she pressed into the curve of his body.

She drew in a deep inhale, loving his smell.

But the scent of your arousal is so much sweeter. He nuzzled her neck. *Like now.*

Her cheeks burned.

"So, when did you two get married?" Dallas asked, shifting in his seat while tucking in his shirt.

"Good question," she said, meeting Cy's gaze.

"On a beach," he rasped. "In a cave. In a shuttle bay. On a viewing deck."

Her heart thundered and leapt with each of his responses.

"She was mine from the moment I met her." He glanced at Dallas then Pierce. His O.D.I. buzzed. *One moment, ensa.* He rose and left the shop.

"Pony, are you sure about this?" Dallas leaned across the table to whisper, "There's something lethal about him as if he can kill without hesitation." Pierce slid his finger along the rim of his cup.

She beamed. "Yes, he can, and yes, he has."

Pierce's face paled. "I... We can't save you this time, Wren."

Dallas slapped him on his back. "I don't think she needs rescuing, what with the full might of Etteria behind her."

Cy returned, shifted the chair to within an inch from hers, and sat. "We will be staying longer than expected."

"Oh?" she asked, tossing a smile at the waitress when she slid their order onto the table.

Malo's Dar Eth was taken. Cy flicked off a dollop of cream and popped it into his mouth, sweeping his tongue across his finger to do so.

Her breath hitched. The world shrank.

She cleared her throat and fanned her flushed hand with the plastic napkin. "With what you told me about him, I pity the kidnappers."

Cy smirked. Indeed. When he met Pierce's gaze, he said, "And I will kill again if anyone threatens my *wife*."

Dallas choked on a slurp of iced coffee while Pierce found the ships outside fascinating.

"Etterians have preternatural hearing," she said, hiding her smile behind her cup.

"Wren Marie Turner, you better start explaining yourself."

At that cultured voice parting the customers like Moses himself had arrived at Demeter, Wren winced.

"Shit," she whispered. "Who called my mom?"

Glossary

Etterians worship one God, one Maker since the universes have only His fingerprint on all of it, a single golden thread through all of creation.

Tokens: an intergalactic form of currency

Kliks: predetermined length of distance.

Durn

An iridescent insect that sheds its carapace in fright – gagoni (gah-go-nee)

Precious – ohara (oh-haar-rah)

Snake/millipede creature – abingu (ah-binn-goo)

True mate – dhutya (doot-yah)

Etterian

Alodon (A-low-donn): who accidentally shot his balls off with his own blaster.

Teacher: lima (lee-ma)

Great teacher: lima kuu: (lee-ma koo)

Directions: semit (semm-it)

Lemon: giyua (gee-you-a)

Young one: damu (daa-moo)

Hatimaye – To bring an end (Hutt-ee-my-ee)

Heart: ensa (enn-sa)

Heart of my heart: ensa ra ensa (enn-sa raa enn-sa)

Beloved: thamani (ta-mar-nee)

Little joy: minus susa (mee-nas soo-sa)

Little cat: minus cesu (mee-nas sess-oo)

Large: magnus (mag-nis)

Orgasm: fulfillment/deite asteri (see stars) / released (day-ta ass-tare-ree)

Starfighter: asteri peju (ass-tare-ree pear-joo)

Collection of glass vials: virak (vee-ruck)

Scum of the galaxies: xemi (ze-mee)

Hair up: malia pa (Mar-lee-a par)

Hair down: malia pado (Mar-lee-a par-dow)

White flower in the royal gardens in Issneen: hahyt (hah-hit)

Tiny yellow flowers with black dots, grows on hedges: anahla (ann-haar-lah)

Lysaran

Visitor: kashi (Kaa-shee)

God: Kaiha (Kigh-haa)

King: Kuna (Koo-na)

Orange fleshy fruit: Lemte (Lem-ta)

White flowers: Myameru (My-a-me-roo)

Precious: Delica (Dell-ee-ka)

Sweetheart: Sali (Saa-lee)

Arum Lily-type flower: D'nastu (D-nass-too)

Love Blossom: aroa loulu (A-row-a low-loo)

Maloidian

Title of respect: lommia (Lomm-ee-a)

Stubborn, lethal tree: tewaa (Tee-wah)

Silent Sirens: Serratu (Suh-rarr-too) Kayarra (Kuh-yarr-ah)

Wine – Jucot (Joo-cott) – purple wine

Staff – Katac (kah-tuck)

Spear - katac-isi (kah-tuck-iss-ee)

Bitch – zseera (seer-rah)

Scientist – kuliriji (Cool-lee-ree-jee)

Yellow-orange gloop like almonds and vanilla jelly – genkoo (ghen-koo)

Squealing boar with massive tusks – migtak (mig-tuck)

Toxic furry pink leaves – sjari (suh-jarr-ee)

Tokauri

/Kulai

Blade – Sulac (soo-lack)

Bone – Ukog (you-cog) - bone from some dumb animal, probably an ukog.

Braided – Gisul (gee-sool)

Father – Danno (dan-no)

Heart – Kassu (cass-soo)

Maker – Mugbu (Mug-boo)

Mother – Manno (man-no)

Sapphires – Buha (boo-ha)

Shit – Saho (sa-ho)

Star - stuon (stoo-on)

Stupid – Ungog (oon-gog)

Vessel/ship - sakay (sa-kay)

Viqrian

Haiz – Haze

Kaara – Karr-rah

Shioll – She-oll

Tagana –Tar-garn-ah

Tarni – Tarr-nee

Viqrian – Vick-ree-in

Yithian

Estuuba – Eh-stew-bah – family

Zedali – Zeh-dar-lee – Black trees without foliage. (They look dead/burnt.)

Pronunciations

Names

Aaro - Ah-row

Adda – Ay-dah

Afax – Ay-fax

Aldur - Al-durr

Alllero - A-le-row

Ariez – Ah-reez

Balllio – Bah-leee-oh

Barro – Bear-oh

Bos - Boss

Bry-dar - Brigh-darr

Brynr - Brin-ner

Cales - Cale-es

Cento - Sen-tow

Cewa – Cue-wah

Citus - Sigh-tuss

Coldar - Coal-daar

Cria - Kree-ah

Criass – Kry-ass

Cylo – Sigh-low

Eriz – Err-iz

Danic - Dan-eek

Deeezo – Dee-zoh

Der – Durr

Diexa – Dee-ex-ah

Diso - Dee-sow

Diyo - Die-oh

Durok – Doo-rock

Eira - Eye-raa

Enyl - E-neel

Eriz - E-rizz

Eysso – Essie-oh

Fyca – Figh-ka

Garix - Ga-ricks

Gayn – Gain

Geffa – Jeff-ah

Hiossu – He-oh-soo

Iddan - Ee-dann

Idon - Eye-donn

Illan - Ee-lann

Jarg – Jar-g

Jokta - Jock-tar

Kanzo - Can-zow

Keelu – Key-loo

Keryr – Kerr-eer

Koddo – Koh-doh

Korre - Core

Kyah – Kai-yah

Ksal - Ka-sell

Lazu – Lah-zoo

Lizu – Lizz-ooh

Lurz - Lurr-z

Malo - Mail-oh

Matir - Mat-teer

Myan - My-ann

Myn-ras - Min-russ

Naio – Nay-oh

Nerx – Nurcks

Nhyht – Night

Nuos - New-oss

Olin – Oh-lynn

Oyaz - Oh-yaz

Prex – Precks

Qaff - Kuff

Ronan - Row-nan

Saan - Sarn

Sena - See-na

Siio – See-ooo

Smez – Suh-mez

Sy'mar - Sigh-marr

Syna - Sigh-na

Tamra – Tum-rah

Taro - Tah-row

Tenu - Ten-oo

Tias – Tee-ass

Tinh – Tin

Trav - Trahv

Vytus - Vie-tuss

Vodin - Vo-din

Ulriq - Yule-rick

Uloz – Oo-loz

Unher – Oon-her

Vorn - Vawn

Vyar - Vie-arr

Xan - Zan

Xeus – Zeus

Yelur – Yeh-lerr

Zaro - Zah-row

Ziot - Zye-ott

Zive – Z-ive

Zucis – Zoo-kiss

Places

Aberdus – A-burr-diss

Argaxx – Are-jax

Berrann – Burr-anne – A waterfall near Nerx's childhood home on the mining moon Fuyra.

Crustiiu – Criss-tee-oo

Doorin – Dure-inn - Caverns of Dooirin

Dyuqa - Dee-you-ka

Etteria – E-tare-rea

Gaelsi – Gale-zee

Galaza – Gah-lar-zah

Gikaet – Gee-ka-ett

Iphara – Ee-far-ra

Knaetian – Nish-shin – Ocean on Yithia

Kulai – koo-ligh

Lysara – Liss-saa-ra

Luchur – Loo-churr

Mascroba – Mus-crow-ba

Sarvis – Sarr-viss

Sosu – Sow-soo

Tokauri – Too-cow-ree

Vahnal – Varr-null – small Etterian village.

Yithia – Yith-ee-a

Battleships

Bronvol – Bronn-vole – Viqrian battle cruiser.

Chikara – Chee-kar-a - Force

Gladio – Glad-ee-oh – Sword

Katvay – Cat-vay - Eternity

Kunakar – Koo-narr-karr - Viqrian battle cruiser.

Kushin – Cush-shin - To Pierce

Ntima – In-tee-mah - Heart

Surata – Soo-ra-tah – Beginning

Usaha – Oo-saa-hah – Endeavor

Vindar – Vin-daar – Endurance

Shuttles/Smaller ships

Celeeri – See-lee-ree - swift

Denessi – Denn-ess-ee - sodge

Eshima – Ee-shee-ma - respect

Kevol – Kev-oll - agony

Kuta – Koo-tah - modular shuttle.

Liri-ny – Lee-ree-nye – freedom

Misaia – Miss-aye-a – memory

Nahatyr – Nah-huh-tier - honor

Sasay – Sass-ay - whispers

Yakin – Yuck-kin - belief

Yarva – Yarr-vuh – Viqrian name for a shuttle/kuta.

Zannwar – Zunn-wurr – Yithian Slave Ship.

Creatures

Abingu – Ah-bing-oo - snake

Asnu – Ass-Noo – buffalo/donkey

Eiltur – Ale-turr

Gracc – Grrr-ack

Ilag – Ee-Lug– leggy slugs that feast on sol.

Kreso – Kreh-soo

Omeika – Oh-may-ka

Pagsu – Pug-Soo - cocksuckers

Reshy – Resh-Ee - huge, like the size of a kuta shuttle, with massive jaws and rows of sharp teeth.

Sogair – Sow-gare

Wilanegy – Will-anna-jee

Znorg – Zuh-norg

Foods

Kreso – Kreh-soo

Lemon – giyua (gee-you-a)

Omeika – Oh-may-ka

Orange fleshy fruit: Lemte (Lem-ta)

Purple wine – Jucot (Joo-cott)

Yellow-orange gloop like almonds and vanilla jelly – genkoo (ghen-koo)

The yellow leaves from Maloid are bitter and poisonous – sjari (suh-jarr-ee)

About the Author

Sevannah Storm is a fiction writer who immerses herself in fantastical worlds both magical and science fiction. She has a flair for the creative having studied art and interior architecture and spends her time drawing, oil painting, and writing. An avid reader from an early age, Sevannah finds her inspiration from various sources: games, novels, music, and the land of make-believe. The unique versus the practical has brought on numerous debates.

In her spare time, she rereads novels that snatch her breath away. Having embraced the social media world, you can find her on most platforms.

Her home is a land south of Wakanda, where animals roam free. Born in Zimbabwe, she grew up in South Africa. The crisp blue skies with cotton-candy sunsets expand her heart and soul, encapsulating a sense of freedom.

Words she lives by: “Know your pothole and dodge it. Don’t work in a pencil factory if you’re a vampire.”

Sevannah loves to hear from her readers. You can find and connect with her at the links below.

Website/Newsletter:

https://www.sevannahstorm.com/

Facebook:

https://www.facebook.com/sevannah.storm

Instagram:

https://www.instagram.com/sevannah.storm/

Twitter:

https://twitter.com/sevannah_storm

Thank you for taking the time to read *Time Forged*. If you enjoyed the story, please tell your friends and leave a review. Reviews support authors and ensure they continue to bring readers books to love and enjoy.

SOUL FORGED

The Gifting Series #1

Know-it-all Oriana agreed to travel with aliens who need women. But she didn't agree to abduction, life/death battles, and escaping with a bossy, arrogant man. She was sabotaged, attacked, and kidnapped, but she is far from beaten. Forced to participate in an alien battle arena with no promise of freedom, she has to forget the loss of her family and focus on surviving.

Enyl has given up hope. His people are dying due to a genetic modification gone awry. Darkness is consuming his warriors, and his world, as he knows it, will end. His father, the king, has rolled out a plan to save them all. But Enyl doubts a solution will be found in time.

And when a compatible female is found...and lost, he must rescue her, a human female capable of surviving despite all odds. However, freeing Oriana serves to anger the aliens holding her captive. Ensuring she is cared for—as per Etterian protocol—he is stunned by the strong connection between the two of them. Such a bond was only experienced between Etterian mates.

Is she his salvation or is that wishful thinking on his part?

Read it here:

https://books2read.com/u/mlAWr9

FATE FORGED

The Gifting Series #2

Jacqueline (Jack) Dunois struggles to find a man not intimidated by her career as a law enforcement instructor, especially in the small town she calls home. She would sacrifice a kidney to find someone who would make her ovaries clap and didn't live with his mother. Then she meets a supreme commander from another world who thinks the stars in the galaxies shine in her eyes... What's not to love about that?

Supreme Commander Ulriq doesn't believe in love, an archaic term for a volatile and untrustworthy emotion that Etterians were no longer subjected to. Until he meets Jack who triggers the Ethera, the soulmate force that irrevocably changes a male when he finds his ideal female. At that moment, his world, his focus, his very loyalty shifts. But when she is taken from him, it is too much to bear. Under the influence of the Ethera, he launches a rescue. He'll start a war and kill anyone who dares stop him, just to have her back in his arms.

Read it here:

https://books2read.com/u/bMY09v

SUN FORGED

The Gifting Series #3

Meeting a drop-dead gorgeous man, who falls onto a knee the first time they meet, sounded too good to be true for Ava. Of course, with her luck, he had to be an alien. Thrust into an unknown alien world, meeting weird and scary creatures, and fearing for her life, Ava tries to survive as best as a hairstylist can.

Kanzo never expected to find a life mate, a Dar Eth. Since he was young, he was taught that pairings were rare with fewer females born. The statistics on finding his Dar Eth would be slim to none. Instead of dreaming and longing for companionship, he focused on being the best male possible, to end his life on a battlefield with honor. But when he experiences the Ethera—the life mate force, and is blessed with his female, he isn't prepared for the level of pain, pleasure, and need she invokes within him.

Unable to save her as she's teleported from him, the dark consuming pain in his chest drives him into a blinding rage. With no idea who stole her or where to begin the search, he will scour the known universe to find her, to hold the female he never wanted.

Read it here:

https://books2read.com/u/3n5vaB

WAR FORGED

The Gifting Series #4

Being kidnapped by aliens does not sit well with Quinlan. Not only would her seven guardians give her hell if she doesn't attempt some sort of escape, but she refuses to be at anybody's mercy. With her practiced military skills, the help of an underground lounge singer and a personal assistant, she takes over the alien slave ship. Not knowing how to fly the damn thing, she sends a distress signal. ...The rescue comes swiftly in the form of a bronzed man with exquisite ice-blue eyes. Leaving her to ask the true question: has she just given up her newfound freedom for a gorgeous man who seems determined to have her for eternity?

As Elite Supreme Commander of the Etterian Forces, Xan answers a distress call in Earth English. That is all he did. The female who captured the slave ship shows remarkable skill, making her a warrior in her own right. Said skills should be respected and honored. Except she is his Dar Eth, calling forth the Ethera—the soulmate bond. How can he protect his female when she can do so herself? What can she possibly need from him? What can he offer a female, not Etterian but human? Not that he can think clearly in her presence when she scents so good and makes him want to kiss all of her.

Maker help him.

Read it here:

https://books2read.com/u/bz1QGD

STAR FORGED

The Gifting Series #5

Macy is feeling a little left out, as usual. Who would have thought moving from one planet to another wouldn't change that loneliness? She is never alone these days since Etterians guard human women with an urgency she understands. But the lack of companionship is like a dark aching abyss inside her chest. On some days, it threatens to implode, and Macy Mitchell would cease to exist. Looming is her impending meeting with King Xeus of Etteria. How is she supposed to keep her shit together when presented to royalty? Not after she ran from the last king she met.

For Xeus, the void expands daily. Duty, honor, concern for his dying people, and endless loneliness fill his life. Having decided to search for pairings among other worlds, he is pleased his son found his soulmate among human women. It doesn't mean that Xeus's loneliness and longing haven't ended until he stumbles upon a crying female. Meaning only to soothe, he is spellbound when her presence brings him peace. Unable to resist, he forms an attachment to a female he can never have

Read it here:

https://books2read.com/u/3nXgp5

SHADOW FORGED

The Gifting Series #6

Forty-year-old Caroline is too old to start dating and too bored with her vibrator, but what other choices does she have. On the day she burns her shirt and breaks a fingernail, she meets Etterian warriors. As part of her job at E.S.A. (Earth Space Association,) she must 'entertain' the hot-as-apple-pie Chief Engineer she suspects isn't who he claims to be.

Operations Commander Malo, Head of Espionage, must act as an engineer and ambassador, hoping to invite human females to visit Etteria and save his dying race. From Princess Oriana, he has strict instructions to distrust humans. What he finds he cannot trust are his emotions and his body whenever in the presence of the human ambassador, Caroline. She does not believe in soulmates or in a forever with him. Convincing her to choose him is the greatest task ever set before him, one he cannot afford to fail.

Until she is stolen from him. He calls in favors, utilizes all his resources to find her. And *when* he does, he is never letting her off his battleship...or his bed.

Read it here:

https://books2read.com/u/bPNd8j

EARTH FORGED

The Gifting Series #7

Guilt hounds Izzy, who caused her sister's injury and subsequent blindness. But no matter how she cares for Simone or what she sacrifices, it doesn't ease the ache in her chest. With Simone and naive Caro, her best friend, Izzy's role as protector is fully realized. The cost? Hiding behind quirkiness, pseudo-joy, and giving up her hopes and dreams. What she needs is a knight in any armor. After all, beggars can't be fussy. She has no idea that armor, in her case, means black military and that a knight could come in any color, specifically bronze.

Oyaz wants to find his life force, his soulmate, and he'd like her to be human. Earth's females are soft, amusing, passionate, and their scents rival a garden of hahyt blossoms. His task is to guard their planet that promises so many salvations for his males. It's a duty he's pleased to perform, one he would die for. When Operations Commander Malo orders Oyaz to retrieve a human female, he's eager to oblige. That it would lead to his salvation is something he couldn't anticipate. What he hadn't planned for is an ambush that costs him more than his memory, the loss of his soulmate.

Now what? Nothing in their training prepared him for this.

And yet, despite not remembering kneeling for Izzy, he longs to claim her with every inch of his soul.

Read it here:

https://books2read.com/u/31V82D

LUST FORGED

The Gifting Series #8

Ex-socialite Leona wants nothing more than to enhance the mechanics within sex-cybs, not to mention improve their performances with their 'lovers.' It's a job where she's safe in an all-woman factory on Callisto, and far from her matchmaking mama. When the chief engineer is incapacitated, Leona's required to gift—her term would be pimp—sex-cyborgs to prospective clients. On an Etterian battleship, surrounded by gorgeous males, she tries not to think of sex when it's her work, especially with the Sub-Commander Aaro whose neon-blue eyes are the stuff of her erotic dreams.

As a diplomatic favor, Aaro must abandon his task to guard Earth, and perhaps find his Dar Eth or soulmate, all to protect cargo en route to many worlds, including the dangerous and unpredictable Yithia. Princess Oriana is most concerned for the two human female engineers determined to ensure the deliveries are successful. A simple enough mission until one human enters Aaro's cargo bay, dropping him to his knees.

But revealing to independent Leona that she's now trapped in a marriage isn't something Aaro can bring himself to do. He violates all he stands for, every ounce of honor by not telling her the truth. All in the hopes that she will choose to love him.

Read it here:

https://books2read.com/u/3LdA1w

FIRE FORGED

The Gifting Series #9

Britt's a fighter and the self-appointed protector of her mom after her father died. No matter what or how, no one gets the best of her. She's strong, self-reliant, and bold with no filter between brain and mouth. So when she accidentally-on purpose pepper-sprays an alien, things can only go from bad to worse. Hell no is she apologizing when she's clearly not in the wrong. She'll just have to stay out of his way on their small spaceship. Easy, right?

Nerx has spent a lifetime in strict control of his emotions, calculating every scenario. His life and grumpy outlook begins to change when he adopts Lily, a human girl. As a father with his daughter's future in mind, he must complete a royal mission to Earth before he retires as supreme commander. A trip planetside ends in blindness, and worse, the woman who attacked him has no remorse. He wants nothing to do with her and plans to avoid her during the trip to Etteria.

Until she triggers the mating bond.

Now he has to somehow convince this shrew to take a chance on him and his daughter. Except, she's not what he expects. She's fierce but sweet, entertaining, and sassy. And the most disobedient woman he knows.

Read it here:

https://books2read.com/u/b56vP

www.ingramcontent.com/pod-product-compliance
Lightning Source LLC
Chambersburg PA
CBHW070602120726
47909CB00007B/2416